This book is dedicated to Aidan Hardt;
For helping to inspire the initial idea, brainstorming with me, and for
cheering me on

Table of Contents

A Selkie's Home

Chapter One - Waves

<u>Morgan</u>

The wound ran almost the length of her entire side. Ever since I had gotten it to finally stop bleeding it had been pink in the middle surrounded by an angry, harsh redness. It was somehow black along the edges, as if the blade had severely burned her skin as it tore through her. I knew that it had to have been a magical weapon that the hunter had wielded— there was no other explanation for why it refused to heal so many months later. I felt I had tried everything to make my little sister better, but even all of what little magic I had in me to use only managed to close the wound. *I'm a horrible sister for letting this happen to her.*

But I had to keep trying. *I could go up to the surface, gather some plants that I know could make a good poultice... but I doubt that would make a difference. Maybe... Maybe if magic had caused the injury, and the weakness it had brought with it, magic could heal it.* I knew of a place on the surface, in the human town, an old library under lock and key... I was pretty sure it might have books that could teach me how to use my magic to heal my sister.

I looked over at her as she lay listlessly, floating in the water next to me. Occasionally she would swim around a little, weaving slowly through the long tendrils of seaweed that stretched up from the sand below us. Her jaw snapped instinctively at a fish as it swam right by her, but it continued on its way untouched. I couldn't let her continue to live like this.

"Adva," I said quietly. She turned her head towards me and looked at me with large, dark eyes. "I'm going to go up to the surface to try to find another way to help you." She opened her mouth to protest but I stopped her. "It'll be okay. I'll be back soon. Stay safe, hidden in the coral and seaweed here. If you smell or hear anything coming, get up into the cave." I nuzzled her gently, and then turned and swam away-- but not before glancing back, and giving her a small smile.

When I neared the shore, I sighed and began my transformation. My body became thinner, longer, gangly in comparison to the seal body I was more used to. I stuck my head up above the waves when I felt my chest tighten, and took a breath. My long hair was plastered against my head and face, and I roughly moved it out of the way.

The small, secluded area I typically chose to surface in was deserted. A pile of large rocks extending out of the water blocked the view of the path that led towards the town, sheltering a small patch of sand at the edge of a forest. To one side of the path, a forest stretched outward. I stepped out of the water, careful not to stub my delicate toes, and ducked behind the rocks. In a crevice between them was the clothing I had stashed here about a week beforehand, the last time I had been to the surface.

Once I was dressed and had gathered a few specific plants, I stepped away from the little seaside forest, hurrying up the small sloped path towards the town and holding my jacket closed tight with crossed arms. The town was bustling more than I would've liked, people filling the sidewalks and carriages and carts filling the cobblestone streets. Horses, strange animals, pulled the carriages and I jumped out of the way as one came careening towards me, heading out of the town. I walked quickly with my head down, ignoring the abundance of sounds and smells that surrounded me as I weaved through the groups of people. I made sure to keep my long white hair tucked into a hat that sat low on my forehead, and fussed with the red scarf around my neck. *Ugh, there's so much unnecessarily restricting, uncomfortable human attire. But since they don't have naturally white hair when they're young, it draws attention to me that I can't afford...* As I moved through the streets of the busy town, I felt as though dozens of watchful eyes were tracking my every move. But it didn't matter. I would do anything I possibly could to help little Adva, but I was beginning to understand why she hated coming up here.

When I finally reached the right building, I glanced around and behind me cautiously. I couldn't get caught, and Adva and I had had a far too close call already, but I seemed to have left the crowd of bustling people behind. I was down a small side street, tucked away from any potential prying eyes. Good. Getting two long, thin pieces of metal out of my pocket, I began to pick the lock open. My anxiety grew until the door successfully unlocked. I slipped inside, closing the door silently behind me.

Inside, the entire building was dark, and towering shelves full of books lined the walls and stood in rows. Luckily I was born quite a ways beneath the waves, so being able to see despite a lack of light had never been an issue for me. I snuck around corners, listening carefully to my surroundings, ignoring the large paintings on the walls and the plush seating that dotted the large room. Before long, I found what I was looking for. Grabbing one, I began to furiously flip through a book about magic. I glanced at the table of contents, and scanned through pages trying to find something that might be helpful that I didn't already know, hadn't already tried. As the seconds passed to no avail, I searched faster as my heartbeat quickened in my chest. *Come on, come on, there has to be something in here somewhere!* Reaching the end of the possibly useful chapter, I roughly shoved the large book back onto the shelf in frustration and picked up another one.

"Hey! Who's there!?" A deep, gruff voice boomed throughout the silent darkness. *Ah, shit. I'm so dumb, why did I do that?* I sighed and put the book I had picked up back down. Peeking around the corner of the shelves, I saw a tall, broad shouldered, burly man with a neat beard and brown eyes to match his hair. He wore a dark uniform holding a lantern that cast amber light around him and created long shadows. I snuck off in the other direction, skirting the perimeter of the room, careful to always keep at least one wall of books in between me and the wandering guard. This guard would probably soon think he had simply misheard something, not a book being shoved back into its place, as I silently left. I stepped out from behind a shelf and opened the door-- only to be roughly yanked backwards by my jacket's collar, then feeling it begin to slip off of my shoulders as a large hand reached out of the dark. *No!* I snatched the edge of my jacket angrily, forcefully pulling the article of clothing away from my pursuer with all of my might and back onto myself.

I didn't wait another second before I pulled open the door and bolted down the street. The sound of the human's thunderous footsteps rushing behind me filled my ears and echoed the sounds of the blood pumping in my head as my heart raced. I ignored all of it, instead focusing on making these awkward long legs of mine go as fast as they could. I made sharp, sudden turns down alleyways and side streets, narrowly avoiding ramming into carts and wagons as people yelled at me and jumped out of my way. I zigzagged and turned randomly, sometimes doubling back or even going in a giant circle. Eventually, when I thought my lungs and my legs were about to give out entirely, the sound of footsteps behind me softened until they were gone.

I stopped running and collapsed on the ground on an empty little dirt road. My lungs heaved, taking in gulps of air while my legs and feet ached and never wanted to move again. But I could not give my little human form, my muscles, what it wanted. It wasn't safe here; clearly it would never be. So I stood, ignoring how my body screamed internally, and walked. *I don't deserve to rest yet anyway. I've failed again.* My mind drifted off, solely focused on taking one step after another. That was okay, my body always seemed able to lead me back to the water without my mind giving any input.

As the sound of the waves and the smell of the sea reached my ears, I sighed in contentment and relief. I took one last glance over my shoulder-- no one in sight. I took the bundle of plants I had picked from the edge of the forest out of my pocket. They looked so small and almost pitiful now, in my hand. But at least it was something to go back with, another attempt: a spark of hope, perhaps. Better than nothing. I clasped them between my teeth and threw my hat and scarf to the ground. Normally, at this point, I'd duck behind something for this next bit, and take care to make sure I could retrieve these clothes later. But this time I didn't care. I was far too tired to care. What more could they do to me, at this point? I was about to be back in my element. Taking off my jacket, pants, and shirt, I dropped all of them except for the jacket on the sand and began to walk into the surf.

As the cold, crisp water surrounded me, the waves rolled into and past me and it slowly climbed up my body as I walked. Once I was waist deep, I dived in, pushing myself further forward and deeper. Oh how terrible the human form was for swimming, but the water felt luxurious. I had been on the surface too long. I felt the jacket that was still in my hands begin to morph, shift, and change as my magic flowed into it. The human jacket turned into its true form-- a large, white as snow pelt covered in black spots --and as I draped it around my shoulders, I turned into *my* true form as well. Legs melded into a tail, arms became fins, and my body widened. My seal skin and I became one, and the black spots scattered across my bright white coat seemed to faintly glow like stars. I closed my eyes in bliss as my body felt warm, the sea salt flowing past me easily and like a second skin. I propelled myself through the water, heading deeper. *Perfect.* With the plants I had picked earlier still encased between my teeth, it was time to head home. My little sister would be waiting for me.

<u>Milan</u>

I walked down the small hill that my village sat on, looking behind me now and again, scanning through the people that milled about the paths as if my Ma might just appear there suddenly and catch me. Pretending that I wasn't doing nothing I shouldn't be, I headed further down.

"Hey there Milan, how's the store going?" A friendly voice jumped out of the crowd as a slightly older man with round glasses and brown hair that was beginning to grey waved me down and smiled.

"Oh, uh, it's goin' good, Mr. Richards, thanks for askin'," I said, caught a tad off guard.

"Where're you headed, son?" He asked, peering up at me from above his glasses. Mr. Richards was nothing but nice-- well, 'cept he was sometimes a little nosey. Most people in my village were like that.

"Oh, nowhere, sir, jus' t' the grocery store to pick up a few things," I tried, patting him on the shoulder. He stumbled for a step but quickly caught himself as I began to apologize. "Sorry sir, y'know I still sometimes don't know my own strength," I forced a chuckle.

"Yes, yes, well, have a good day, say hi to your Ma for me," he said, waving me off as he turned back towards the rest of the village, up the hill. I watched him go for a few steps before relaxing. *Phew.*

After that, I decided to use the tree cover that lined the edges of the small slope, hurrying away from my little village. Towards… the *ocean.*

The sound of the lapping waves gently hitting the shore came to me before I could see the water past the trees, and instantly I felt calm. The trees opened up in front of me soon after, and I stared at the perfectly blue, soft water as the sun hit its surface and shone like gems. I stepped onto dusty light sand, feeling myself sink in a bit, and headed to the edge of the water. Plunking myself down, I dipped a hand into the clear ocean water. It's beauty always caught my attention, and it's sound and just being by it made me feel warm and soft like nothing else.

"I'll never understand how all the folks up there can hate this," I said quietly to myself. But that wasn't the most true. I didn't remember the day the ocean rose up and swallowed our village, only bits and pieces, but everybody else couldn't forget it. Maybe that was why all I could see was its goodness, and all they could see was what it broke and changed. I had been just a youngin' at the time, maybe ten years or a little more ago. It caused a lot a destruction, and death… But I don't remember much a that either. We went and lived in another town for a bit while our village was fixed up. When we got back it still took some time for things t' get back t' normal… in a way, we're just in a different normal now. I lifted my eyes up from the sand and the edge of water, out over to where the water eventually touched the sky.

"They're all scared of you now, always on edge by you, avoidin' you, worried that at any moment another wave is gonna come and swallow the village again. I don't think we'd make it past that one more time... I can understand their fear, but I don't get it." My voice went out over the waves, the constant sound of moving water echoing in my ears. "T' me, the ocean is… you're beautiful." I let my eyes slowly drift over the water, as the sunlight bounced off of it and flickered in it's tiny waves. "If it wasn't for the cold wind, I'd sit here all day… Well, if not for that, my jobs in town, and the fact that I've already been caught and told off for getting too close to here too many times already. I've barely managed to get them to believe my 'xcuses as it is. Honestly I think they believe what they want t' be true 'bout it all. 'Bout me."

"MI*LAN* WHAT ARE YOU DOING YOU'RE GONNA GET YERSELF *KILLED!*" the shrill voice made me jump. I quickly scrambled to my feet, spinning around to see my Ma standing a little ways up the hill towards town with her hands on her hips and a glare in her eye. I stepped away from the water and walked up to her, looking down with my hands behind my back. I didn't meet her eyes, even though she only came up to my elbow. Her white hair was in a messy bun, as if she hadn't had time to do it up properly that day. I kept my gaze down near her feet, where her loose flowery dress almost touched the sand.

When I got to the top a the hill where my Ma was, she reached way up on her tiptoes and pinched my ear, causing me to yell in pain and surprise; Ma only does the ear pinch when she's really not happy. She dragged me back to town like that, making me walk all hunched over. As we walked she scolded me and talked about all her other problems that had piled up that day. Apparently, the hunters were having trouble finding game, the roof was leaking again, Little Suzie's cat was stuck in a tree again, a tree had fallen and had to be moved, and now her only son-- who could easily help solve each of those problems-- was not only nowhere to be found, 'pparently nearly causing her a heart attack, but I was by the water. As she scolded me I couldn't help but think about how I could probably lift her up with one hand, yet she was the one dragging *me* by the ear. I quickly stopped that thought in its tracks and tossed it away-- the last time somebody had disobeyed my Ma, they didn't stick around to tell the tale.

"--And Milan Joseph Carter, ya know *better* than to be down so close to them waves, and hey don't look so pouty, that water is *dangerous!* You've seen what it did t' us, how long it took us to recover! It took your whole life! An' if that damn sea decides outta nowhere to come for us again you can*not* be so close! You must stay up in the town with us where we will have time to safely escape, and you have jobs to do all the time, and--" My Ma could go on for a while once she got going. But now that we were getting back into town, I pulled my ear from her grasp and stood up, stretching my back. I apologized to her, but I just got told to go help out as she stomped off muttering about how I said that last time and 'what do I think I'm doing'. *Sigh.*

As I wasn't being watched now, I turned and looked back over my shoulder. The hill my village was on wasn't very steep. I stared for a moment at the long stretch of water down the hill behind me. I could still smell the sea salt, could still feel the breeze on my face. Something in my chest wanted to go back to it. I don't know. I forced myself to turn back and head further into the village before anyone noticed my gaze, refusing to look back or peek until our buildings blocked the view entirely.

But it was time to get back to work-- moving boxes, doing the heavy lifting for everything in town, and maybe I would be able to fit in doing a quick shift at my Ma's storefront after everything else. Even if it wasn't the best the world had to offer, it was what I had to do.

Adrian

I strode along the sand, doing my last round of the city for the day. The sandstone brick walls that surrounded it rose up next to me looking as if they had erupted from the sand itself, perfectly sculpted. The world was dark. Not a sound stirred from beyond them, and no sunlight reached us this far down at this time in the evening. Cylindrical towers rose up even higher on the walls periodically, each one with a flat covered top on which stood more guards, surrounded by battlements. The city itself was composed of majestic, beautiful buildings. They were all made of the best marble and sandstone. Elegant and sometimes extravagant details were etched into railings, and the frames of doors and windows.

As I admired it all, a small current drifted past me, brushing against my cheek and lifting my roughly shoulder-length black hair to trail behind me for a moment. It slid easily against and past the armour I wore, and I made sure to keep a grip on my spear, its blunt end in the sand at my feet. I let a small smile cross my face-- I enjoyed the feeling of the flowing water around me, and as the current passed, I gazed upward in time to see a small school of fish swim by, far above me. The quickly fading sunlight of dusk glinted off of their scales, and I could see it sparkling on the surface in the distance. Streaks of pink and yellow appeared in the ever-distant sky as the dark purples and blues of night began appearing. A small final shine of light closer to home caught my eye, as the transparent spherical barrier that created a ceiling for Myrddin past its towers and walls reflected the light for a split second. At midday, the sun easily brightened the entire city. At dawn and dusk, it barely reached its peak.

Dusk. My shift was over for today. As a fellow knight approached me to take over my post, I gave him a nod and headed back in through the main gate. I walked through the sandstone streets as the people of Myrddin slowly began to wake up and fill the city with its familiar sense of life. A few hours ago, these very streets would have been filled with smiling people, music, and laughter. Now, I simply received greetings and smiles from the few still roaming about. I did not know any of them personally, but my armoured uniform provided me immediate respect from the people. Occasionally it bothered me; I was no more special than any of them, I simply existed in a lucky family, trained and taught from a young age.

I ducked into the knight's quarters briefly, where friends of mine were either waking up or heading to bed. I wished a few of them a good night or good luck, but instead of staying to chat or heading to bed, I changed out of my armour and into commoner's clothes before discreetly slipping back out into the streets. I was much more comfortable in the plain, brown and white flowing robes anyway. Even if I had only briefly been the status they denoted when I was young. Before my mother married.

I checked my pockets. *Good.* With that, I walked swiftly through the dark streets, avoiding eye contact. A stark difference from when I strode in wearing my armour, but in Myrddin your perceived status affects much. I walked with my head down until the elegance of my surroundings began to fade. Until carved marble with smooth sandstone foundations became rough, cracked rock and sagging roofs. There, I slowed my pace, and peeked at faces, but still walked with a sense of shyness. In this place, this far section of Myrddin that The Crown liked to pretend did not exist… here I was, in a way, more truly recognized.

Calls of "hey, Adrian! Guys, Adrian's back!" reached my ears. Sometimes I still wondered if giving them my true name was such a good idea, but I reminded myself that as long as they never learned my last name, and I played the part well, they would not know of my true status. It seemed no matter which clothes I wore, or where I was, I was always playing a part. A part where the people I interacted with, even if I called them friends, only knew some of me. Whether knight or peasant, neither were fully who I am.

Friendly, smiling faces I recognized welcomed me back and asked how my trading and hunting exploits had been going. I smiled and chatted, but was interrupted by little ones ramming into my legs excitedly. Even their scales almost seemed to shine with the joy that was beaming out of their eyes… Even though they wore tattered clothing. The three of them wrapped their webbed fingers around my leg and jumped and chattered to me happily, updating me on their young, simple lives. I smiled, genuinely now. The gills on their necks and fins on their legs were growing nicely. *Soon they will be racing around through the waves with them instead of only chasing each other across the sand,* I thought to myself.

I began handing out fish I had kept wrapped up and in the folds and pockets of my robe to those crowded around me, ignoring their polite opposition and insisting they take. Every one of them needed a little help more than I really ever had. Yet, most of the time, they were all genuinely happy. Each was content with what they had, counted their blessings, and they did not stress much. Did not worry. They had enough to get by, a roof and walls, and family. None of them really cared for much more. Whenever I visited, I could not help but notice this, the simplicity of it all, and compare it to the extravagance of the side of town I came from. Greed only seemed to increase the more one already had, the higher up you were on the social ladder the higher you strived to be. I looked around as I thought this. My peers might see only filth and struggle here, but I saw a simple joy and genuineness that I actually envied. A true sense of family as well.

<u>Lorelai</u>

I couldn't help but notice the creaking sounds that the wooden boards made as we tipped back and forth. The gentle rocking was becoming annoying as well as I stared, hands at my sides, at the pitch black ceiling above me. Though I like the sea and all, I guess, sometimes it would be nice if it just… stopped moving. Hm. I could probably find a spell to calm the tides. But did I care enough to put in that effort for a moment's solace? No. No, of course I didn't. Perhaps it was simply nearing time to get off this damn boat. As far as I knew, we were nearing the waters of my prey's territory anyway.

With that, in one swift, fluid motion, I threw the blanket off of myself to one side and swung my legs off the hammock to the other, and stood. Only to feel a blunt pressure against the top of my head, causing me to curse and bend as my hand flew to my head. *Oww! Goddamn guest cabins and their low ceilings…Ugh.* I moved my hand down to rub my forehead and my eyes with a sigh, before slowly, carefully standing as tall as the room allowed. I hunkered over to my work table, feeling ridiculous as always at the fact that I was unable to stand upright in my own --albeit temporary-- living quarters. My work station was a cluttered mess, full of parchment written in the script of a long dead language, various gemstones, assorted gold jewelry I never wore, two spare daggers, and a near empty ink well with a feathered quill protruding from its top.

I scooped up a few gems as well as a small cloth bag from a drawer and headed out towards the ladder that led up to the deck. I couldn't last a minute longer in that dark, stuffy, cramped cabin. But as I left, I placed two fingers on the outside of the closed door. A runic symbol appeared, looking as if it had been painted onto the wood, and glowed blue, letting me know that no one would be able to enter in my absence. When I removed my hand, it disappeared. I headed down the hallway.

As I lifted the trapdoor at the top of the ladder that divided below deck from up top, a pleasant chilled breeze drifted across my face, gently pushing my eyes closed and lifting the very corners of my mouth ever so slightly upward. I continued upwards after a brief moment's pause, and climbed out onto the deck. I scanned the area; no one was up or milling around yet, the deck of the schooner empty except for one lone person still on watch up at the helm. I gave him a nod and headed for the far opposite side. This crew was used to my insomnia at this point. They knew that I know what I'm doing on a ship, and trusted that I wouldn't mess with anything or go where I wasn't supposed to. Or even if there was no real trust, per say, they had agreed to at the very least put aside their preconceived negative notions about me and give me my privacy after a coin pouch had traded hands. Not that a small merchant vessel would have any intriguing nooks or crannies to get into anyway.

I walked up to the edge of the deck and leaned against the railing. The waves nudged against the ship's side below me, rhythmically swaying the boat. The days and *days* of the utterly *eternal* shifting and rocking was not only a nuisance to my work, but also only increasingly got on my nerves. The smell of the sea salt filled my senses, and was an irritating smell in such high quantities-- sea salt was a useful tool but futile if inaccessible. But regardless my gaze was lost for a few moments in the almost hypnotic rising and falling of the tide against the wood. When I finally tore my eyes from the sea's grasp, I lifted them towards the sky instead. The stars shone, dotting and filling the entire sky, creating a vast network of tiny lights. I personally found their aesthetic rather overrated and dull.

I sighed, and reached for one of the gemstones and the cloth bag concealed in my robes. I chose a green, smooth and polished stone from the ones I had grabbed; aventurine. Keeping the small stone in my palm, I opened the small cloth bag and took out a length of white string and a sewing needle. Carefully, using my body to hide what I was doing from the watchful eye of the crew mate also on deck, I slowly pushed the sewing needle against my index finger, causing a tiny well of blood to appear. Slipping the aventurine back into a smaller, more easily accessible pocket, I ran the length of the white string through the bubble of bright red blood on my fingertip, twisting and pulling the string, running it back and forth, until it was dyed entirely red. Once the blood had served its purpose, I waved my other hand over the puncture. The red string dangled from my hand as a quick flash of golden light flew out of my palm and landed on the lightly bleeding hand. A moment later, the bleeding stopped. I wiped away what was left on top of the healed skin. Then, I tied the crimson string around my aventurine, almost silently muttering a simple incantation for luck, before dropping the stone with the attached string into the waves.

I pulled a handkerchief out of my pocket, wrapping up the sewing needle and discreetly wiping the spots of blood from my fingers that came off while tying the string. Pushing everything back into my clothing, I abruptly turned back away from the sea and headed back down into my quarters. *Perhaps now I'll mix a few herbs together with an incantation to lull me to sleep for the night...I'll need all the energy I can get, as tomorrow we should be in the proper area for me to get a good bit of hunting done...*

<u>Adrian</u>

It was long past time to head back to the knight's quarters before any of my peers became suspicious or confused. I had accidentally fallen asleep for the night in one of my friends' homes in the lower area of Myrddin. If I was not back at the knights quarters soon, they would ask questions. Although I enjoyed aspects of spending time in the lower area of Myrddin for sure, I had duties--a life--elsewhere.

Once I was in a more middle-status neighborhood, I quickly ducked into an alleyway to change back into my proper status' casual robes. Passerby wouldn't be a problem once I was no longer wearing the poor status clothes and they were tucked away-- the last thing I would want is to be questioned because I owned both types of clothing. Once changed, I stepped out of the shadows, my demeanor switching back to the confident stride of a knight. I sighed, and wondered idly if I would always feel like I was pretending. Would any clothes ever actually fit me?

Pushing those thoughts away, I kicked off of the ground and swam the rest of the way back. My fins sliced through the water, propelling very quickly with ease, as I found the feeling of the ocean rushing over my scales and through my gills refreshing. Not really feeling up to small talk or sleeping anymore, and as a result not really wanting to get to the other knights so quickly, I decided to take a longer route than normal.

As I swam quickly through small streets and alleyways, I was not really paying much attention to my surroundings. That is, until the sound of crying stopped me dead in my tracks. I found myself in a dingy, empty alleyway somewhere near the edge between the middle-status and upper-status neighborhoods. I spun around, the water rippling around me; it was now the only sound that reached me. The crying had stopped. Slowly, I backtracked through the lane between homes and buildings. After a few moments, I picked up the sound of a small whimper, which then crescendoed back into crying. I lifted various bits of items, parts, things thrown away and discarded. Under it all, I discovered a tiny baby girl, barely wrapped in a thin dirty rag-- and she was cross-eyed, unable to look directly at me. *Uh oh.*

I immediately realized exactly what had happened, and in response I couldn't help but glare in the vague direction of the near upper-class neighborhoods. I spat in their direction in anger. Such an act would get me severely reprimanded if someone were to have seen me, but I was alone. And, looking back at the young, shivering, toddler… I was considering much, much worse. The right thing to do, according to the law of the Crown, anyway, would be to leave the child where I found it. Where it would likely die. Well, actually, the right thing to do according to the society of my people would have been to keep going and pretend I had not heard anything in the first place. In fact, as a knight, killing the child myself right there in that alleyway would be more acceptable and *much* more legal than the ideas that were popping into my head more and more the longer I crouched by the little girl.

Obviously this girl had been abandoned. The Crown… has a lot of strong opinions. One of which was that any child deemed "undesirable", or worse, were to be treated as though they had never been born at all. Left in the dirt. Unless the family in question wanted legal action taken against them. The Crown refuses to have '*stains*' on or in its city, they say. Simply thinking of the terms they all used made me want to punch someone in their scaly goddamn face. Upper classes are not a huge fan of girls, either, with only men allowed to be heirs and all.

But even though it was treasonous to think like this… they did not deserve this. The law was being unjust, and cruel. I mean, what did this poor adorable little kid ever do to deserve death?

I stopped.

Footsteps. Chatter.

Someone was coming.

I had been here far too long, if someone were to find me with this child… nothing good would come of it.

I looked down at the girl again. She had wide, brown eyes and was shivering.

So with that, I scooped her up, tucked her into my robes, and ran down more alleyways and tiny side streets.

I did not know where to go-- until I did. I could not raise a child, especially an "undesirable" when I always have other knights breathing down my neck. Knights that would do the legal thing in this situation… But every fibre of my being told me that the legal route was so incredibly *wrong*. I could not. Instead, I snuck around but had to move quickly. I went the opposite way from where I had been heading initially, now going back towards the less wealthy areas. I stayed in dark alleyways, sticking to the shadows. My mind was on red alert, aware of every sound coming my way. I finally made it to a home I had not visited in a couple days, at least. The owner was a good friend, and this was an emergency. Still, I felt a bit bad about barging in like this. The house was a bit run down, as all of the homes here were. I rapped on the thin door urgently. A woman with dark hair in a messy bun and bags under her eyes answered the door after a minute. When she saw me, her features darkened. Her eyes darted back and forth with fear as she scanned the alleyway around me, searching.

"You're in your knight uniform," she muttered urgently through gritted teeth.

"I know. It is urgent," I whispered back. With that, she quickly ushered me inside. She began to offer tea, and what little food she had. Her two children began to swarm me. However quite quickly the little ones sensed what must have felt like coldness towards them, as I ignored their advances, and they stepped away confused.

"Whina…" I said. There was no time for pleasantries. She stopped immediately and looked at me more closely, concerned. I hesitated. But then lifted aside a fold of cloth to reveal the little brown haired baby girl in my arms. She was asleep, somehow.

"Adrian…?" Whina was confused. She ushered the other curious children out of the room. I did not speak again until they were both out of earshot. I plopped down in a chair, suddenly feeling worn and defeated. So tired.

"She's an undesirable," I said. "I found her abandoned in an alleyway-- with the *trash.*" The disgust was evident in my voice. Whina looked shocked, and now she had to sit down too.

"Adrian!" she said, her tone somewhere between scolding and shocked. "...you will get yourself *exiled*-- or worse-- if anyone finds out." Her voice had fallen to a whisper.

"I know."

We both looked at each other, then down at the baby girl asleep in my arms with a small smile on her face.

"*Please*... take her in. I can't leave her to die simply because an unjust rule says so. Your mom made sure I did not die when they made a mistake. Now I need you to carry on that legacy. *Please.*"

<u>Morgan</u>

Adva watched me as I swam back and forth around our little clearing among a forest of kelp, gathering a few items. Her eyes moved slowly, tiredly, as she lounged. With everything we would need in a little pile, I swam up to her and nuzzled her face as her eyes began to droop closed.

"Come on," I whispered, giving her a small nudge with my nose. "It'll be cool up on the rock, that'll feel so nice for you," I coaxed. Slowly, I managed to get her to get up and, with some assistance, to swim up to the surface and flop onto the ground of the little sea cave we had claimed. I went back for the items before joining her. Then I turned into my human form. My body stretched and morphed back into a thinner, taller body. Once fully transformed, I was sitting cross legged on the cold rock with my seal skin in my hand. A small breeze blew through the cave and I shivered violently, unclothed and no longer with my seal blubber to warm me. Magic coursed through my hand and into the seal skin, turning it into a warm sealskin coat with fur trimming, which I then put on. Adva sighed.

"Why did you choose to make it a *sealskin* coat? It could've been any kind of jacket or sweater, even a blanket…" She looked up at me with dark, sad eyes. "Those things always make me think of what they'd do to us if they found us," she said plainly. I looked at her.

"Would you rather it be a human jacket? At least this way it maintains some of its integrity," I said, and with that turned towards the items I had brought up; the plants I had picked, and a rock with a flat edge and a sharp point. If there was one thing human bodies were good for, it was using tools.

"Besides," I added as I began to turn the plants into a paste, "they'll never find us again." *As long as I stop making stupid mistakes.* Adva remained silent for a few minutes. I kept working in the quiet, and she surprised me when she finally responded.

"Maybe they won't, as long as I never go into town again. One of the arms of my human form hasn't been working since this injury anyway. And maybe if I hadn't gone into town with you while hurt, it never would've happened in the first place." I stopped and turned to look at her. Her head was laid down on the stone beneath her, the white fur of her seal form standing out brightly against the dark rock, causing the pattern of black speckled across her to be seen better than normal.

The triangle of larger spots on her fin were hiding most of her horrible wide cut along her side as her fin laid over top of it. She used to love learning about human society… before one human had ended our lovely pod and given her a gruesome, ugly wound that refused to heal. Her breathing was always a bit laboured since, as she now had a hard time even when resting.

"That one time in town wasn't your fault," I said, turning back to the plants, and crushing them more forcefully now. "And as for your health, I am *going* to get you better one day, I swear it."

She didn't say much more for a while after that. I had been searching for a cure for many months now. I would find a way to cure her if it was the last thing I did, but I wished I could cure her guilt for almost getting us found out, too. Wished I could restore her curiosity, her vigor, her joy. Heal her grief. But one thing at a time. One thing at a time. First… the unhealable injury, and the sickness it had brought with it.

I was abruptly brought out of my thoughts as I felt a small, wet nudge against my bare leg; Adva had leaned over and was poking me with the edge of her tail to get my attention. I turned to her expectantly..

"…What was the human town like this time of year?" She asked the question hesitantly, as if she was afraid to even consider her old fascination with what she now thought to be a dangerous place. A small smile tugged at the corners of my lips. So I stopped what I was doing, and I went and sat cross-legged by her head, the coat wrapped loosely around my small frame. I weaved a scene for her, as I sat there and scratched her chin where I knew it felt good as a seal, and her long whiskers tickled my arm. I told her that the leaves on the trees were more green than the brightest kelp or coral, and that the branches reached so high into the sky they seemed to nearly touch the clouds. I told her that the town had planted flowers along its roads, which were blooming with an incredible myriad of colours. I told her that the human's clothes were comfortable, that the sun actually felt nice on my skin, and that the humans were kind, clean, and quiet. I told her that they had giant, brightly lit, cozy rooms full of towering piles of knowledge and stories.

Maybe I wasn't being entirely truthful, but Adva needed a ray of light. She didn't need to know that I had broken into a dark room, snuck around, been yelled at and chased out. She didn't need to know that the town was still the dusty, dry, noisy grouping of buildings it had been when she had seen it, or that all human clothes always felt itchy and constricting. As I spoke softly to her, trying to paint beautiful scenes, her eyes drifted shut and her breathing became slow and relaxed. I only stopped when I was sure she was fast asleep.

Gently, I applied the cold plant paste to the gash on my little sister's side. I let magic flow into the paste as I held it, hoping with all my might that the natural healing properties of the plants plus selkie magic would help. Her skin was hot to the touch, especially around the wound, and I knew deep in my chest that this wouldn't be nearly enough. We would be lucky if it did much of anything more than I had already managed to do. I sighed; I would have to go back, back to the surface. But regular human knowledge wasn't doing us any good. This injury was magical, that much was obvious, and as the months had passed since the raid on our pod that had caused it, Adva was only getting more sick. I imagined that her incredible amounts of bottled up grief, plus a few touches of guilt, somehow had a little something to do with her worsening physical health too.

I needed better solutions. I needed more magic, stronger magic, *different* magic. Something. My gaze drifted outside the mouth of the cave, over the strengthening waves, and towards where I knew land would be. I needed a magic user… maybe even a human one. I shuddered. But after losing our entire family and pod, and then later being exiled from a normal seal pod-- for being too sick, too different, drawing too much negative attention...And the few hidden cities populated by sea creatures believing the rumours and stereotypes about selkies instead of *looking* at the sick and injured orphan and sister in front of them… The ocean didn't have our answer. Which left only the land.

I rubbed the edging of my seal skin jacket between my fingers absently. It had almost been taken from me the last time I had ventured onto the land. I hated it there. But if I lost my seal skin, my life might as well be over. I wouldn't be able to get back to Adva, I wouldn't be able to be myself, Adva would be all alone and getting worse… I couldn't take that risk. I had always thought that my seal skin was safest with me, where I could protect it. But the reaches of the ocean are vast, with countless nooks and crannies and hidden spots. Perhaps it would be safer in one of them, considering how that hadn't been the first time I had almost been caught or found out by humans. I didn't seem to be good enough at keeping it free of danger. I certainly couldn't leave it with Adva; she wasn't strong enough to protect it, it would only put a target on her back to leave something seen as valuable to humans with her.

It was decided then. I would swim out, and find the perfect hidden, secluded, and covered spot to leave it. It would have to be somewhat near a cave or edge of land, considering how terrible human lungs and limbs are underwater. Secure enough that the waves or a curious passing animal couldn't grab it. I could do that.

I gave Adva a kiss on the forehead. She would know where I had gone when she woke up-- I think we both knew the poultice wasn't good enough. The sea cave was secluded enough to be safe, and she could always return to our home in the kelp on her own. I wouldn't be gone too long.

Turning back into my seal form, I took one last look at my little sister and the sea cave she slept in. Her breathing was calm and a slight smile was on her face. I slipped into the water silently, and left.

Milan

I'd been living in my little village and helping my Ma out in her shop my entire life. Everyday was almost always, roughly, the same. No surprises. Everybody else loves it that way. But one day, something new happened; a ship docked at the edge of our little beach I was always being pulled away from. I had never seen a real ship before, and this one was but a baby sailboat, but I was more excited than a rabbit in a carrot patch. Of course, I had to hide my feelings. The last thing I needed was another scolding from Ma, especially only a day after the last one. All my friends and family were mighty suspicious of the man who got off the boat and walked up our hill. *I* had to stop myself from accidentally bowling him over or pestering the man with questions about what life was like at sea.

Turns out, the man was younger than I was by a few years, and was simply bringing letters and parcels between his rich family and their rich family friends. That definitely took the edge off of my excitement, I'll admit. He was just stopping by the village to grab a quick bite to eat before continuing his journey. He headed towards a cluster of our shops, and it looked like the whole village was watching him go, all curious. Strangers don't tend to stop by our tiny little neck of the woods. But as the gaze of everyone else followed this boy into town, mine drifted back… to the boat. Seeing my chance to go right up to the water and *see a real boat up close*, well, I couldn't help myself, I had only ever seen one from a great distance before. So, I crept up. I slid my hand across its sleek sides, nudged it and watched it shift on top of the water. I don't know how long I spent admiring the thing, but it must have been several minutes, 'cause before I knew it, someone was calling out to me. Presumably to punish me for being not only near the water, but on a *boat*. Except this time, it was a voice I didn't immediately recognize.

I spun around, my hands flying up in defense, my mind already whirling to try to come up with an excuse for my actions. Then I noticed that it was just the boy, and he was alone. He chuckled, and apologized for startling me.

"You're a fan of boats, huh?" he asked, walking up to me next to it. I paused, surprised. I had never even considered the question before, it was outrageous to.

"Yea, I...I guess I am."

"You ever been on one?" he replied, hopping up onto the deck of the sailboat. I shook my head. He gestured back, motioning for me to join him. My eyes widened and without even meaning to, I looked towards my village, where everyone had gone.

"...I don't know what your people's problem is with strangers, but I promise I won't set sail and steal you or your stuff. Heck, look at you, I couldn't kidnap *you* even if for some crazy reason I wanted to. My father also frowns upon inviting strangers to sail far away with me. *But,* none of your people will be heading back this way for at least a few minutes," he said.

I was *so* tempted. The boy stood up on the little boat, towering over me now, and gazed out and up at my village. He held onto the mast to steady himself, and as the wind blew through his hair I was imagining me in his place. Out on the open sea, the wind in my hair and the sun bouncing off of the ocean water that surrounded me. *Ahh...* I jumped onto the boat, making it lurch and surprising the boy, who just managed to keep his footin'. I nodded to him, and he smiled back. I carefully, oh so cautiously, walked up to the far edge of the boat. The one farther from the shore. I lost track of how many or how few minutes I stood there, feeling every little shift in the tide beneath me. The sun hit my face, hit the water too, and I smiled. I suddenly realized… I was only a few feet off of the shore of my home, and already I had never felt so free.

It was far, far too soon before the boy was telling me that my people were coming back. Probably looking for me. Again. I tore my eyes from the sea. Again. And stepped off of a boat-- for the first time-- and onto the shore. I gave my thanks to the boy, and was about to head up the hill so I wouldn't be caught by the water's edge again, when to my surprise the young boy stopped me.

"The last time I saw anybody look at the sea with that much *love* and admiration… and longing... it was after my dad had had to retire from sailing," he paused there, looking me dead in the eyes. "I don't want to step on your toes, and I don't know anything about your village," he continued. "But I do know that a passion like that should never be stifled."

His words surprised me so much that I didn't know what to say. I simply nodded, and he nodded back, and his gaze let me go. I headed up the hill. But as I reached its peak, I took one last look back. Just in time to see the little sailboat, with the young but wise little sailor, drift back out to sea. And I felt… a familiar ache in my chest. Except this time it refused to be ignored; it didn't want to go away.

I woke up from a nap later in the day and the sad, unnamed ache was still where my heart was supposed to sit. I couldn't shake it. Before I even really knew what I was doing, before I had even admitted my decision to myself, I was putting my things in a bag. All I knew was that I couldn't go another day, or another night, living the boring life that was expected of me and hiding my true thoughts. Something in me was snapping. Yet not in that anger way, just that, well, it was all finally enough.

My Ma walked in as I was finishing packing up my belongings. When she asked me what I was doing, where did I think I was going, I stood up and faced her with tears in my eyes. That stopped her in her tracks. I sat her down, and held her tiny hands in mine. I told her that it was time for me to leave. That I loved her, but I wanted to do more in my life than just be her son and work in her shop, or work carrying lumber. In a rare moment of understanding, the tears in my eyes were reflected in hers. She hugged me and made me promise to send letters from wherever I ended up, and to take care of myself, not take food from strangers, and to never forget about her or the tiny village I had always called home.

"I could never forget about y'all," I replied, holding back tears as I wrapped her frail little body in my embrace.

I guess maybe she had never really believed my excuses about why I was always down by the sea after all.

<u>Lorelai</u>

Typically I spent my time during the day in my quarters, as there were always men running around all over the deck during daylight hours. They often did not take kindly to me, making horribly rude comments behind my back about either my gender or my skin colour. *Idiots.* It would take every ounce of willpower I had not to immediately blow them off the ship entirely or whip out my sword and a snarky remark. I could easily defeat them if I wanted to. But, nevertheless, I was free to wander the ship as I pleased, and they *did* give me a cabin fit only for someone of a much shorter stature than me. Really it was more of a cuddy, hardly deserved to be called a full cabin... I could only take so much crouching, crawling, hitting my head, or lying in a thin hammock with a constant slight swing. *Ugh.* Attempting to get any of my work done wasn't easier or any more of a pleasant experience. So I decided to go up during the day to be able to actually stretch my legs and get some fresh air.

I was walking around the deck, minding my own business while all of the crew members avoided my gaze, when abruptly a loud sound from below deck went off and shook the entire ship. Crew members grabbed onto anything they could reach to steady themselves, a few of them holding onto each other or managing to keep their footing as the boat rocked heavily for a few moments. I stood appearing calm and collected. *Shit… nothing on a normal old merchant boat would ever cause that.* For a few seconds after, nobody said anything. It felt as if no one was breathing, and that in all the world only the sea still moved. Then, all at once, commotion hit. People yelled and ran around, most of them swarming to down below deck where the sound had come from. I stood amidst all of it, like the eye in the storm.

I wasn't sure what to do immediately. I was pretty certain I knew what had caused the issue, and that meant trouble for me. I must've made an error with the strength and size of the defense spell; this wasn't supposed to happen. But it was already far too late to stop the entire crew from seeing the scene that surely awaited them. I didn't even realize I had reached for the inside of my boot until I felt the familiar texture and weight of my dagger in my hand.

I listened as angry, incredulous cries erupted from below deck. They cried out in anguish at the sight of their fallen friend who had been unfortunate enough to try to go where he shouldn't have, especially when my spell strength was off. I heard them settle into a mutter in the distance, accompanied by shuffling and the creaking of wooden boards. I could see in my mind's eye what they were finding, and my grip on my dagger tightened. My work, my spells… The thundering sound of many furious men running back towards the ladder and clambering onto the deck before me was next. I stared them down as they shifted to surround me, but not before an incredible cry erupted from the group of them. It was filled with anger and a hint of sadness as they screamed in my face,

"WITCH!"

They weren't wrong, but that was no way to treat a lady, especially a guest.

Suddenly I was being surrounded by swords. I smirked. I tossed my dagger high in the air, sending it flipping. They couldn't help but watch it soar. It came back down quickly, and when it did, it was the length of a small sword. It was also in my hands, the blade near a pirate's neck. To their surprise, I stepped back and clashed swords with the fellow instead. I'm not in the business of killing humans-- at least not for no reason, not if there's another way out. While fighting off one of them with my blade against theirs, I muttered under my breath and flung my free hand out to the left side in a flourish. My crystal necklace warmed against my skin under my clothes, and the three men to my left were thrown backwards, off their feet, landing and hitting their heads hard enough on the wooden deck that for now they remained still. This briefly created an opening in the hostility surrounding me, I went for it, able to only for a moment create a shield around myself from their advances, feeling the familiar but growing heat on my collarbone.

I spun back towards my attackers.

"You fellas want to see what a real *witch* can do?!" I spat angrily. For a second, this made them hesitate. Then, per the captain's orders, they came at me once more. I felt they weren't putting every ounce of strength into it anymore though; perhaps they were beginning to second-guess taking on and attempting to kill a feisty sea witch out on her own domain. *Ah yes,* I realized. *The sea. A perfect weapon.*

Without hesitation, I glared at all of them.

"Tip for you boys, next time, don't disturb a witch's things," my voice was dainty and sweet, catching them off guard.

With that moment of time, I grabbed my necklace out from under my shirt, my ears barely catching the sound of it's thin metal chain scraping against the metal choker above it. Even chaos and murder attempts against me couldn't stop me from noticing that sound when my necklace slid up, apparently.

I held the pointed crystal talisman at the end of my necklace fully enclosed in my palm. I began to chant, a deep, loud, guttural chant in a language that no one else but me had spoken in a long, long time. My eyes fluttered closed. I opened them again when I felt the wind begin to stir a little stronger, and clouds drifted over the sun, casting us all in a shadow. My blue grey eyes began to glow a startling, icy blue as I felt the heat of my talisman grow uncomfortable, nearing painful, in my palm. The wind picked up, lifting my hair up to frame my face as if it was beginning to float. The waves grew, tossing and lurching the ship, making everyone else stumble and fall, unable to reach me, while my feet stayed moored on the edge. I never stopped chanting, my piercing gaze unfocused.

The men cried out in surprise and anger, the captain shouted orders, trying to be heard above the increasing wind. I barely heard any of it. It all might as well have been very far away. Instead, the sound of the waves filled my ears, blocking out every sound except for the beating of my steady heart that echoed like a war drum in my ears. The sea spray and strong wind didn't faze me as the heat of my talisman in my hand neared burning. The ship lurched and rocked drastically. The sky was grey then as waves began to rise higher and higher, splashing on the deck before me. One giant wave crested behind me, and I turned, and jumped into the storming sea. When that wave fell, I was gone.

Leaving the pirates in the storm they provoked.

Chapter Three - Foreign Waters

<u>Milan</u>

When I left my village… I wasn't totally sure where to go at first. But if I knew one thing, it was that I wanted to sail. It was a lengthy trek to the main harbour-- t'was a ways from the tiny bay near my village. I had to stop to rest up, but when I finally got to the waterfront the next morning… I couldn't believe my eyes. Ship after ship, of many different sizes and types, stretched out in a line before me. Their sails towered high above me, and as I looked at them-- beautiful, clean, billowing freely in the sea breeze, a wide grin spread all across my face. But the pretty sails were quickly forgotten when my gaze caught the gorgeousness of the sea past them. The little lapping waves near my home were nothing in comparison to the white tipped, perfect blue ones that seemed to continue on and on forever here.

As excited as a kid in a candy shop, I went to approach the workers of the closest ships. I wanted to join them, so I asked if they were hiring. Some, at first, pretended they hadn't even heard me. Many, many others scoffed and turned me away when I admitted I had no experience sailing. I began to feel a little bad about the whole thing. *What am I thinkin'? No one's goin' t' take on a big guy from a tiny*

"Ey! Ey you! Big guy over there! Yeah you! Come here!" A short, kinda scrawny guy in a sailor's uniform was jumping and running, weaving through the people on the docks and waving. Apparently, he had been trying to get my attention while I had been busy walking away in my worries. I paused, watching him quizzically as he made his way over to me. *Wait!* I realized. *This could be good...* I was getting excited again now, but I tried to calm myself.

"I hear you've spent the past hour around here looking for a sailing job? I hear from my buds you don't know how to sail, which, by the way, is maybe something you should've figured out before looking to get a job on a boat. But! My fellow crew recently lost a couple members, and we could use some muscle," When he said that, he stabbed a finger at my bicep and smirked. A giant, wide smile covered my face.

"I take it that's a yes? Wonderful! So big guy, what's your name?" he asked, beginning to lead me towards his ship.

"M-" I automatically began, before stopping myself.

The question, which should have been a simple one, stopped me in my tracks. I didn't really, uh, feel much like a 'Milan' out here. Milan worked for his Ma, never left his village, and only loved the

ocean in secret. Milan had only ever seen one teeny bit of it. But now…
now I was staring out at moving water that reached the horizon and
seemed to touch the sky. I was about to board a ship! A real, bonafide,
large, *ship*, which I was gonna be a member of! Milan never would
have done that. Milan just would've dreamed to. But the boy was
looking at me all curious now, as I was taking a moment too long to
answer.

"... Miles," I heard myself say. "Yeah, Miles!" I said, more
confident now. I had traveled miles and miles to get here, and I
imagined I was headed to maybe become a person who was miles
different from Milan the sheltered village boy. I liked it. It fit. The ship
crew boy chuckled to himself quietly.

"Nice to meet you, Miles."

Adrian

I was getting my things together for work and getting dressed
the morning after leaving Whina's house, trying not to think about
much, when I overheard other knights saying something that chilled me
to the bone. They talked of a newly open case they were working on.

"-Yeah, a woman was charged with harbouring an undesirable
this morning. Poor hag's probably going to be killed." Their tone was
nonchalant, apathetic. Casual.

I froze where I stood as my heart and mind began to race. *Dear god what have I done to poor Whina? And they find out so soon?* But their conversation was not over yet. The other knight responded,

"Oh yeah, definitely, once we find her."

A large breath released from my lungs in relief. I listened in on the rest of their conversation as discreetly as I could. They said that someone had heard crying in an old alleyway, only to figure out where it was coming from in time to see someone *in a knight uniform,* with a muscular build and shoulder length black hair quickly fleeing a now silent and empty back alley. When I heard this, I could feel the colour draining from my face. Blood pounded in my ears, but I kept listening. The witness reported it, only to have someone else report a few hours later that they thought they saw a tiny girl with crossed eyes and difficulty walking playing on their neighbors porch. *Whina.*

Without thinking, I left, and swam as fast as I could. I did not know where I was going, but I could not stay surrounded by knights for a second longer with such an accurate description of me swimming around their minds in that context. Somehow Whina must have realized she had been spotted and fled with the kids just in time… I was not sure I would be so lucky. Not that she would be in such a good place right now either wherever she had decided to go. I rushed through the streets, hardly able to think or focus as my chest tightened and I nearly ran over several people.

Two spears clashed in an X in front of me, nearly slicing my nose. Knights, technically my peers, stood in front of me with their helmets down, their faces hidden. I spun around, only to find two more broad shouldered knights, also with their faces obscured, rapidly closing in behind me, swords drawn. *Swords? Instead of spears? Did they really think I was going to attack them?* I was weaponless, defenseless--I had not yet grabbed them for the day in my panic. A deep voice boomed from under one of the helmets of those with swords, declaring that I was being arrested, brought to see the High Council for a first level count of treason for disobeying a high law of the Crown. I recognized the voice. We had been friends, brothers in arms. Now we were criminal and authorities. He said that if I fought back they would not hesitate to restrain me, or protect themselves. *Ha. 'Protect themselves'. I knew what* that *truly meant.* My gaze was drawn to the large, gleaming swords.

My eyes dropped to the sea floor. I raised my arms in surrender, turned around, and put my webbed hands behind my back. The knights closed in, and I felt the cold, rough clasp of metal being snapped around my wrists and tightened a little too much. They dragged me to face back in the direction I had come from, and for the entire walk, spear tips dug into my back and every other person around moved aside to stare and whisper in shock. After all, I was still in my knight uniform.

They brought me to a building that towered over all of the rest in Myrddin. It was made almost entirely of pure white marble, complete with a domed roof made of glass and inlaid with gold. Below that, extremely detailed and realistic carvings of heroic Myrddins of the past circled the building high above where I stood in clasps. It was the building of The Crown. Most people of Myrddin would never enter its walls— how ironic that breaking the higher laws would allow one escorted access. I had been inside once before though; when I was knighted. This time was an opposite, stark difference from the fanfare and ceremony of that day. All that could be heard was the echoing steps of the knights boots up the stairs, and the hushed whispers of anyone in the area. The water surrounding me felt thick with tension and as still as ice.

I was led through their great halls, over red carpets and past magical torchlight. I was pushed up staircases, and forced—shoved—to the ground before the very throne I had once excitedly kneeled before to be given an honour, a title. The throne was gold-plated, and the man who sat upon it was equally as extravagant. The Crown wore flowing red and dark purple robes that draped over his frame and drifted gently up and down in the water. A gemstone-encrusted crown sat on his light brown hair, with gold and silver bands weaving throughout the headpiece. His green triton scales reflected the sun, and I could not help but notice some of his scales were iridescent as their rainbow reflection caught my eye. For a moment, I was in awe at being face to face with the all-powerful, all-mighty Crown.

But his eyes… I had not gotten a good look at his eyes the first time we had met, so much had been going on. There seemed to be nothing special about them at first, they were green with hints of blue. But now, when our eyes met as I knelt before him, I saw a deep *hatred* inside him. And more anger than I had ever seen in someone, actively being held back. It shocked me. But I had a feeling it had less to do with me, but more so with who I had saved. When the Crown himself finally spoke to me… disdain and disgust filled his voice. The entire time they read about my crime and spoke down about the young children whose only crime was being different, but whose punishment was supposed to be death… I said nothing. And thought only of the adorable, sweet little girl who would have a life now because of me. The only things I had to say to the Crown would only get me more counts of treason. *How could anyone have so much hate within them that they order the deaths of countless innocent children? How could such a triton be revered?* I did not meet his gaze again.

"Adrian Cadmus. Once a valued knight, for your crime of treason and disobeying my word, I should have you killed immediately on public trial to set an example…" My eyes widened in horror as my legs began to shake beneath me. "However," he continued, "You did good work for me for years, and I am not cruel." The Crown's words surprised me, but at the last words I held back a scoff. I knew of the rumours about him. "So, I will grant you mercy. You are to be stripped of your title and belongings, and exiled permanently, at once. You are to wander the ocean depths, forever ostracized, and never allowed home. We will tell the city you have been killed. But be forewarned; regardless of your exiled status, you are still a subject of the Crown of Myrddin. Break more of our laws, and you will receive further punishment. As you know, spies who are faithful to me abound outside these walls." He hit the bottom of his bejeweled staff on the ground when he finished, causing a deep thud to echo through the chamber.

Then they took my uniform, left me in rags, and discreetly threw me out the back of the city. The city whose walls I had never ventured from before.

But now, all of a sudden, I found myself outside the glowing lights of my home. The sudden change in water pressure made me feel light-headed, and I could hardly see for a moment in the darkness. I was alone, cold, soon to be thought of as a dead criminal by my family and friends, and doomed to never be accepted by any other creature or community of the deep. I fell to my knees with my face in my hands as the weight of what had happened crashed down upon me.

<u>Morgan</u>

I had just secured my seal skin in its hidden location, after searching for quite some time and finally finding an acceptable spot. I was swimming as quickly as my little human limbs could towards the surface-- luckily I was, of course, an expert at holding my breath underwater. But the waves began to pick up, a little too much, unexpectedly. Enough so that they shoved me away from my goal- *shit*. I had always been able to see a sea storm coming miles away, but as the waves only continued to become more chaotic, I had to admit that one must be coming. No storm had *ever* appeared so quickly and forcefully, with such lack of warning, in all of my decades of living. The waves pushed me and tossed my small human form back and forth, and I felt my chest tighten and begin to hurt, as my heartbeat began to rush. I was pushed down, my vision became blurry, and I fought desperately against the water I usually called home. I was no match for it. This had never happened before-- then again, I had never been in a storm as a human, much less while underwater. This storm was moving through the area *fast*.

The reality of the situation began to dawn on me as my head felt fuzzy and black spots appeared on the edge of my vision. My heart was racing now, thumping loudly and forcefully in my chest. My body screamed for air, my brain screamed for peace, as my mind raced. *I am going to die here. I am a selkie and I am about to drown, I can't do anything right, and Adva will never know what happened, and she will die and my body will never be found and--* My head ached and pounded, as the black edges of my vision slowly encroached on more and more of my sight. The water continued to throw me around so strongly that I no longer knew which direction I was supposed to be trying to head in. I felt betrayed by the very element that had always been home. Before the darkness swallowed my vision whole, I could have sworn I saw a blurry, tall humanoid form appear. They saw me and swam through the rough seas with ease, heading below me. *No... my skin...* but before I could even be sure that it wasn't a hallucination, the black overtook me and I lost consciousness under the roaring waves.

<u>Miles</u>

The young lad brought me aboard the wonderful ship, and on the inside I was jumping and hollering with glee at seeing a true, large beauty of a ship up close and in person and to even be *on* one! 'Course I had to contain myself, got to make a good first impression. They showed me around, made sure I knew not to touch certain things, and left me to swab the deck. I didn't mind, they could tell me to clean the floor by licking it and I'd do it with a smile, as long as I got to stay on the ship when it set sail.

As I was cleaning, I was really the only one paying any attention to the ocean's edge. So when what looked like a person, a man, dressed only in sopping wet rags was left behind, limp on the sand, as a wave retreated once more, I didn't believe my eyes at first. Nobody else reacted; nobody else had seen right away. After a moment I realized my eyes weren't playing tricks on me, and called some of the others and ran off the boat towards the person. The others on my boat hesitated, their eyes shifting between one another, but I had to check on the poor person.

But, before I reached him, he lifted his head and coughed loudly, spitting up water. Immediately now, others began rushing to the guy's aid. *What took ya so long?* I easily dragged him out of the water, and then knelt by his head while others began to crowd around and somebody hollered for a medic. The man looked to be in his mid-twenties, with dark skin and shoulder length black hair. He had some muscle to him, but not a ton. Green eyes stood out, looking back at me curiously. Whoever he was, he didn't look like he was from around here. He still seemed pretty out of it, as he looked around at all of us and at every little thing with wide eyes.

The captain decided to bring him up onto our ship briefly, as it was the closest place out of the water and off of the sand, where the medic could take a look at him when she arrived and he could warm up. I carried him up onto the boat and sat him down on a bed in one of the unused quarters below deck, and one of the others wrapped a blanket around his shoulders. The medic showed up around then, checking his pulse and such. He stared at her and flinched a little in surprise when she put two fingers to his neck, and stared at *everything* with this look of wide-eyed disbelief-- he even looked down at himself the same way.

But when they tried to ask him basic questions like his name and whatnot… I'm not even sure how to describe what happened there. He opened his mouth, but instead of a response, out came a long series of sounds that included clicks, whines, and something that was kinda like a quiet shriek? It all had a sort of upbeat tone to it, but it was definitely the weirdest thing I had ever heard in my life. Now it was everyone else's turn to stare in shock and surprise at *him,* and when he looked around at all of us then, he silently closed his mouth and his shoulders shrunk into him, his gaze falling down to his hands in his lap. He fiddled with the blanket. *I wonder what on* earth *is going on in that head of yours right now…* The medic, confused as any of us, tried to gently ask him where he was from, but he just looked at her and made more click and whistle-like sounds, a genuine, questioning look on his face. When the medic's face was again filled with confusion, he let out a tiny sigh. The way this guy tried to speak was unlike anything any of us had ever heard of.

A memory suddenly came to mind; my old Papi, telling me stories from his years of travelling the countryside as a youth. Long, long, before our townsfolk became afraid of the sea. When I was just a little tyke, he had told me all sorts of wonderful stories about strange creatures he had stumbled upon. Even ones that looked like humans, but weren't, not really. Everyone else thought Papi was a little crazy, but he had told me that every word was true, and I believed him. He even lent me books talking all about 'em. But there was no way this nearly-drowned man could… could not be… or could he?

It didn't seem to matter too much to everybody else, as he was left for a few minutes in the mostly empty ships quarter we had put him in, leaving one person to keep an eye on him. The Captain of the ship met in his office with the first and second mates on what to do with the guy now. People slowly went back to work, while gossiping heavily about the whole situation. But I couldn't just forget, or put it to the back of my mind and go back to work. I tried, I really tried to focus on polishing and swabbing for a couple minutes... But before long, I noticed no one was paying much attention to me, so I slipped below deck. I had an idea.

When I went to the room they had left the guy in, I cracked open the door to see the man from the sea sitting by the porthole, wrapped in the blanket, very closely examining a copper piece with a smile on his face. The crew member who had been left to watch him sat in a chair by the door on the opposite side of the room looking bored. When I told him I was switching with him he was happy to not question it, leaving me to sit in his chair and close the door behind him. The man stared at me from across the small space with wide, questioning eyes.

"You must be mighty scared," I said. He didn't respond. Slowly, I took a piece of blank crumpled parchment out of my pocket and stood up. "I'm jus' gonna go over to that desk there by ya and see if there's a quill and some ink, okay?" I wanted to warn him before I moved towards him; I've been told that I can be a bit scary when I never meant to be. He nodded excitedly, clicking and whirring sounds coming out of his mouth. *How does he even make those crazy sounds,* I wondered while getting up and going over to open all the drawers in the back of the desk.

"Ah! Here we go!" I exclaimed, having found what we needed. The sea man jumped to his feet, throwing the blanket off of him-- only for me to look back a second later after hearing a heavy *thump.* I tried to not laugh, but the poor man was briefly sprawled out on the ground! He must have slipped on the edge of the blanket. He quickly and awkwardly clambered back up to his feet though, a few little quiet clicks escaping him, and jumped over towards the desk. I decided to ignore this interesting way of moving in the small space, and handed him the parchment and quill. He picked up the quill, fumbling with it for a moment, and dipped it in the ink. He was holding it pretty oddly, but that was okay.

"What's your name?" I asked him, motioning to the paper as if I was writing. His writing was slow, big, and very messy-- but it was in English, luckily. I watched as he struggled to keep the quill still and controlled in his hand.

"If you don't mind my askin'... how'd ya learn to write like that? Who taught ya?" I gently prodded. Writing, or at least writing in English, was clearly not something he did often. I was hoping that might be a clue towards where he was from, maybe even why he turned up half drowned. He stopped what he was writing and paused. He restarted below what he had already written. 'Books' it simply said. After showing it to me, he finished writing what he had been trying to say first. 'I am Adrian' the paper said.

"Adrian! Your name's Adrian?" I asked. He nodded excitedly. "My name is Milan, but I'm gonna go by Miles around here. Nice to meet you Adrian!" I said, extending a hand to him. He stopped, and looked down at my hand, his brow furrowing, his head tilting as you could see the thoughts moving in his head. I chuckled, causing him to look up at me suddenly.

"Your hand, Adrian," I said, nodding to the hand he was supposed to use. He looked down at his own hand and raised it, looking at me quizzically. I slowly reached for his wrist, and lowered his hand to my still extended one, and gave him a hand shake.

I shook my head, grinning. After letting go, I motioned back to the paper and asked him where he was from. His face darkened. Somehow I had been expecting more confusion, but he had a strong expression of knowing, remembering something negative. Then his face fell even a little more, towards sadness, and he scribbled onto the parchment. 'Nowhere, now'. He handed me the piece of paper with the response, and then sat back on the edge of the bed, wrapped himself in the blanket, and stared out of the porthole at the ocean. I hadn't meant to upset him.

I left after that, leaving Adrian the quill, parchment, and ink. I felt I should go tell the Captain what I had discovered-- but the ideas of him maybe not being human were gonna be my secret to keep.

Chapter Four - Surge

<u>Adrian</u>

What even possessed me to decide to turn into this human form? I do not think I have ever even used it before. Most creatures of Myrddin do not have one, or even have anywhere near the capabilities for one; one of the many "perks" of being high status, I guess. Ha. Nothing about being high status in Myrddin was a perk. Except for the food on your table and the roof over your head. The clothes on your back though? A curse. I know these awkward, clumsy, ridiculous forms were only supposed to be used in specific emergencies, like if humans ever invaded or something, but hey, being exiled was an emergency to me. If only I had remembered that these damn things can hardly swim or even breathe. Besides, humans are really weird and inept but they don't seem so bad. They took me in, gave me this--what, blanket? Blankets are *not* this soft but okay. I wonder if they will let me keep it?

My thoughts were interrupted by the door to the room they had put me in creaking back open. I turned to see a man dressed in a different uniform than what everyone else here wore. He had on a long, dark jacket with yellow-gold edges and buttons. It was open over a plain shirt and pants, and he had a silly large hat on his head. He was the only one who wore the jacket or hat, and they seemed to listen to him, so he must have been an authority here. I wondered how far his authority extends.

"COME, SEE REST OF BOAT WITH ME? TIME FOR YOU TO LEAVE SOON." He was speaking slowly and very loudly, while making big hand gestures. He definitely did not ever do this with anyone else here. *Huh.* I mean I could understand him fine… Surely he knew enunciating like that would not make a difference? Regardless, weird good authority is still good authority, so I got up and followed him.

"No, no, please, leave the blanket here," he gestured to the oh so soft blanket still wrapped around my shoulders and back towards the bed. *Oh.*

After I put it back down, he led me without speaking through a hallway with several doors, and then up a ladder. *Wait. Humans have stairs, right? Do they know about stairs?* But I was already nearing the top of the ladder. I climbed out onto the wooden floor, and when I looked towards the land I could not believe what their structures looked like. Somewhat similar to ours, however somehow much less elegant and pretty than higher Myrddin, yet also more put together and cleaner than lower Myrddin. Fascinating. Look at that they even figured out glass windows at some point, good for them!

Wait. What was that smell? I looked around for the offending odor and quickly found it-- one of the men on the boat was taking a break, eating some sort of weird thing with rotten fish in it. I raised an eyebrow. *Humans are so weird.* None of them even seemed to notice the stench of rotting fish. *Ugh.*

The authority of the boat took me over to sit down with him on some barrels--again, weird choice but okay-- and pulled out a piece of parchment and an ink and quill. *If they keep insisting on knowing where I am from I might just tell them and see what happens at this rate.* He passed it over to me-- and suddenly I had a question. It was really bugging me. I scribbled 'Do you like eating rotten fish?' on the parchment before he had a chance to ask me a question, and handed it back to him. He took it, and made this deep, repetitive sound with a big smile on his face. Miles had done a smaller version of it before, I still was not sure what it meant. He showed a few others, and they all made similar loud, repetitive sounds. If they had not been smiling I would have been worried.

"No my boy, no of *course* not! Do your people do such a thing? Surely that isn't good for you either?" he managed to eventually answer. A look of disgust crossed my face and I shook my head vigorously. *We are not* animals. *But wait, it is not good for them either? So then why was that guy--* I saw someone with the same type of food, also reeking the offending odor, head towards us. The authority figure's attention looked to it expectantly. *But, wait, no, you cannot just-- are they trying to poison him?!* I leapt to my feet, lunging towards the food, but my weird human feet slipped out from under me and I fell face-first flat on the wooden floor. As I was falling, I managed to reach forward and slap the disgusting food out of the giver's hand as I had wanted to, bringing it down with me. The weirdly shaped thing protruding out of the middle of my face hit painfully on the wood. *Oww… At least I got the food out of his hand, I suppose.* I glanced up, rubbing my--what was it? Right, nose-- everyone was staring at me again. At least this time I could explain. I clambered to my feet and scribbled down on the parchment 'the fish in those meals is rotten'.

The authority figure looked very confused when he read my message this time.

"Are you sure? How do you know?" he asked, incredulous. I poked the strange human nose on my face-- that's normally where I would smell through. *Not sure why the protruding skin and such is necessary though, makes for quite a painful landing.* The authority figure got a look in his eyes I didn't recognize.

"Your name was, what, Aidan? Adrian?" he asked. I nodded at the last one.

"I guess multiple people feeling sick today wasn't a coincidence… Can you always tell so early and so easily when food is rotten?" he asked. I paused.

'If it is from the sea. Can you not tell?' I scribbled. The authority figure did not respond, instead he looked at me with thoughts in his eyes that I could not read and a slight smile on his face.

"…Do you have anywhere you should be going back to? Because if not, that could be useful for us-- if you want to stick around."

My eyes widened in disbelief. I was shocked he was serious. When he handed me back the parchment, flipped over, he could probably barely read my very quick, excited scribbles of 'Yes! I will stay! Thank you!' The man smiled at my enthusiasm.

"Good," he said, "Because we set sail this afternoon."

<u>Lorelai</u>

I walked across the smooth but uneven stone, freezing cold against my bare feet, my beloved boots long since abandoned to the rough waves. I ran my fingers through my sopping wet hair, attempting to shake out the sea salt and regain some semblance of a good appearance. The only sounds I could hear was the water dripping off of my own body, the waves behind me, and a small wind whistling through the cavern. I shivered. *I'm soaked, I'm freezing, and now I'm stuck in a damn cave unless I get back in the water. Ughh... The only good thing about those filthy pirates discovering that I was a witch was that now I finally have peace and quiet... Well, that and the fact that I picked up another thing as a result...* My gaze drifted over towards the corner of the tiny cave where I kept my now meager belongings, and a smile crept up my face. My new little piece of luck also laid there. I was absolutely certain that the day I would be able to use it would be the best day of my life.

A small, constant flow of heat still emanated from my necklace and warmed my collarbone. *I never did get the storm to cease, did I... Well, It's no easy task. However, a constant stream of power going is not good right now, no matter the size...* I wrapped my hands around the talisman. *...And it has been quickly moving away.*

<u>Miles</u>

The first few days on the ship with it actually sailing were incredible. I started learning the ropes of the ship, how to sail, how things worked 'round here. They also kind of put me in charge of checking in on Adrian every once in a while. Make sure he didn't get into no trouble-- he never really did, 'cept for touching the occasional thing he shouldn't've, but he was good about remembering what not to touch once you told him. Everything was going swell, until one day I noticed Adrian desperately trying to show a note he had written to everyone on board, and no one was paying him any attention.

I walked up to him--he's a nice guy, just doesn't speak the language, y'know? Doesn't mean he should be ignored-- said hello, and checked the note he was pushing. 'A bad storm is coming' it said. I looked up; there wasn't a cloud in the sky, it was a beautiful sunny day. And the other actual sailors he had shown the note to could usually read the signs for these kinds of things in time, and they had ignored Adrian. I looked down at him, and he looked genuinely worried. But when I asked him how he was so sure of this, he wrote down 'I can tell. I can feel it.' Which. Uh. Wasn't exactly the biggest vote of confidence. I wanted to believe in the guy, I really did, but I had no more pull here than he did.

So, before long, I had to leave him to it. He seemed a little hurt that no one believed him, but… what was I supposed to do?

Adrian

No one would listen to me. Ridiculous humans, do they not know that the weather, the ocean, the sky, all acts far beyond what they can tell? Everyone went to sleep that night except for me and one person on watch besides me. Because of this, I noticed when the waves began to move only a tiny bit faster. I felt the difference on my skin when the wind barely started to pick up. After that it was not long before the waves were thrashing, hard and wild, and the other crew member went to go get the authority-- who everyone called "Captain"-- and wake others. I was intrigued to see how they would handle a sea storm when they were at the mercy of it all, floating on top of the water and surrounded by wind. I knew I would be fine no matter what, though I really hoped they would make it through as well. Not listening to me, not knowing, didn't deserve a severe punishment. But there I go again thinking like a traitor to the Crown. Perhaps it was inevitable I ended up here.

<u>Miles</u>

I was roughly shoved awake by a crew member as calls of "batten down the hatches!" and various other yellin's filled m' ears. I got up quickly, only to see people hurrying around, heading up on deck. The boat lurched and I had to catch m'self from falling. Reluctantly, not sure what else to do, I followed the others up.

Everyone was rushing around, the deck was wet, slippery, and full of noise and commotion. People yelled orders and responses back and forth, and I could hardly make heads or tails a any of it. Dark grey waves tossed the boat around as if it was a toy. I decided to try to stay out of the way, clutching onto railings with all my might and trying to slowly get back to below deck. I was no use here, so I might as well get out of the way.

But before I could get anywhere, I saw something-- someone, I recognized. He was almost like the eye in the storm of frantic people, as he stood surprisingly calmly there amidst it all, just...watching. Not the least bit afraid.

But then there was a burst of lightning, the crack of thunder.

A single bolt.

It hit the right spot.

To knock over the boom.

I watched as the rain, the waves, and the running crew members slowed down around me.

It was heading right for him.

I ran, sprinting, slipping, yelling.

And when Adrian was knocked off a' his feet and over the edge of the railing

Into the waves

I followed him in, leaping over the railing and into the waves.

He didn't deserve to die.

Chapter Five - Fathom

<u>Adrian</u>

I had been standing on the ship when something slammed into me. It hurt a *lot*, but I was quickly distracted from the pain by the feeling of my body tumbling over the railing and hitting the surface of the water. I was very quickly overtaken by the waves. All of the sounds of the busy deck suddenly sounded incredibly distant and distorted, almost gone entirely. The cold surrounded me and pushed me, and with my mind in a daze the presence of the ocean felt… comforting. Soothing. As my eyes drifted shut I heard a seemingly distant splash, one my mind did not really comprehend in the moment.

I awoke feeling gritty and dry-- sand. I coughed up some sea water and in that moment I felt as if my human form was separate from me, doing something *it* had to do, not necessarily something *I* had to do. I felt a large, gentle hand on my shoulder and looked up to see Miles to my right, sitting up on the edge of the shore next to me. He held a small, golden, circular locket in his other hand, and it was open to reveal a waterlogged picture of an older lady. I refocused on his face.

"Are you alright, Adrian? It was hard to find ya in the waves for a bit, ye didn't have air for a while…" he said, concerned. I did not know what he was talking about. I felt perfectly fine, simply a little sore where the ship log-like thing hit me. *Wait, how did I make it to land? Was Miles tossed off the ship too?*

Abruptly, I heard the sound of sand or branches or something shifting, movement, and my eyes flicked to an edge of the treeline about six feet away. A few branches still moved after having been disturbed, but there was nothing there now.

But that was not all there was to see on this beach, as I saw a form out of the corner of my eye sitting next to me on my other side on the sand. I looked-- and was shocked to see a girl sitting up in the sand, wrapped in nothing but Miles' overshirt. It was sopping wet and clung awkwardly to her body. She stared at us with wide eyes, and then looked back out towards the sea. She had long, white hair, and very dark coloured eyes. She looked young for a human. The extreme contrast of the light hair and dark eyes made her seem almost ominous somehow, and as she looked out at the ocean, something clouded behind her eyes.

"Yeah…" said Miles. "We have company. Meet Morgan. She washed up here 'cause a' the storm, too, she was awake already when I noticed her-- and she don't really talk much so far." She looked at me. *Does not really talk, huh? Well considering I am now out of parchment and ink, that fact might actually help us get along. But where on earth did you come from?* No satisfactory answer immediately came to mind.

With, I suppose, introductions done, and everyone more or less okay, Miles slowly clambered to his feet and attempted to brush some of the sand off of his soaking self to no avail. Shrugging, he headed off towards the treeline. Where did he think he was going? I glanced at the young woman next to me on the sand. She was already looking at me, as though analyzing a specimen's usefulness. I didn't feel like it was quite time yet for one on one with her, to say the least, so I got to my feet and hurried after Miles.

Together, the two of us wandered through the trees, staying near the beach, and picked up fallen twigs and branches and such. I had seen trees several times since coming to land, but I still could not get past how magnificent and pretty they were, with their bright green leaves and thick, textured stems. The only downside of trees was that I kept stumbling over their big roots curving out of the ground, but I could usually manage to steady myself on another tree, or Miles, and not fall all the way on my face this time. At one point Miles was about to break a branch right off of a tree and I slapped his arm and glared at him-- taking part of the plant off of the main stem would kill the piece. He seemed to sort of understand and left it, and we continued to pick up fallen pieces. I was not really sure what the purpose of this all was, until, that is, I shivered violently when a chill breeze hit the soaking clothes I wore. Miles noticed and said,

"Don't worry buddy, we'll make a fire and you'll get nice and warm." So fire was the purpose. *What, you mean the tiny magical flames that were on torches in Myrddin for light? Those would never keep us warm…*

When we got back to the beach where we had all washed up, Morgan had not moved from the spot she had been in when we left. She sat barely beyond the edge of the waves, hugging her knees to her chest and staring out at the water. Miles was messing with the sticks and leaves and things we had gathered-- really mostly him, he kept tossing mine away when he thought I was not looking. For some reason. He had been weirdly particular about which sticks to pick up and which to not, but they all looked the same to me. I glanced back over at Morgan. A wind was coming off the sea, and I could tell even from where I stood that she was shivering violently. I wanted to help but I could not call to her, at least not in a language she would understand, and I was a little hesitant to approach her. She seemed… unhappy. Angry. I was not sure, I still was not great at telling human emotion.

"Guys! I'm going back into the woods for a few minutes, just need a few more things for the fire, I won't go far, you both stay here!"

It was Miles' voice, bellowing from the edge of the treeline. With that, he set off.

Oh… now it is just the two of us… wonderful…
I paused. I looked down at the pile of dry sticks and branches and leaves, and then over at the brooding woman who refused to leave the seas edge, or speak. Thus far anyway.

Reluctantly, I walked up to her and slowly sat down next to her, with ample space between us. Her gaze did not shift and she gave no reaction.

Several minutes passed in silence. She did not move a muscle. Except when she shivered.

Carefully, I reached out my hand. Nothing. I moved it closer, and closer, and poked her in the arm-- only to quickly pull my entire self back. I stared at her, waiting.

Slowly, ever so slowly, her head turned to face me.

"Are you always such an awkward dunce?" she asked, her tone blunt and abrasive. I blinked. Then slowly shook my head side to side. "… What's your name?" She sounded almost curious now. I paused, looking around. Picking up one of Miles' sticks from the pile, I drew my name out in big letters in the sand. Morgan stared at me the entire time, and I couldn't really decipher what the look on her face meant.

"You can't speak, can you." It was a statement, not a question. I shook my head no. It technically was not true, but as far as humans were concerned, I could not speak any of their languages. But in the languages of the sea and its inhabitants? I have always been fluent.

She pointed at me, before touching the fingertips of one hand to her head. Then she pointed her finger on either hand and moved them around each other in a circle, before creating little L's with her fingers that moved away from each other. I stared at her. I do not think I had been *that* confused since first coming on land. Seeing my confusion, Morgan sighed loudly, throwing her head back before looking back at the ocean again.

Hesitantly, I went and sat back down next to her, looking at her confused. Had I done something wrong? She leaned back and laid down on the sand. Her feet were in the water at times, and her hair was getting covered in sand--as was Miles' damp shirt-- but she did not seem to care. After a moment's pause, she turned to look at me.

"You must be a damn good listener if you've gone all this time completely unable to speak," she said.

"HEY guys I'm back! Glad to see e'rebody's still alright." The sudden presence of Miles' loud, cheery voice caught my attention.

He walked back over to his pile of sticks and branches, holding long roots and more branches, arranging and messing with all of it. I went over to try to help, or watch, leaving Morgan alone once again by the water's edge.

He cleared an area that was away from the edge of the forest, and made a small pile of pieces of the giant stems of trees, with dry leaves and small sticks. Around that he then used the bigger pieces of wood, placing them around the pile in a square and then building that up to be taller until the pile in the middle was fully encased. Placing a final piece with a notch in the middle that he had set aside in the centre, he put a stick on it and… began rubbing it very quickly between his palms? *I-- what? What is he doing? What is this supposed to accomplish again?*

Suddenly, a tiny bright piece of light appeared out of nowhere, and when it hit the dry leaves and twigs Miles had put there, it began to grow very rapidly. I watched in awe as a small flame appeared, eating the small pieces and growing bigger to eat more. It moved and grew as if it was alive, slowly devouring the bigger pieces of wood now. I had to lean back, as the tall flames flicked hungrily in my direction and emanated heat. It moved constantly, yet stayed amongst the wooden pile Miles had created. How it constantly danced and flickered, as if it was searching for more to consume, was mesmerizing. Not only did it release enough heat to warm us all, it glowed brightly too. This was almost *nothing* like what I had always thought fire to be.

"Careful, you're going to get your nose burned off at that rate, dunce. You act like you've never seen fire before." I turned away from the flames, surprised to find that at some point Morgan had come and joined us. She looked at me pensively. Before I could think of a response to her remark, one came from over the other side of the flaming pile.

"Yeah, Adrian's like that at times. Very… excitable, let's say, but don't call him a dunce please, it isn't very nice," Miles interjected cheerily.

Morgan only looked at me through suspicious, slitted eyes, for a moment more before ignoring us both again.

The sun went down as we all sat there, each staring deep into the flames. For quite a while all you could hear was the crackling of flames in front and the waves behind me. Until out of nowhere, Miles began to sing a simple, slow yet happy song. At first Morgan glared daggers at him, but he never even seemed to notice. He sang almost… wistfully, and when he finished, a small wind came off of the sea and blew the flames all around. They settled, and as they did, Miles stood up.

Miles ended up sleeping on a row of logs and leaves, while I preferred the soft sand. He was worried I would get too cold, but I managed to shoo him away, after showing him that I would sleep in a hole in the sand with a thick, sandy blanket if it would put his mind at ease. He was definitely confused by this, but ultimately decided to let it happen. Morgan, on the other hand, slept by and under a thick tree, with nothing covering her.

<u>Morgan</u>

I woke up feeling itchy and more uncomfortable than I had ever felt in my entire life. For some ungodly reason, I was covered in *leaves,* even though the tree above me hadn't lost any noticeable amount. I threw them all off of myself, creating a significant rustling sound. But neither of the other two I was now stuck with moved. I glanced over at Miles. *I don't think I will ever understand how humans sleep comfortably with so many long, gangly limbs.* I had woken up several times throughout the middle of the night, so clearly I couldn't manage to do it myself. Now, though, it was almost sunrise. Making sure to give the buried-alive one with only his head poking out a very wide berth, I walked down the shoreline for quite a distance. Until I turned a corner and couldn't see him anymore.

I sat for a moment, enjoying the peacefulness, before glancing back to make sure they were both definitely asleep. Satisfied, I turned back to the sea and called gently into the waves. After a few minutes, I saw him-- a little speckled seal's head, poking out of the edge of the water, eyeing me.

"Thomas, it's me. I need a favour. You know I wouldn't be asking if I wasn't desperate." The seal sounds squeaked out of my mostly-human vocal chords as if my voice was cracking, but I knew it was intelligible. The seal hesitated for a moment. "Buddy, we were friends-- you owe me one after saving your entire pod from that orca," I insisted. With that, he came as close to me as he could without entirely coming out of the water.

"Remember where Adva and I usually hang out these days? It's about eight fathoms deep into the kelp there, with the cave?" I asked, and he nodded, even though he was never a fan of me using human terms. "I need you to… check in on her, okay?"
Thomas glanced down the beach where Adrian was apprehensively, before turning back to me and quietly barking,

"What happened?"
I sighed.

"I lost my skin. It was stolen." Thomas' little seal eyes grew wide in disbelief and fear, but before he could say anything I interrupted.

"I'm going to get it back. No one has tried controlling me yet."

"It's one of those two down the beach isn't it? You know if you get them into the water I bet my pod and I could--"

"No. Thomas, stop. It's not either of them. These two seem…
okay. For now. They think I'm human and it's staying that way. Check
in on Adva and keep your little mouth shut about this, okay? Please?"

He paused, thinking. Finally, he agreed, and I urged him to
hurry back home. As he disappeared into the sea, I felt an ache of
longing that I couldn't go with him. *I was such an idiot to think that
leaving my skin was a good idea.*

Before long, Adrian and Miles woke up. The big one announced
to us, in his booming voice, that we should all, together, head into the
woods to find food and supplies to catch food. I'd find both of those
things in the ocean, not the woods. Everyone knew that. But my options
were basically, go with them and keep tabs, or stay by the sea alone.
Which was making me feel pretty bored, and even homesick. I hated
being alone with my thoughts. Silently, I trudged after the others.

I stopped paying much attention to where we were going as
Miles led us seemingly randomly deeper into densely spaced trees and
uneven ground. I grumbled, annoyed, to myself as I focused on keeping
up with their long strides and not tripping on anything. When the land
increased in altitude, that didn't exactly make my life any *easier,* either.
I was doing much better than the mute one, though, who kept repeatedly

tripping on every little thing *right in front of me.* I did my best to bite my tongue, lucky for him.

I felt my head ram into his back and stepped back, only to finally try to get around them both when I heard yelling past the big one in front. A woman's voice was yelling at us, and Miles sounded terrified and surprised. When I finally got around both of them, I saw a very unexpectedly tall woman with wrinkled clothing, short messy black hair, and dark circles under her eyes. She was almost as tall as Miles, which I didn't think was possible in human women, and was pointing a dagger at him. She was a lot thinner than him though, and was standing next to a small, hidden opening in the rising cliff face. The weirdest thing about her, though, was by far the strange metal choker on her neck. I couldn't see any fastener to be able to take it off or put it back on, and could just barely make out that there were etchings of some kind in the metal. I didn't recognize any of it. The chain of a necklace hung under the metal choker and disappeared under her clothing. I leaned past Miles, who was trying to talk down the crazy dagger wielder, to get a better look at the opening of the stone wall she was guarding-- and I saw that it extended quite far into what would be complete darkness for humans, and opened up into a cave.

The lady turned the dagger on me suddenly. I realized I definitely should be feeling fear being faced with death via a human with a glorified knife, but at first I didn't really care. Until an image of Adva, sleeping peacefully in that cave with a fresh poultice on her wound, flashed in my mind. It was the image of the last time I had seen her.

If this freaking human gets that dirty knife one breath closer to me I swear to god--

"Don't! Back off! There's nothing in there for you! Go away!" the lady had been yelling at me.

"We don't want any of your damn dirty belongings, *hag*," I spat in reaction.

"*Morgan!*" Miles scolded through gritted teeth. "It's okay, we're not going t' go into your cave, and we're not going t' hurt ya. We're stranded here too. How long have you been here?" Miles said gently to the woman, who turned the dagger back on him.

"Exactly as long as you, you fool. The same storm that swept you all up is also the reason I'm *stuck* here." She said. Miles blinked. She looked as if she had been here for weeks, or longer. She looked exhausted.

An idea seemed to spring on to Miles' face. *Uh oh.*

"...When did ya last eat?" he asked the woman, who was beginning to lower her weapon. She glared at him without answering.

She looked so tired I imagined she hadn't been able to search for or catch or hunt anything, which would mean it's been at least a day.

"If ye come with us," Miles continued, "Ye can have cooked fish to eat and a warm fire to sleep by." *What? No, that's a terrible idea. She'll kill us in a crazy rage in our sleep. Or eat fish we need. Or worse, try to have actual conversations with me.* I thought to myself, glaring daggers of my own at the oblivious giant. *I feel like I need to give Miles a talking to about inviting crazy weapon-wielders, who live in cracks in the wall, to come with us.*

She was basically eye level with our gentle, cheery tall one. She thought to herself for a minute, glaring at all of us and sizing us up. But then the dagger was back up, and steady now.

"I don't need anyone's help. I don't need your fish, or your fire, I need rest and for all of you to go *away*," her voice was steady and calm, but clearly edged with anger. Without another word, she slipped into the crevice in the rock that was a cave, and disappeared from view.

When we got back to the shore, I quickly left the others and decided to climb a tree. I had figured out how to do it so that I could hide from humans during my brief land visits. It served basically the same purpose now. The big one, Miles, spent his time creating a fishing rod out of roots and a stick. I'd never get over how stupid and silly looking fishing rods are. For a while, the other one-- what was his name again? Adrian?-- swam around in the ocean. At times, it looked like he was trying to catch fish in his hands or even his *mouth,* and I chuckled to myself when he came up sputtering and spitting out salt water. But after that, he came out of the water. Didn't seem to care that he had soaked his clothes again. Curiously, he didn't stay by the water or around the area. No, he looked around, and when it was obvious that Miles was completely preoccupied, and I was out of sight, he headed down the beach. This guy was… abnormal, to say the least. Even for a human. Silently, I slipped out of the branches and crept after him, staying hidden amongst the tree line.

Before long, he bent down at the water's edge, his shoulder length dark hair moving in front of his face. I didn't need to be able to see his face to realize what was happening when all of a sudden, he made clicking and squeaking sounds-- that I recognized. The crazy-- *thing,* guy, whatever he was-- was speaking *fluent dolphin.* I couldn't speak it myself, but I knew it when I heard it. I couldn't believe my ears. Sure enough, the small, long, grey nose of a dolphin poked out of the water after a few minutes. Adrian made more dolphin sounds at it, and it clicked and squeaked right back at him. *I'm sorry,* what? *I mean I had my suspicions, but now, this… There's no way this guy is human.* The dolphin's chatter sped up as it looked right at me, and suddenly

Adrian spun around. He stared at me, our eyes locking. His eyes widened as his mouth dropped open a bit, and he stood up, frozen in place. I stepped out of the treeline, arms crossed. Adrian's mouth began to move, but he stopped himself, and no sounds came out. The dolphin disappeared. Seemingly dumbfounded, he mimed bringing food to his mouth and eating it.

"I don't care why you were doing it. I just want to know *how,*" I said.

But before Adrian could think of a way to give me any kind of answer, we heard yelling from down the beach. Turning, we looked to see a large, impressive ship heading directly in our direction. Not far down the beach I could see Miles jumping and shouting and waving his arms like a lunatic at the ship. Adrian took one glance at me, and then another at the deep mess of trees and bush that covered the island. I grabbed his arm before any more thoughts could fly through that little head of his, and yanked him in the direction of the humans and the ship.

"You're not going anywhere, *fish boy.*"

Chapter Six - Ahoy!

<u>Miles</u>

I was minding my own business on the beach, trying to remember if I had ever been taught a method to make shelters, when I finally raised my eyes away from the surface of the water. There in the distance, I saw brown wooden hulls, with glorious hints of gold. A flag flapped in the wind, and the ship's figurehead of a mermaid woman, with her mouth open and her hair flowing, was pointed right in my direction. I honestly didn't believe my eyes. But it didn't disappear, it kept coming and was headed straight for us! Seeing it made me as happy as finding a barrel of water in the desert. I got so excited, I couldn't help myself and I ended up jumping up and down and hooting and hollering to make sure the people on the ship knew that there were people stranded.

As it got closer and closer, I laughed in excitement and relief. Never had been a fan of island life. I was jumping around when I noticed Morgan coming back, dragging Adrian by his arm. But Morgan stopped suddenly, staring at the farthest tree line. I looked, just in time to see the scraggly and haggard woman we had found in the bush before, heading directly for me. With crazy looking eyes hell bent in my direction as she stumbled toward the surf, her necklace scraping horribly against that odd metal choker, I took a quick couple of steps away from her. But she wasn't looking at me after all, she was staring at the ship, as a smile formed under her wild, knotted short dark hair. Morgan and Adrian approached a little bit cautiously with her there. But the woman paid all of us no mind.

The large ship came up fairly near to shore for its size, it's long side facing us. The sounds of talking, calling, and clambering could be heard coming from atop the deck even though it was still a far ways from shore. To my surprise, a long wooden board began to extend out of the upper edge of the ship, studded with pieces for grip to walk up it. The board just kept coming, and coming, and coming. Adrian walked up next to me on the beach, staring. I didn't know if he was thinking now that this was normal, but I hadn't ever seen anything like it before in my life. The edge of the board hit the sand and wedged a bit into the ground.

I glanced over at the woman from the forest apprehensively, who was on Adrian's other side. The end of the board was closest to her. What I saw, though, when I looked over is very far from what I had expected to see. As I watched, the woman gasped, her eyes wide in sudden realization. She waved one hand, gesturing at herself wildly. In awe and shock, I stood there as she changed— but not into anything else, simply a very put together version of herself. Her hair was neat and brushed now, ending at around her chin. Her clothes were mended and clean, a green jacket over a white shirt, blue jeans no longer ripped and dirty, everything done up. She even seemed to have a full face of makeup on after. Was that… had that been… *magic?* I stared at her with my mouth hanging open, unbelieving. *There's no way...*

Suddenly, her face went as white as a sheet, and she crumpled and fell to the side, Adrian quickly catching her in his arms. A tall, handsome man with dark brown hair, a long red and gold jacket, and a confident smile appeared in front of us up on the ship. He showed up *just* in time to see the woman crumple, while the rest of us stood around.

"Lorelai!" He exclaimed, his smile disappearing as he ran as fast as he could down the entire board and scooped up the woman out of Adrian's arms with surprising ease. *Wait, this guy knows this random woman?* He turned around and headed back up onto his ship, calling out to us at the last second—

"Oh, come aboard, friends of Lorelai are friends of mine." And then he was gone, disappearing onto the ship.

Adrian, Morgan, and I all looked at each other confused, before Morgan shrugged and climbed aboard. We followed.

"Sweetheart, why aren't you wearing any clothes?! Are you okay my dear?" A friendly and concerned woman, a member of the ship's crew, ran up to Morgan. *Uh oh.* Somehow we had all kind of…

forgotten? Gotten used to? That she was just wearing my undershirt that was long enough to cover everything. We waited there for a minute as the woman ran off, dragging Morgan by the hand and whispering worriedly in her ear. Morgan pushed her off but went with her. The two of us, Adrian and I, generally stayed together onboard the fancy, beautiful ship. But for once my attention wasn't focused on the new ship I was aboard. Instead, my gaze was torn between the mystery ship captain carrying off the woman, and Morgan being led away for clothes. When she came back, my undershirt was gone, and instead she wore a white shirt, a brown tan jacket, and pants that were too baggy on her short-ish legs.

"... do ya like it?" I asked hesitantly. She huffed and headed in the direction the tall man had effortlessly and quickly taken the woman— below deck. I stopped her and insisted on going first. Just in case. So with Morgan and Adrian in tow, I headed down. The lower deck was filled with bedrooms. I peeked into a few with open doors as we passed and saw that they all had two small beds, a dresser, and a small bedside table. *They can afford actual beds for everyone instead of hammocks... Damn.*

We found them pretty quickly. The man had placed the passed out woman-- who was 'pparently named Lorelai-- on an empty, clean bed in the back of the lower deck. He sat on the edge of her bed and smiled down at her, and his hand lifted to gently tuck her hair behind her ear, seemingly automatically. Morgan fake coughed at that point, loudly, as the three of us stood in the doorway peeking in. When the man noticed us he stood up abruptly, clearing his throat and avoiding our gaze for a second-- especially Morgan's, who stood there staring at him with her arms folded across her chest. After a brief moment, he gathered himself and stood confidently again. After meeting and holding Morgan's gaze silently for a moment, he turned his attention to me and smiled.

"So, what brought the group of you to that particular island? How do you all know Ms. Lorelai?" he asked politely.

"How did *you* even find us?" Morgan's tone seemed almost accusatory, and I gently shushed her and told her to be nice, as he had saved us after all. She gave me a look in response, but said nothing more. The man smirked.

"I know Lorelai quite well," he replied.

The little conversation was interrupted as a ship medic gently pushed past us in the doorway, before nodding respectfully to the man, and crouching near Lorelai. The medic woman carefully held up Lorelai and slowly poured a vial of light green liquid into her mouth before laying her back down. She nodded again to the man, who smiled at her, and we parted to let her leave.

I felt a small poke on my shoulder from behind, and glanced back to see Adrian peering up at me. He pointed to the man, then to me, then back to the man, then to myself, himself, and Morgan in turn.

"...Is your friend mute, or shy?" the man asked, peering at Adrian curiously.

"Mute." Morgan said immediately.

"Sorry, sir, we were wondering, uh—what's your name?" I asked.

"Oh, I'm sorry, of course, can't always assume she would've mentioned me-- My name is Nicodemus Galanis, and this is my ship, Miss Medea. Welcome aboard."

"Good t' meet you sir, my name's Miles!" There was a pause then, as no one immediately jumped to introduce themselves next. I glanced over at Morgan, who was still glaring at Nicodemus with her arms crossed. *I wonder what her problem is...* "... and this here is Adrian, he don't speak but he can understand and write," Adrian leaned past me and waved in response. "And this lady here is Morgan," I continued. "... she's nice once ya get t' know 'er." She turned to me and raised an eyebrow, but I ignored it and shook Nicodemus' hand as he chuckled to himself.

"Well!" He said, clapping his hands together, "We should leave Ms. Lorelai here to rest up in peace, don't you think?" He then began leading us out of the room and down the hall, adding, "Unfortunately I don't have enough spare rooms for each of you, but tonight one of you can share with Lorelai where she is now, and the other two can share another room," he pointed to a room as we passed it. "In the meantime, there is a common room you may occupy, and you are free to wander the ship except for the crew members rooms and my quarters, which is where I will be if you need me. If you need minor assistance, ask Leo, my first mate— he's the one with the red bandana. Now if you'll excuse me-" When he finished, we were at the end of the hall below deck, and he climbed the ladder faster than I would've thought possible for someone of his height, and disappeared above deck.

Adrian and I exchanged confused glances at the whole situation, while Morgan pushed past us and climbed back onto the deck.

Lorelai

I slowly opened my eyes and blinked. There was a slight sway… I was on a ship again. *Sigh*. Then, all of a sudden, my memory came rushing back to me; stopping the storm, being too drained of magic and energy to get off the nearby island, re-cooperating in a cave… those three annoying people finding me. And then…

I sat bolt upright, my head swiveling as my eyes scanned my surroundings. Seeing that my bag was still strapped across my torso, I grabbed it and threw it open. I dug around for a moment, and then sighed in relief and flopped back down to a lying position. It was still in there, my things hadn't been touched. And Nico's ship. I was on Nico's ship, in a spare cabin below deck. He had made sure I was alright. *Of course he did...* A small smile tugged at the corners of my mouth as I remembered him, and our last meeting. It had been months ago. *I suppose it is about time to see him again anyway, hm? I could use the relief.*

Speaking of relief, I slowly realized that I actually felt quite *good.* My body no longer ached, my muscles no longer cried out in exhaustion, my headache was gone. Instinctively, my hand reached for and fumbled with the talisman that hung from around my neck. It was back to a normal, room temperature. *Good.* My head was still upset with me for sitting up so quickly, though. I wasn't completely "recharged" yet, but because of whatever assistance Nico had given me, I was much closer in less time.

Slower this time, I sat up and swung my legs over the side of the bed. I paused to make sure my hair was still in order after the glamour spell that had sent me over the edge to fainting. Standing up, I headed off to go above deck. Time to see my dear Nico once more. I smiled.

I opened the door to his quarters, and there he was. Standing behind his desk, facing away from me. I closed the door behind me.

Hearing the door, he turned, and smiled a wide, bright smile at the sight of me, his pale blue eyes sparkling. I couldn't help but mirror his smile— I couldn't remember the last time I had smiled like that either. Probably the last time Nico and I had run into each other. He walked around the left side of his desk towards me, and I walked to my right, smirking. We walked a few steps more, circling, unable to pull our eyes away from the other.

"Don't play games with me, darling," his voice drifted, deep and glazed with honey.

"Who's playing?" I twirled a strand of hair around my finger in faux innocence.

He smirked, and a twinkle in his eye informed me of his next move. He began to walk towards me, and I met him in the middle of the space between us. Our lips met, and his hand was in my hair, clenching, and his other was on my lower back. Our kissing increased in intensity, as if we had been starved in the months between our meetings. Our bodies and hips pressed against each other, and his hands began to lift my shirt.

I stepped back, my hands flying to either of his shoulders, and suddenly we were standing my arms length away from each other. A storm of worry, concern, and questions spun inside his eyes, but I spoke before he got a chance to.

"We can't do this, right here, right now, not yet, sorry— I'm, I'm a little frazzled, we can have all of our usual fun later, I just, um, I really spent myself magically and whatever you gave me really helped but my heart is racing and I feel—" Nico pulled me into a hug abruptly, and I stopped. He was so warm, so strong, so familiar against me. With his arms around me, soft and strong at the same time, I felt safe. Relaxing into his embrace, we held each other for a moment. I was briefly reminded of the countless times he had reassured and calmed me in the past, whether it was before a match in the Arena when we were young or right before a particularly difficult monster hunt. He was always there for me. Slowly, he stepped back, and his hands slid down my arms reassuringly until our hands fit together. He looked at me.

"You need to rest. I understand."

"You always do. Always have."

A smirk cracked his soft demeanour.

"You know, nobody ever really sees you- what was it? *Frazzled*?" I dropped his hands immediately and glared at him as he chuckled at my expression. "*There's* that Lorelai back," he said.

"*What* Lorelai?!" My voice came out slightly too high, and I crossed my arms. He laughed then, not a chuckle this time, but nearly his full laugh, and it filled the room. My features softened, and I couldn't help but think about if it had been anyone else laughing at me, there would've been a sword tip to their throat before they could get much laughing out.

Once it died down, he finally answered my question.

"The Lorelai everyone else knows. The always glaring, pessimistic, attitude you. But *I-,*" he paused for dramatic effect and sauntered back around to the other side of his desk, sat down in the plush chair, and as he continued he propped his feet up on the desk. His voice became a loud whisper as if it was a secret. "I know there's a soft heart under it all, as well as a *tiger.*" He ended with a wink, and I laughed and sat on the desk in front of him. I hadn't laughed in a long, long, time either. Not a real laugh anyway.

<u>Adrian</u>

Miles and I ended up finding the common room, which was below deck. The ship was so large, if the common room had not been on the first lower deck where we had been shown earlier, it would have taken us a while to find it. *How on Myrddin does such a large vessel, with multiple lower decks, still manage to float and sail?* It astounded me. As I was distracted by my thoughts, my foot slipped on the ladder coming down and narrowly avoided hitting Miles in the head! I was able to recover fast enough that he did not notice, though. It was interesting, him explaining to me how to play a card game, the only hard part being trying to ask him a specific question. We quite quickly came up with hand signs, gestures, to mean each of the, ah, suits of the cards. I quite enjoyed coming up with these signs, so after several minutes of playing with the cards I grabbed paper and an ink quill. We spent a significant amount of time then, writing down words, phrases, and names and assigning hand gestures to each. Some we had already established by our previous communication efforts, but this would make speaking much easier from now on, which would be wonderful.

After doing this for quite some time, Miles decided it would be a good idea to check in on Morgan and see what she was up to. We did a quick look around the first of two lower decks, since we were already there, and then went above deck. There wasn't very much on the ship above deck, so it didn't take long until we found her, peeking into Nicodemus' quarters.

"*Morgan...*" She jumped at the sound of Miles' voice and looked embarrassed. "What're ya doing?" He sounded somewhere between suspicious and a scolding parent.

"I-uh- nothing, it's none of your business what I'm doing!" I looked at her doubtfully. She sounded like a teenager.

"Ugh okay fine, I just wanted to know what is up with those two, I mean don't you think it's suspicious that they both show up at the same time and know each other? Something's fishy, I swear." Realizing the irony, she smirked at me before continuing. "But I haven't been here long and all they've done is talk and laugh, I can't hear what they're saying… did either of you notice that when we all got on the ship, the crew was more wary and confused about *us,* and meanwhile didn't even bat an eye at their apparent captain carrying an unconscious woman aboard?" She asked.

I looked at Miles. He looked at me.

"Did you notice?" I asked in hand signs. He shook his head.

"Did you?" He signed back. I shook my head no as well.

"Woah, woah, woah, hold up what the hell is going on here? What's all *this*?" Morgan exclaimed. She gestured randomly and in our direction.

"We made gestures mean words, so that we can speak properly. I can teach ya it if ya want."

"UGH!" She groaned, tossing her head back. "You mean like *ASL?*" We stare at her. "American Sign Language? A *real, legitimate,* widely used language of hand signs?!" She seemed frustrated.

"Never heard a it before," he shrugged apologetically.

"Me neither." I signed flippantly.

"You're both ridiculous. I can't believe you two sometimes. I'll be in the common room, *for time alone.*" And with that, she stomped off.

There was a moment of stillness. I broke it by turning and heading towards the side of the boat. For once, it was Miles following *me,* even if only briefly.

My gaze looked out to the sea, as side by side we leaned against the edge of the ship. For a moment, it was mostly quiet aboard and I could hear the waves against the side of the ship.

My mind slowly drifted to Myrddin. It was far from perfect, not even all that moral in the end, but it had still been home... or had it really? I never felt like I completely belonged anywhere there. No role fit well like it seemed to for everyone else.

I turned to Miles— only to find that he had already been looking at me. My face was not amazing at hiding my emotions, I knew, so I was not very surprised when he asked, in our new hand sign language,

"Where is your home, Adrian?" He looked at me intently.

I glanced back out at the sea. Then turned, towards the ship I stood on. Morgan was below deck, and Lorelai was within the Captain's quarters. I looked at Miles— who had never doubted me, or hesitated to help. Where was home, he wanted to know. *Good question.* But that was not the answer he was searching for. I turned back out towards the sea, for a moment. He wanted to know where I came from. I felt I owed him something, some knowledge of my previous life.

"I am from a place…" I paused, my hand signs hesitating. "A

place where most everyone is happy. And everyone has a...role." I made up the sign for "role" on the spot, so afterwards I pulled a piece of paper and writing utensil out of my pocket which I had grabbed as we left the common room. I wrote "role", handed it to him, and did the new sign again. Miles nodded in understanding, but his thoughts seemed to be distracting him.

"I'm from a tiny village," he said. "A village where e'ryone hates the sea, 'cause it destroyed a lot, years ago. But they were all always happy with that sorta life, never lookin' back t' how it had been before." He turned back to the ocean, and his face that had darkened now cracked a small smile. "I had always been different in that way, deep down."

I tapped his shoulder to get him to look at me.

"The sea is... gorgeous," I said. I smiled back at him, and we both nodded and smiled in a moment of shared realization; we had both finally found a person who loved the ocean like ourselves, who really understood. I had wanted to say that the sea was amazing, incredible, or something even better, because it was so much more than just aesthetically pleasing. But our language failed me. That was okay; one day, maybe just maybe, we would be able to do the ocean justice with our new way of communicating.

The sound of someone ringing a bell took our attention. Most of the crew headed below deck, so we followed. We were then led into a part of the lower deck which we had not yet been in-- the second lower deck. The room had two large rectangular tables with chairs. A crew member passing by welcomed us to 'mess', whatever that meant, while another yelled to someone else for more chairs. Miles seemed quite happy, and sat down at one of the tables, and I sat down next to him. The crew left space around us. Before long, Morgan walked in and sat across from Miles. We looked at her. She looked at us.

"I *guess* I'll let you teach me the stupid new sign language," she grumbled— and Miles lit up.

Lorelai came in last, her face alight with a genuine smile and the last bit of a laugh as she tore her cloudy sea-grey eyes away from the man she entered with-- Mr. Nicodemus Galanis, who appeared to be Captain.

"Why Ms. Lorelai, is that a *stain* on your shirt?" he asked her. I could not tell if he was teasing or genuine. I did not see a stain, personally.

"If there is it's *entirely your fault,* you pig-headed buffoon," she replied. *Wow. I* really *can't tell if* she's *teasing or genuine.*

"Slob."

"Idiot."

"Tease."

"Narcissist."

"Aw GEEZ go back to your little room already, or sit down and shut up, ya damn weird lovebirds," an older crew member from the other end of our table yelled. *Lovebirds? What?* My thoughts were interrupted when the room immediately erupted into laughter. The pair smirked at each other and sat down to my immediate left.

Lorelai sat next to me, and gave me a small smile, and I smiled back big in return. I had not noticed before, but she had a really beautiful smile. She turned back to face Nicodemus, and I turned back to the rest of our group. Morgan had still looked a little irritated, sitting quietly by herself, until Miles started talking to her nearly nonstop about various marine life. Surprisingly, she seemed to enjoy the company this time.

Food was served, and I stared down at it. It was a liquid in a bowl with things floating in it. And what was the stick with a tiny bowl on it and the fancy spiky stick for? *Hmm..* I dipped my fingers into the liquid.

"Ah!" It was hot! Why was it hot? *Oh no now people are looking at me weird again...*

"Its food," Miles whispered directly into my ear so others wouldn't hear. *Oh. Okay.* I tried lifting the bowl to drink from it, but

Miles stopped me. *Every time I think I'm getting the hang of things, but then...*

Chapter Seven - Caught

<u>Morgan</u>

As everyone left the dining hall, I grabbed Adrian's arm and dragged him to the common room while I ignored his tapping on my arm and everyone else headed either to bed or above deck. I shut the door behind us, and then spun towards him.

"Alright fish boy, drop the act! You're not some innocent idiot who can't speak, you *were speaking fluent dolphin* to a dolphin before we left the island. You're obviously not human. So what. The hell. Are you."

Adrian stared back at me, flustered, and grasped for words without making a sound. For a moment I considered telling him that if he could speak seal, I could understand him. But I thought better of it. If no one knew my true identity, that was the safest. Even if he wasn't human, that doesn't necessarily mean he could be trusted. If anything, it means he probably couldn't be… right? He made signs and gestures with his hands, fast and confused and worried, but I didn't know their silly little language yet. I sighed and gestured to the paper and quill and ink that were ever present in this common room. He nearly dived for it, and began to scribble furiously. Then, suddenly, he stopped. He turned back and looked at me. Then ripped off a piece of paper and handed it to me.

"If I tell you what I am, I will surely end up dead. Humans want to kill what they do not understand. No offence," it said in a messy scrawl. I held back a smirk.

But when I looked up at him, my face fell. He looked… scared. Worried. I sighed. Ugh. *Maybe he is just a poor idiot boy, whatever he is. Or maybe now I could figure out where he is actually from, and why he was here with us.*

"I'm not going to hurt you. And I won't tell a soul, no one, I promise." He hesitated "I'm… curious. I guess. But you can trust me. There's more to me than a bad attitude. And besides, you could always escape into the sea I bet. No land creature would speak dolphin," I tried to give a small encouraging smile and to keep my tone gentle. After days of always being at least a little annoyed it wasn't the easiest feat. But somehow, I seemed to have convinced him. He handed me his paper.

"I am a triton. Tritons are-" I immediately stopped reading and dropped the paper.

"A *triton? Really?* Of all things you're a goddamn triton?" I exclaimed. He stepped back, and signed again with his hands, before remembering and scribbling; 'You know what tritons are?' I ignored the paper. I couldn't believe he was a triton of all things, he *had* to be the one non naturally hostile sea creature that hated selkies. We had never been allowed into their oh so fancy holier-than-thou marble city, nooo of course not. Stupid scaly fish people with their spears and--

"Wait. How the hell do you have a human form?" I suddenly realized. He blinked. Stood there for a moment, staring at me. Then, slowly, giving me a wary look, he flipped over one of the other pieces of paper, wrote on it, and handed it to me. 'I was of high enough status to receive one,' it said. *What?* We gave each other weird looks; for once, his wasn't of confusion-- mine was. He looked wary.

"...Why are you here?" I asked plainly. He again hesitated, but ultimately decided to write, ripping up pieces of the paper. The small piece he handed me said only one word.
'Exiled.' I stared at him.

"For wh-" he handed me another piece of paper he had already written on.
'For saving a young girl.' *What? What the hell? What kind of place...* I handed him back the papers instead of finishing my thought.

"Well I guess now I've *really* got to learn you and Miles' little sign language. But I'll keep your secret." With that, I left, heading to my--and unfortunately also the tall woman's-- room.

When I got there, I noticed that the room was empty. I crawled into bed and under the covers, and laid there. Staring at the ceiling. The sun set. I heard some noise from the hall as more people headed to their rooms. After a while, it quieted down. Silence. Darkness. Slight sway. I stared at the ceiling. I rolled onto my side. Other side. Arms in front of me, or against my sides, or above my head, lying on my back, my stomach. *Ugh.* Getting comfortable was impossible. I imagined being a seal, lying in a warm, comfy heap with other seals, Adva by my side and the sound of the waves lulling me to sleep. *Sigh.* Imagining it didn't help. It only made me feel homesick. *I'm the worst caretaker for her. But I miss her so much... God, how long have I been lying here awake?* Worry about Adva began to grow on the edges of my mind, so I threw the blanket off of myself and got up. The tall woman with dark hair had never come to bed. *She's probably with the Captain again.* I left the room, and headed above deck.

The sea breeze cooled my face and swept up my long hair, sending it flying. I noticed that someone else was up here, on the other far side of the deck. I recognized the woman, Lorelai, even though she was facing away from me. *What is she...?* I watched as she seemed to be almost... dancing? But not quite. Her short hair whipped around in the wind, as though the air was moving faster on that side of the ship. She moved elegantly, her arms flowing as she leaned, stretching one out towards the sea. As she lifted her arm high above her head, a stream of seawater followed, as if pulled. It arched over the side of the ship, suspended in mid-air and reaching for her hand. She stood on her tiptoes and began to spin, her one hand still in the air, and the water spun with her. It surrounded her, creating a whirling vortex that, before long, I couldn't see the woman through. She reappeared, facing to the left now, and threw her hands out in front of her. The water went flying in a direct, fast shot off the side of the boat. Then, with a small flick of her wrist, a small amount of water returned, and she shaped it into a sphere. Twirling her finger, the suspended ball of water spun. She flicked her wrist to her left with a snap, and suddenly the little ball of water came flying directly towards me. Before I could react, my new clothes were drenched.

"Hey what the h-" I stopped as I noticed the woman smirking at me as she walked towards me. The strange etchings and engravings in her thick, metal choker seemed to almost be shining a little, glistening, in the moonlight.

"I don't like being *watched* unknowingly," she said, her eyes narrowed. "You were one of those three who found me in the forest, weren't you? Nico told me about how he let you all on-board as well…"

"You're a magic user, aren't you? There was right before we got on the ship, and now…" my voice trailed off. She gave a slight smile.

"I'm no ordinary magic user," she replied, holding up her hand. As I watched, water appeared out of nowhere, floating above her fingertips, and became a tiny self-contained wave. After a moment, her hand clenched into a fist, and the water broke, splattering on the deck. Her grey eyes bore into mine.

"I'm a sea witch."

We looked at each other for a moment.

"Why are you telling me this?" I asked. It was dangerous to be so open about something like that— many humans want witches dead. Though I wasn't even sure myself what made a witch different from any other magic user. She leaned in, making me a bit uncomfortable but I didn't back up. She grinned a small, devilish grin, and for a split second I thought I saw her eyes become a bright blue. But it was so fast, I couldn't be sure.

"Because you and your little friends are no threat," she whispered. Turning away, she headed back towards the entrance to the lower deck.

"Wait." The word left my mouth before I gave it permission. She paused, but did not turn around. "I… I need your help. Magical help. I want to make a deal." She slowly turned on her heel.

"What *kind* of deal."

"I will do anything you want, as long as you can heal my sister." The sea witch smiled, her eyes dancing in the darkness.

"*Anything?*" She implored.

"Anything."

<u>Lorelai</u>

I woke up the next morning after little sleep as usual. The mattress underneath me was too firm, the swaying of the ship nauseating, but the blankets in Nico's guest and crew cabins *were* more comfortable than I was used to, I must admit. I slipped out of the room quietly, not wanting to wake the girl who slept fitfully on the other side of the small room. I knocked on the door to Nico's cabin, despite it being early. He answered anyway, already dressed and polished. Even I rarely saw him unkempt in any way.

"We need to talk," he said. I stopped in surprise; I thought I was here to talk to *him.*

"...yeah. Is everything okay?" I asked as I slipped inside and closed the door behind me. His face was void of emotion. When I asked the question, he shifted and avoided my gaze. Turning back to rifle through papers on his desk he asked me,

"First, what brought you to me this early in the morning?"

"We have to change course, head to a different destination." That stopped him. He finally turned around and met my gaze, an eyebrow raised. "I made a deal with the girl, Morgan, last night. We have to head to that little town, Cobalt something or other, so that I can acquire some rare spell ingredients." His face finally glowed slightly with interest.

"What for, my dear?" he asked.

"Oh, her sister is magically injured or something," I said absently, brushing it off. "But if I help her, which shouldn't be too hard at all, then she's willing to, in return, help me with a certain problem involving…" My voice trailed off, and I gave him a knowing look.

"No," he said, aghast. "No way anyone would agree to that, I thought you were *kidding* when you suggested that as a solution!" His tone was exclamatory and surprised, but his face was impressed.

"Well what can I say, the girl must be desperate. So, anyway, what did you want to talk to me about?" His face darkened.

"Adrian." He said grimly, staring me down. Unflinching.

"... What about him? I've barely interacted with the boy." I didn't understand what he was getting at.

"Lorelai-" he heaved an exasperated sigh and put his head in his hands. "Lorelai, dear, come on, surely you've noticed?" I said nothing. "Lorelai… he's clearly not human. So you've either lost your edge or--"

"Woah, hold on, what do you mean, of *course* he's human, he's just a little dumb, not from here, mute. That kind of thing." I peered at Nico. He really believed what he was saying. *Hm.*

"Lorey he didn't understand that soup was food," he stated plainly.

I had no idea what he was talking about. He then informed me that at dinner the previous night, he had overheard Miles tell Adrian, after he had dipped his fingers into the hot soup, that it was food, as if Adrian didn't know that on his own. How had *I* not heard that? I had been closer than N- *oh right. Nico's sensitive hearing. How could I forget.* I tried to argue that that didn't mean he wasn't human, but even to me my voice sounded flat this time. He continued to point out that Adrian kept making ridiculous little mistakes and dumb decisions, and that neither of us knew anything about him or his origins. But I was stubborn. Despite the evidence, I refused to believe that I, a highly accomplished monster hunter, could have been right next to a monster without realizing or even doubting them.

I shot back at Nico that he had to be wrong, that there *had* to be another explanation, that there was no way. Raising his voice to match mine, he insisted that I was being blind and had lost my edge, that it was glaringly increasingly obvious that he was not human in some way, and how could I not see that? We argued, our voices raising as we slowly became more and more in each other's space. I was taller than him by a bit, but he had a large presence, and would never be intimidated— especially by me. Our frustrations with each other grew, both of us too stubborn to ever back down, until he yelled;

"YOU HAD NO PROBLEM BELIEVING *I* WASN'T HUMAN!"

Everything stopped. I took a step back. We stared at each other. He was breathing heavily. The world was so incredibly silent. He lowered his gaze to the floor.

"We agreed we would never bring that up again." My voice came out as a whisper. His eyes flicked back up to my face.

"But you still haven't let it go, have you."

I left. I tore out of that room where the air was tight and heavy, the sea breeze hitting me for a moment before I was back below deck. I went to my room, where Morgan was pretending to still be asleep. It was still early. I could sleep some more.

I stared at the ceiling.

<u>Miles</u>

After that evening where my buddy Adrian, uh, got confused, at supper with the soup-- we touched land three mornings later. In the meantime, Adrian and I spent some time teaching Morgan our own sign language. I tried asking around where it was we were docking, but the crew were a tad bit done with me after I had spent a lot of time following and watching them in the past days. I just wanted to learn how to sail, that's all! So, reluctantly, I approached The Captain. Surprisingly, he remembered my name, and told me and the others that we were going to dock in Cobalt Bay, a small seaside town.

"You and your friends will be assisting Lorelai in gathering some supplies-- for the ship. The crew and I are busy onboard, you understand."

When we did arrive at the town, Miss Medea was by far the biggest ship in their small harbour. A few people recognized the ship, what with its golden trimmings, large flag, and a figurehead of a woman with her legs melding to become one with thrashing waves. Captain Nicodemus must have docked here before, as people greeted us and asked about him as we left the ship. I greeted them back and introduced myself, but Lorelai whipped her head around and snapped at them, ordering them to leave us alone. The gentleman I had been talking to gave me an apologetic glance, and they all quickly backed off.

The town was simple, but had a charm to it all. Small houses that were white, beige, pale blue, black, brown, and grey, were piled close to each other, but many had brightly coloured doors. Trees dotted the sides of gravel roads, and small signs poked out into the street from storefronts. People mostly walked the streets, greeting each other as they went, but I also saw one person trot by on horseback! I had only ever been told about and seen photos of horses… They were much taller than I had expected! But they were pretty, and strong animals by the look of it.

"Uhhh… Lorelai, was it? What exactly are we here to get? And why are we all needed for this?" Morgan's voice interrupted my thoughts and drew my attention back to the group. Without a word, she handed each of us a piece of parchment. They all had one edge torn, with curled edges and were yellowed with age. Each piece had a detailed drawing on it of a flower.

"We need these for something important. You should be able to find your item either in a store here, or in the surrounding flora. It will be faster if we split up into pairs, I will go with Adrian. We'll meet back here in a few hours. Do it and I'll get Nico to bring you to wherever you want to be." She paused, looking between Adrian and I. "Oh don't be *pouty,* you two needed to be detached from the hip at *some* point," she sneered.

I turned to Morgan. Lorelai's offer of travel didn't appeal to me much-- there wasn't only one place I wanted to be! Except if you count on a ship… But I was happy to help with whatever anybody needed anyway.

Both pieces of parchment we had were drawings of flowers I didn't recognize. As Lorelai walked off with Adrian following behind, Morgan insisted that we search just outside the town for the flower first. Heading out, I tried to start a conversation, but as per usual Morgan wasn't the most chatty. She looked at the ground, and together we searched in silence. Before long, we had wandered a small ways away from the edge of the town. Morgan's head shot up abruptly, her gaze locked on something. Urging me to follow, she headed quickly for whatever had caught her attention so strongly. She led me to a large pile of rocks poking out of the side of a small cliff edge that we were below, and pointed upward.

Near the top of the cliff, growing out of a crack in the rock, was a flower. It had the same pointed petals and details, with a single leaf coming out of the stem. The petals were pink with a yellow centre between them. The picture was an amazing likeness.

"That's the drawing, isn't it?" she asked. I had been able to see the rocks from where we had been before, but how on earth had she spotted the small bit of pink from that distance?

"Yes, but, Morgan--"

It was too late. She was already trying to climb the rocks, finding footholes and gripping edges so tightly her knuckles went white. Before I could stop her, she was already too high for me to safely drag or lift her down. I was forced to stand there, helpless, watching as she struggled to find her way up. I was tempted to climb the rock wall after her; I could lift myself up easier than she could. But would the rocks support both of our weight?

Her foot slipped, and she dangled there for a brief moment held up only by her hands--which were about to give way. She scrambled, and I stepped towards an edge that was jutting out near the ground. Her foot found a holding, though, just in time. I released a breath I hadn't realized I had been holding. She was almost to it now, so close. I held my breath as she got closer and closer, my eyes darting between her hands and her feet, wishing with all my might that she wouldn't slip or lose her grip. Unable to find a higher hold, Morgan stretched one of her hands higher, her fingertips brushing the pink petals.
All of a sudden a thought struck me-- why on earth did we even need this plant? For the *ship?* Why? Surely it was not worth risking her safety for.

Morgan gasped, and my eyes shot up to her just in time to see her hand slip from it's edge as her other hand picked the flower.
I stared in horror as Morgan began falling, flower in hand. I started climbing, bounding up the rocks as fast as I could-- heading for the large slab of rock she was falling towards. The sun shone in my eyes for a moment, as I looked up to see her hair drifting like waves of snow as

her arms and legs hung above her as she fell. I had to focus. I tore my eyes away from her, instead finding edges to hold onto and forcing my body to move fast. It felt like forever.

In truth, only seconds had passed before Morgan slammed into solid rock. I reached her soon after, and her chest was heaving as she tried to get the air back into her lungs that had been knocked out. I gently lifted her into a sitting position and held her as she breathed. I looked her over for obvious injuries first-- and saw a small red circle seeping through the bottom edge of her pants. I laid her down and shifted, inching carefully on the side of a tiny cliff, until I reached her ankle. Slowly, gingerly, I lifted the clothing away from the injury. What I found was a gash, seeping blood-- she must've cut or scraped herself on a sharp edge as she fell. Sighing, I ripped a long strip of cloth off of the bottom of my shirt. *At this rate, this girl is going to cause the loss of every shirt I ever wear...* 'Course, I didn't really mind. But as I wrapped and tied up her ankle in the strips of cloth that had been part of my shirt, I noticed something odd-- dark black speckles, spots, on her skin around and a bit above the gash. I had never seen anything like it before. *That can't be good...*

With the injury wrapped for now, I scooped her up into my arms, and she yelped in surprise. From there, I held the small girl with one arm as she wrapped her arms around my neck tightly and buried her head in my shoulder. Using one arm, occasionally two for a moment, during which Morgan also wrapped her legs around me-- I made our way down the side of the pile of rocks, incredibly slowly and carefully. Eventually, we made it to the ground. To my surprise, Morgan didn't even try to hop down back onto the ground and walk. I had been sure I would've had to argue with her and convince her that she couldn't walk on that leg or on one leg, but as I started walking, she didn't budge from her place in my arm and around my neck.

Once we got back into the town, I asked for directions and quickly made my way to the medic station for the people here. They weren't busy at the time, so Morgan and I were soon led into a smaller room for help. After I put her down, I was told that non-patients were to wait in the other room unless they were family. *But--*

"Miles. It's okay, I'll be fine. I'll be right out. Go," Morgan lightly urged.

I didn't want to, but I went, sat down, and waited. And waited. And waited. Staff bustled around. *This is taking too long...* And so, when the amount of people in the room had thinned, I snuck around the corner.

Sadly, I'm not the best at sneaking around.

"Sir! *Sir!* You can't go in there right now! Do you have an appointment? Sir!" a voice called out after me. I ignored it, and only moved faster. I reached the room Morgan had been in-- and saw a group of people down the hall with weapons in their belts and across their backs silently hustling out a back entrance. Something was wrong. I threw open the door, and the room was empty.

Turning, I charged after the group. But they were fast, and knew what they were doing. A horse-drawn carriage was waiting just outside, and I froze in my tracks for a moment as I caught sight of Morgan-- wrapped up in netting, tied up in ropes, and not awake. They tossed her roughly into the back of the carriage. I yelled, and ran at them, and managed to catch them by surprise enough that one crumpled under my fist. I stopped-- I had *never* hit anyone before. Ever.

Five other people whipped out daggers and swords, pointed in my direction. I stepped back slowly, my hands up. After two lifted the hurt one into the front of the carriage, they all hopped in, one by one, until only one weapon was pointed at me.

"No point in trying to protect a *selkie,* it'll only attack you in the end," the man said, before jumping into the carriage.

They rode off, leaving me standing there feeling confused and lost. A *selkie?!*

I had to find the others.

We *had* to find Morgan. I didn't care what the man had said. So what if she wasn't entirely human? She still didn't deserve whatever they wanted to do to her. I knew it wasn't gonna be anything good.

Chapter Eight - Shadows

<u>Adrian</u>

The two of us walked through the busy streets of the small town with silence between us. She looked in store windows and at their signs, I looked around elsewhere. Carriages were pulled by tall, odd animals with the top half of a hippocampi and— strangely —a similar bottom half, with legs and a tail. *How crazy looking.* The stone streets were reminiscent of the lower area of Myrddin, but the structures were in quite good shape. Past windows, people did all different things, and items I had never seen before lay inside on shelves.

I glanced at Lorelai as she walked beside me. I wanted to try to strike up a conversation with her, but that may have been difficult even for someone who could speak. I could not even do that… Perhaps she chose me simply because she knew it would guarantee quiet. I turned back to the windows.

Several minutes passed. I was not sure how many, before something on the distant edge of my hearing caught my attention. I stopped, puzzled. People behind us nearly ran into me, but I ignored them, closed my eyes, and listened intently. It was a voice, making quite a commotion in the distant streets as it drew closer.

My eyes shot open. *Miles*. He was distressed, and yelling.

Lorelai looked back at me, realizing I had stopped. "What the hell are you doing?"

I ran up to her, and held one hand up high to indicate height, one to each side to indicate broad, a gesture to indicate yelling. I pointed down the street. She regarded me with confusion, and disinterest. I hopped in place, gesturing wildly down the street. Why was she not getting it?! We had to *go*, Miles was in trouble!

I sighed.

And then took off down the street.

She yelled after me angrily, but all I was listening to was Miles' call. I ran past carts, nearly got hit by a carriage, tripped and scrambled back to my feet, pushed through people, and became frustrated at my inability to swim through air. I could not even call out back to him—not without risking and likely dooming my life.

It did not take me too long to find him; the town was not very big. As his form finally appeared through a crowd, he noticed me, and ran towards me, grabbing my arm. Abruptly, I was dragged into an alleyway.

"Is Lorelai still with you?" Miles asked, panting. I nodded, and pointed a thumb behind me before gesturing vaguely over my shoulder.

"What's wrong?" I signed, as he looked around wildly. Was he… *afraid?*

"They took Morgan!" He blurted, still breathing heavily. *What?!*

"Who?! Who?" My hands moved frantically. *Oh god.*

"I don't know!" He cried.

Something behind me caught his eye. I spun around. But it was just Lorelai, glaring angrily at me with her arms crossed.

"Can you two *really* not be apart for *one hour* before you f-"

"They took Morgan."

Silence. Then, fury began to grow on Lorelai's face. I was surprised, and Miles and I both took a step back.

"Who. *Who* took her." Despite the fire across her features and her hands curled into fists, her voice was ice cold.

"I-I don't know, they had weapons, and were silent, and called her a selkie a-"

"*What.* No. You must be wrong. You *must* be-" her fist slammed into the closest wall with a sound of anger, followed by a grunt of pain. Miles echoed my flinch.

"We have to find her." She was definitive.

"Really? You'll help?" Miles asked excitedly, but his voice was edged with caution.

"Yes. We have a deal, and I require her to be able to fulfill her end. She can't if she's being sold for parts." Turning, she marched quickly off down the street.

Miles stared at me wide-eyed.

"*Parts?*" He squeaked.

I stared at the empty space where Lorelai had been. *Morgan... was... a* selkie, *this whole time...* My brain had absolutely no idea how to process this information. I did not know what to do with it. I slapped my forehead. No wonder she knew what a triton was! *Oh no.* My face fell. *She probably thinks I hate her.*

And what on Earth did Lorelai mean by 'parts'? She was a person— well, a selkie, apparently— not a *thing.* You cannot sell a person for 'parts'.

I looked at Miles, who was now pacing nervously. His eyes were wide and filled with fear.

You cannot *sell a person for parts... right?*

…

But maybe with a selkie you can.

I yanked Miles' arm out of the alleyway after Lorelai. She was the only one who was not scared. Angry, but not scared. Maybe she knew what to do to get Morgan back safely. She was on the sidewalk--

fast walking away from us. *What?* We ran after her, and caught up quickly.

"Where are you going?! What are you doing?" I tried to ask, my hands flying in big, fast motions as I made sure to keep up with her. But she did not even turn her head to look at me.

"What're y--" Miles started.

"I need a drink. And a walk. To get out of my head, calm down, and think about what we can do now," Lorelai interrupted. She must have correctly assumed our questions.

So off we went. Miles and I focused on keeping up with her long stride, pushed into silence by the angry, storming feelings coming off of Lorelai. I was still surprised she was so upset by this; I had not thought that she cared about Morgan much. Although she did claim it was simply because of a deal the two had. I had no knowledge of such a deal. I peered at Lorelai out of the corner of my eye, and saw that her head was down slightly as thoughts ran behind her eyes. Her face was in a permanent angry scowl. *Would simply a broken agreement cause such a strong emotional response? ... Perhaps it depends on how important it was to her.* I turned my attention back to where she was leading us. We headed down a main road before heading directly for a certain building as soon as she spotted it. I could not tell how it was any different than any other store around, though.

Inside, the large room was dimly lit, with a very long counter to one side and little tables with chairs scattered across the room. Behind the long counter were rows and rows of liquids I mostly did not recognize in bottles made of glass instead of seashell. *What kind of store is this?* Lorelai went directly to a table in the far back corner, marching forward as people moved out of her way as soon as they saw her. Miles and I slipped into the space created in her wake. The spot she had chosen was dimly lit, mostly hidden in shadows where the lights did not quite reach. Lorelai sat down and immediately pulled a scrap of paper out of her bag along with a quill and inkwell and began writing furiously. For a bit, we sat in uncomfortable silence as she ignored us and continued whatever it was she was writing down.

Finally, she put the pen down and addressed us.

"I've done some thinking… I think I know where to find Morgan," she said. Immediately Miles smiled hugely and started to get excited again. But something kept me feeling uneasy.

"Really? Where? How? When do we leave?" Miles asked.

Lorelai mostly ignored his questions, and her lips pursed in discomfort.

"I've heard rumours, stories, with elements of truth in them... From other hunters," she paused, the air abruptly tense around us as she glanced at me briefly.

"Wait, what?" I interrupted.

"Oh, really? What did ya hunt? You don't really seem the type to hunt waterfowl with a gun--" Miles said excitedly. I was still staring at her, Miles' next words not fully registering as thoughts ran through my head. *Surely she does not mean... I mean, I heard tales of 'hunters' in Myrddin, people that would hunt down and kill our kind and others. They were, supposedly, one of the main reasons we had to stay hidden inside our city at the bottom of the ocean, but I always doubted if they really were out there...*

"I did not hunt birds or any sort of game you'd be familiar with, Miles," Lorelai said. She glanced around the dimly lit store. No one was near us. She looked at me again for a fleeting second before turning to Miles. She leaned in, and lowered her voice to say; "This may be hard for you to believe, but I hunt *monsters.*"

Oh my Crown, no!

I stood up, the chair I had been sitting in screeching as it was pushed backwards. Miles looked at me, his eyes widening in a mixture of emotions-- realization, surprise, maybe even fear? I could not be sure. Something seemed to be clouding behind Lorelai's eyes as well. I could have sworn I saw her hand drift towards one of her sheathed weapons, and I turned and ran.

Once I was out of the store I did not know where to go. People were everywhere, staring at me, questioning looks on their faces. I could feel my heart beating in my chest. I headed off to run, to who knows where, but suddenly someone grabbed my wrist from behind. I spun around-- it was Miles. He had followed me out, a look of deep concern on his face. Lorelai slipped out of the doors behind him and took several steps away from us, her arms folded.

"Hey buddy, it's okay, let's go somewhere a tad more quiet and talk about this, okay?" His voice was calm, reassuring. I looked at Lorelai. She put her hands up, an annoyed look on her face.

"I'm not going to do anything!" she said. I narrowed my eyes. Pulling my hand free of Miles' grasp, I asked;

"Why not?"

"He-- he says, uh, 'why not?'" Miles translated for me, looking uneasily in Lorelai's direction.

"Like Miles said, let's talk," she replied smoothly.

<u>Lorelai</u>

I wasn't sure where we could find more privacy than the dark back corner of a bar in a small, only vaguely familiar town, but I had to lead the boys somewhere. *Never did get my drink either…Would the bartender find it suspicious how Adrian ran out of there? Hm. I'll just find another bar, surely there is one.*

After a few minutes of walking, I found one. The two men with me didn't say anything from behind me about the fact that I was insisting on meeting in a bar. Smart of them. We settled back in a booth, and it was almost as if the 'outburst' from Adrian had never happened. But, unfortunately, it had. I would be forced to explain myself. But, of course, humans don't typically react with fear when told about my job-- so I suppose there was my confirmation; he wasn't human.

The two of them were already talking amongst themselves, in their own little hand sign language. Frankly I was happy to not be immediately barraged with questions or accusations. Miles and Adrian turned to me. Adrian looked a bit uncomfortable in my presence, his movements were tense and he avoided direct eye contact with me. You could almost see the cogs turning behind his eyes.

"Alright… Adrian wants to know if ya had anything to do with Morgan bein' captured," Miles said. That surprised me.

"What? No! Of course not, I'm going to find her, remember?" I said, before leaning back and folding my arms.

"Do ya really know where she might be?"

"Yes. It's likely they took her where I think she is. I know hunters." I glanced at Adrian again. This time, he was staring at me with an icy hard look. I stared back. "So Nico was right, then?"

That caught him off guard. He blinked, and looked confused. He raised his hands and began to sign, but I didn't bother waiting for a translation.

"Nico told me you weren't human. I shouldn't have doubted him. He's a hunter too, you know," I tossed out casually. Alarm struck Adrian's face and he signed frantically. I couldn't help but smirk. He was so easy to get a rise out of. Before they could ask more questions, I decided to get to the point already. We were losing precious time to find Morgan-- who was the key to my plan. I turned to face Adrian and lowered my voice. "No, I'm not going to kill you, but Nico probably would. If he knew for certain. You're…" I paused. His blue green eyes bored into me. I couldn't think of the right word. "...Harmless. Enough. Maybe you could be useful in getting Morgan back. But Nico? All he would see was red if he knew for sure you weren't fully human." I leaned back, glancing between the two of them. Adrian still seemed agitated, nervously messing with the ends of his hair at his shoulder and fidgeting. *Maybe I shouldn't have told him that… We will still need to get back on Nico's ship…* I sighed.

"Look, Adrian," I said. "I will make sure that Nico doesn't hurt you and retains his doubts about your... non-humanness. As long as there is a *possibility* in his mind that you are an innocent human, he won't hurt you." Adrian visibly calmed, but he also blushed briefly before taking a breath and turning to face Miles. *Hm. Odd.*

When Adrian signed, he didn't bother directing it to me.

"He's askin' why ya want to save a selkie when wouldn't you normally hunt them down?" Miles asked for him, obviously a bit uncomfortable with the question. *Good, back to the topic at hand.*

"I told you. We have a deal. It's a rare circumstance, and a very important deal to me. That's all you need to know. Now, are you men in, or am I searching for Morgan by myself?" I asked, laying down an ultimatum.

"I feel terrible for lettin' her get caught, and can't help but worry about what they might do t' her if we don't save her. I also got nowhere else to be, so I'm in," Miles piped up right away. We both turned to look at Adrian. He glanced between us both before giving a small shrug. He signed.

"He's in!" Miles exclaimed. He gave Adrian an excited bear hug.

"Shhh, keep your voice down! Look, we are wasting time and Morgan is getting closer every second to an untimely death. I was shown that there is a place that is a main hub for hunters to hold, store, and bid off their…" I glanced at Adrian. "...Wares. Particularly the wares that are still alive."

For a moment, neither of them said anything. An uneasy feeling settled over the group of us.

"... do ya know how t' get there?" Miles finally broke the silence.

"Where the hunters gather tends to change frequently, but I know where to find the person who will know where it is now," I smiled. "It is going to involve quite a bit of walking, though."

<u>Miles</u>

Lorelai had somehow gotten The Captain to leave without us in a pretty short conversation that Adrian and I weren't hearing. He seemed a tad frustrated, maybe even angry, but she calmed him and sent him on his way pretty quickly.

So with Lorelai in the lead, the three of us set off on foot. I knew I wouldn't mind plenty of walking, after all I had walked all the way from my little village to the big main harbour, but I hoped the other two would be alright with it all.

I turned to Adrian and tapped him lightly on the shoulder.

"Hey buddy, how ya doin'?" I signed.

"Good.... worried about Morgan."

I nodded sadly. I was really worried about her too. Maybe she didn't care much for *us,* who knows, but we were worried about *her.*

I looked back up at Lorelai, who walked silently ahead of us. *I wonder if she cares, even a little, 'bout Morgan. I know she said that they have some sorta deal or somethin' that she wants done, but I'm gettin' a feelin' that we're gonna be travellin' quite a ways for this. And Lorelai may have t' fight to get her outta there. Surely that much effort ain't done just for a silly deal? What could they even want from each other?*

We were walking through some forest a ways outside the town we had left— I felt pretty comfy in forests after helping hunt for my village for years. Though I did always feel a little bad about killing the poor things... but we had to eat.

I shook my head. I was getting distracted again.

"Uh, um... Lorelai?" I tried.

She stopped walking, but stayed looking ahead.

"What."

"Why, uh, I mean no disrespect, I apologize, but, uh, what *is* this 'deal' you said you 'ave with Morgan? She never mentioned anythin' 'bout a deal with ya..."

I could hear my heart beating in the silence that followed. Lorelai didn't turn around. No one said anything. Finally, I peered around her, wondering what on earth she was looking at. I didn't see it at first glance, but there, hidden in a patch of dense trees in the middle of a forest, was a small, cute wooden home.

"Hm, I had no idea this was here… I meant to pass through, but who would choose to live in the middle of the woods? Let's go check it out," Lorelai said, before dashing behind some trees and slowly heading towards it. *Guess my question ain't bein' answered…*

Adrian and I looked at each other. He shrugged. We quietly followed her, as I wondered what all the sneaking was about. Though maybe she was always this careful about approaching something unknown.

Wait. A thought struck me. *Is she plannin' on breakin' in t' this home?!* I never did get an answer to that one, because as Lorelai neared the little house ahead of us, a woman sprang out of nowhere and pointed a sharp spear tip at Lorelai's neck!

On the other end of the spear, was a woman with medium length brown hair, and eyes that reminded me of the ocean when it seemed greener. Her loose clothing swayed in the breeze. She stared hard at Lorelai— at all of us. But then that's when I saw it-- the small movement in the bushes, dark brown eyes appearing next to the woman.

The large, pitch black dog came up to about the woman's waist. I slapped my hand to my mouth to stop myself from making noise at the sight of the puppy. Even though the little puppy was baring its teeth, snarling, and growling at us. It was still just *so* cute! *Look at those big brown eyes and little nose!*

"Who the hell are you and how did you find me?" the woman growled, her voice low and menacing. To my surprise, Lorelai still smirked even though there was a weapon against her. Adrian peeked out over my shoulder from behind me.

"We're just passing through," she replied casually. Adrian's hands were on my shoulder as he looked past me, and when he saw the growling dog, I felt him tense.

"Don't expect me to—" the other woman's words were cut short as Lorelai grabbed the spear with both hands, and tried to twist it suddenly out of her hands while one of Lorelai's feet raised and kicked the stranger in the knee. Her leg buckled, and before I really knew what had happened the spear was in Lorelai's hands. She pointed it back at the woman where she now knelt in the grass. The big dog launched itself forward towards Lorelai, moving so fast it was a blur. It grabbed her arm in its mouth. It's teeth sunk into her skin as she gave a small yell of pain. She tried to shake it off, but the dog held fast. I could see Lorelai grimacing in pain as blood began to soak through her jacket sleeve. *No, she is not allowed t' get injured!* I ran forward and grabbed the dog around the belly with both arms. I hesitated, not wanting to try to pull it off of her in case it just made the injury worse. Lorelai waved her hand and made a forceful gesture at the dog's face, only for water to suddenly splash in its face. As the pup was surprised it's grip loosened and I pulled the dog off and to the side. It swung it's body and head back and forth trying to bite me, and I managed to avoid it all, but before long had no choice but to put the dog back down on the ground if I didn't want to drop and hurt him, or get hurt myself.

This other lady, now standing, whistled and pointed to the side. Her dog ran to the spot and sat down. Still growling. The new lady then focused on Lorelai, and quickly made some weird gestures with her hands while muttering under her breath. Lorelai started wriggling, her arms pinned against her sides by… nothing? Until she simply burst free, to the new lady's surprise. Adrian stepped out from behind me and we both stared in awe as Lorelai would push the new lady around without touching her, a flick of her wrist causing the stranger to go flying. The lady would pull shiny rocks or powders or strange leaves out of the belt around her waist, mutter something strange, and Lorelai would fumble around all confused and maybe unable to see for a minute. It was incredible what they were doing!

But then… before long, their respective magical gestures started to make cuts and bruises appear, and they'd have grunts of pain as anger burned in their eyes. It scared me. I'd never seen Lorelai like this before. The dog was staying back, but its teeth were still barred as it stood ready to fight. *Why are they even doin' all this?*

"Stop it!" I cried, while jumping forward and grabbing Lorelai's wrists. "Why are ya even fightin'?!" All of the commotion stopped very suddenly then.

"... You're not from the Navy?" The lady eyed us all with suspicion. *The what now? Why would the sea army for the big cities be all the way out here?* I looked at Lorelai, who seemed to be slightly confused and wary now herself.

"No. We're not. Who *are* you?" Lorelai asked.

"You're the one ambushing my home. Who are *you?"* the lady retorted.

"Someone who isn't about to let a weapon be pointed a--" Lorelai snapped, but I interrupted her.

"Hi, I'm Miles, and this here is Adrian— he's mute," I said, jumping forward and shaking the lady's hand with a smile. "And this is Lorelai!" Lorelai scowled at me. I never did understand why she was so *angry* all the time. "We were jus' passin' through this forest wonderin' why somebody would be livin' all the way out here by themself!" She gave me a look, and I realized I was still shaking her hand with both of mine. *Whoops.* I let go.

Her gaze raked across all of us, and settled back on Lorelai.

"Well *he's* certainly not from The Navy, despite his build," she said, gesturing at me. She stared hard at Lorelai. "I would apologize for the harm my dog caused you, except he was simply protecting me from people who were, again, sneaking up on my home. And as far as he could tell, attacking me." She crossed her arms. For some reason I couldn't figure out, Lorelai smiled.

"Of course, my apologies," Lorelai said, nodding deeply. The lady's eyes narrowed.

"So if you're not with the Navy, what is that metal brace-like thing on your neck and, more importantly, why is it engraved with magical runes? Where did you get it?" The lady asked, peering closely at Lorelai's strange metal choker with suspicion. Lorelai's smile fell.

"I made it myself," she said simply.

"*What?* There's no way--" the lady started. But as they had been talking Lorelai looked down at her arm, as the dark red spot continued to grow on the sleeve of her green jacket. She rolled her sleeve up as well as she could, trying to avoid touching the wound. The lady stopped talking. Blood dripped onto the grass, and I had to look away. As I eyed my shoes, I saw a bright yellow light appear out of the corner of my eye. Peeking back up at Lorelai, I saw a golden, shimmering light drift out of her hand and land lightly on her wound. I hate the sight of blood, but I couldn't look away as the bite marks closed, entirely healing over. The light disappeared, and with a wipe movement from her still hovering hand, all of the blood on her arm and soaked into her sleeve was pulled out, falling onto the grass. Leaving her clean and healed as if nothing had happened.

All three of us-- Adrian, the lady, and I-- stared in shock and awe.

Someone who can do that, who can heal terrible pain at the drop of a hat, and control water and air… is crazy powerful. Surely I can't just call someone so powerful only their name, people like that usually have titles… but Lorelai doesn't, does she? Well. Maybe I can show her my respect by calling her Ms. *Lorelai… she is a Ms. is she not? Didn't The Captain call her that once?*

"How on earth did you do that?!" the lady cried. Ms. Lorelai glanced back up at her, and shrugged. The lady paused. "So, you're not with the Navy, and you *weren't* ambushing me?" She asked, looking to me for the answer. *Why is she looking at me?*

"Um, uh, well--" Being somewhat in charge of the result of what was happening, even for a second, made me nervous. I glanced at

Ms. Lorelai, and she turned and glared at me. "Y-yes. Yes." The lady looked back to Ms. Lorelai.

"Good. Now, can you heal animals like that?" she asked. The question surprised me-- it seemed to surprise Ms. Lorelai as well. Our eyes moved towards the large black dog that sat at her side and watched all of us. She noticed. "He has a wound I worry might be infected. If you can heal him, I will help you find your way through these woods quickly and get a roof over your head for the night," her eyes ran over all three of us again as she offered, before returning the steady eye contact with Ms. Lorelai.

"Sure, anything for a pretty face," Ms. Lorelai said, winking at the other woman. The lady looked a bit confused and maybe even suspicious at Ms. Lorelai's comments-- but then her cheeks turned red as she held back a smile. Ms. Lorelai approached the dog, and the lady muttered;

"Down boy." Her dog visibly relaxed, but still eyed Ms. Lorelai as she knelt next to him. The lady bent down at her side and gently pulled one of the dog's back legs out from under him, revealing a deep cut on the leg.

Ms. Lorelai moved her hand over the wound, this time much closer to the injury than she had on herself. I could only make out a small peek of the beautiful magic past the women, but I could tell that the lady was as amazed as I was. *I had no idea magic was real before this, before meeting Ms. Lorelai... I can't believe they can do all this... How's it even possible?*

They stood back up when Ms. Lorelai was finished, and the dog's leg looked good as new.

"We should be heading off now," Ms. Lorelai said, as if what she had done was no big deal. The lady stuck out her hand towards her.

"I'm Velia. It's good to meet you," she smiled. Ms. Lorelai looked down at her hand, and decided to shake it. Velia turned towards us. "It's good to meet you both too. Now let's go, we need to get going if we want to get to a good place to sleep before it's dark." With that, the two women started walking.

Adrian and I listened to the two talk and followed behind them. Just like Ms. Lorelai, she liked to keep details to herself. Velia told us that she preferred living alone in the woods, though I can't understand how that could be true. Ms. Lorelai told her that we wanted to pass through to the next nearest settlement— and no details beyond that. *Hmph. Why all the secrecy?*

"W-Well, can we at least know your dog's name?" I asked. Velia looked at me.

"His name is Colby," she said plainly. I gasped.

"Colby! Colby, Colby baby, c'mere!" I called to the large puppy excitedly in a high-pitched voice, crouching.

"N- *Augh!*" She groaned as her dog came leaping towards me with a huge smile on his face. He pushed me to the ground without meaning to, and licked my face with his tag wagging wildly as I pet him. Adrian leaned down and patted his soft head, then crouched and rubbed behind his ears with both hands, smiling. He stood and smirked at me as I began to try to gently push Colby off of me to stand up.

"Heel!" Velia called out, and Colby ducked his head and hopped back over to her, tail between his legs, before sitting beside her. Despite her tone, she smiled slightly at me and patted her dog's head.

We walked for a while in silence. Velia moved along the uneven ground easily, confidently, with her steps making no sound at all. Colby kept up with her and walked just as silently, almost becoming a shadow himself. Adrian and I stayed in the back of the group-- I made sure to help him not fall over when he tripped. Every once in a while, the doggy would glance back at me and I would give him a smile.

"What do you think?" Adrian asked me, before pointing towards Velia.

"She reminds me a lot a Ms.Lorelai so far," I signed back.

He nodded. "But can we trust her?"

"Well, we're trusting Ms. Lorelai," I motioned back, giving a small shrug. But his worry still concerned me. "She seems nice enough, helpin' us out through here. We *did* sneak up on 'er before," I reminded him. "And… she has a pup. How bad can she be?" I grinned.

Eventually the sky began to darken. But then, little lights appeared ahead of us too. We broke out of the edge of the treeline to see a quaint little town, with homes and shops made from dark wood, and lamps hanging off of the outside of them, to light the road. Velia turned to us.

"I'll help you find the tavern. I need somewhere to stay for the night now too, those woods aren't very kind at night… Can we share a drink before we part ways?" she said, looking at each of us in turn but gained a shy little smile when she turned to Lorelai. I looked at Ms. Lorelai hopefully. Adrian did too. She looked at Velia, then at Colby who sat by her side, then at the two of us.

"Please ma'am? Velia seems quite nice, I'm sure she was jus' protecting her home from strangers before," I said. Velia nodded.

"Alright sure," Ms. Lorelai said. The other three of us smiled at each other.

Lorelai

The local Inn's bar was a bit too brightly lit, with far too many other people in it. I much preferred bars that were dimly lit, not crowded, sitting in a soft booth in the back, either sipping and planning, or drinking and eyeing up someone attractive to talk to. *Though perhaps I could still do the latter...* My gaze drifted over to the attractive young lady we had found in the woods, Velia. The three of them chose a table that felt very out in the open. Velia went up to get our drinks, during which point the two boys communicated silently with their silly made up hand signs, while I scanned the room. There was a group of men jostling each other and laughing uproariously near the bar, an awkward couple on a date in the far corner, several people who were likely here after a day at whatever boring middle-of-nowhere small town job they had. *Ugh.* No one else here was particularly interesting.

Velia returned. Her dark green robes edged with black had tiny swirling purple designs that you could only see when she was close. I was surprised I hadn't noticed them before. She passed us our drinks. Adrian made strange motions with his hands. An apologetic look crossed Velia's face.

"Don't worry I'll translate for us!" Miles piped up again. Apparently Adrian was trying to ask about the Navy Velia had mentioned. He likely simply did not know what the word meant, but I was wondering something about that as well. *How much does she know about what the Navy does? ... And does that have something to do with why she was hiding out in the woods?* Her face darkened. She lowered her voice and leaned in. I did the same.

"The Navy…" she began. "If you don't know what they really do, behind closed doors, all the better. They're greedy, they come out of nowhere…" suddenly she stopped, shaking her head and leaning back. "Too many ears here to talk about anything like that. Be happy you don't know— ignorance is bliss." I detected a hint of bitterness to her voice. I was intrigued, to say the least. I had never before met anyone else who had any idea at all about the more… *dark* side of the Navy. I would have to find out what she really knew, specifically.

She turned to me, a glint in her eye all of a sudden as she smirked. The edges of my lips reached upwards.

"I have a *wealth* of questions for you though, Lorelai!" She smiled. It was a nice smile.

But then she asked me about my magic, how it worked. Had I really been *manipulating air and water* back there? Why did I not seem to need material components? The questions bubbled out of her, her excitement and interest blatantly apparent as she sounded nearly incredulous. My heart began to race, my chest tightening as if a metal claw was around me and squeezing.
And then.

"*How* do you harness and use your magical power? It's different from anything I've ever seen!" Velia exclaimed.

The bar disappeared.

A voice I hadn't heard in a very long, *long* time echoed in my brain.

"*How* do you harness and use your magical power?! *How?!* By dominating the Gift I've given you, being it's *master*, you insolent twat!" *Insolent twat. Insolent twat.*

His anger. Rage. My heart raced, my legs were shaking. Weak. He reached for me.

"No, no, nonono, *no* don't, I-I'm sorry, I can't-"

"Ms. Lorelai! Lorey! It's okay, you're okay, you're safe, no one is going to hurt you…" A gentle hand was rubbing my back. It was cold beneath me. I pulled the large cloth tighter around me. I was rocking back and forth. Slowly, I stopped, and lifted my head.

Miles and Adrian were kneeling next to me. Adrian's hand was the hand on my back. Miles' hand was on my shoulder. Velia's dog was sitting next to me. We were outside. I was sitting on a patch of grass in the dark, the lamp hanging off of the bar above me casting a soft amber glow. Everyone's shadows surrounded me, like manifestations of their worry. Velia's robe was what was wrapped around me. She stood nearby, watching me worriedly with fear edging her eyes. She simply wore a white undershirt and tight black pants. As I looked up at Velia, she came closer and sat in the grass next to me. She put a hand on my knee and said quietly,

"Are you okay? I'm *so* sorry, I didn't mean to—" I raised my hand to stop her.

"It is not your fault," my voice was quiet. I lifted my gaze to meet her eyes. They were green with hazel flecks. "Thank you for lending me your robe."
I tore my gaze away to turn to Miles and Adrian.

"Thank you," I whispered. Adrian nodded, still clearly worried. Miles smiled.

"I carried ya right outta that place as soon as I realized ye weren't okay. None a them in there saw ya past me!"
I put my face in my hands and sighed. *I wish you all hadn't seen this, seen me like this… I had been doing so well for years, how did this happen?…*

Abruptly, I clambered to my feet and handed Velia back her robe. My expression was steeled.
There was no way to go but up; forward.

Chapter Nine - Tongue Tied

<u>Morgan</u>

The wooden boards beneath me and around me bashed into my back and head, over and over and over again. My mouth was dry, and my long white hair was tangled in knots all around me. My head pounded. Everything ached. The injury I had gotten from falling from the damn cliff face created a small pool of wetness by my foot. I couldn't see anything. I thought about how I had heard Miles when they had first forced me in here. *Had he really come and noticed before we were gone? Was* he *why there had been a delay in between stowing me and leaving? What had he done, or tried to do? ... ... Was he okay?*

...

And how would they ever find me?

Minutes turned into an unknown passage of time that felt like an eternity. Did I fall asleep? How could I have, in that state. I couldn't even sleep normally in my human form. My mind wandered in circles. Absolutely no light ever filtered in between the boards.

Eventually there was commotion, sounds of multiple people moving around, talking, taking things out of a different part of the carriage. I was shaken out of whatever sleepy mental stupor I might have been in-- or maybe I was simply losing too much blood, not sleepy. It was hard to tell. I closed my eyes and tried to listen, tried to stretch my senses past the walls of the carriage that was my cage. And that was when I finally heard it-- beyond the noise of my captors, I heard the sea. Blissful, quiet waves lapping against the shore. I could *just* make them out. For a moment the familiar sound almost gave me a touch of relief, until my mind caught up with me and I realized: the sea was now only another means of death or transport, instead of the home and welcome escape I had previously always known it as. And if we were truly at an ocean, I was likely being brought too far away from the others for any possible rescue.

It was up to me, and me alone. My life, and Adva's, were on the line. *Oh Adva. She has no idea what has happened to me...*

It could *not* end like this. Not if I still had a single unbroken bone in my body— not if I could fight.

I could hear my captors moving towards the back of the carriage. *They must be hunters, who else would capture me like this? Especially right after a human saw my spots...They gave me away...Now is my opportunity to escape.* Shoving my hair back, I pushed myself up and had barely enough room to crouch right in front of where they would open the back to get me. I waited, aching, as my heart pounded quickly and the pain in my skull followed it. When the boards finally creaked open, they were fast, and a large thick sack was pulled in my direction. But I was prepared. Before the sack could incase me, I leapt out with all my might, falling right into one of them and successfully knocking him on his back. I stood over the man, snarling at the other hunters who surrounded me. I felt a strange, slightly painful stretching feeling in my entire jaw-- and when I tried to close my mouth, I felt something I had never felt before. Or, at least, never while in my human form. The hunters yelled in surprise, a few jumping back yet all of them unsheathed daggers from their belts.

The large, razor sharp canine teeth I used as a seal to hunt fish, squid, and even occasionally penguins if I travelled up north, had appeared. Grown right into my human mouth when I needed them most.

I snarled and growled, baring my teeth at all of them. One lunged forward with a dagger-- I grabbed his hand before he could hit me. A roar only a seal would make, deep and throaty and loud, bellowed out of me in his face. Shifting my grip to the hilt, I threw his dagger out of his hand and onto the floor. It went skidding off to the side. When the next hunter out of a total of five came at me, I managed to kick his feet out from under him and send him sprawling. Jumping over him, I aimed to run. Run away as far and as fast as I could and hide. But before I could clear it, the man grabbed my ankle from underneath me and a female hunter next to him simultaneously swiped my side with her dagger.

I collapsed with a heavy thud, a bleeding side, and a re-opened bleeding ankle. I grabbed my side with a groan, as the hunter I had fallen onto ensnared me in his grasp. I struggled on top of the man to get free, but I had no chance before multiple others roughly pulled me up and bound my wrists behind me in rope. I snarled and spit and swore and cursed, still struggling against them, but they ignored my threats. One of them grabbed a shotty bandage and a dirty old shirt from inside the caravan, slapping the bandage onto my side wound and tapping it. A single strip of cloth was ripped from the dirty shirt and was tied around my injured ankle.

One of the hunters, a man who must have been standing back while the others attacked me, stepped forward. I hadn't even noticed him standing there before. He had a dark, neatly trimmed beard, and a pirate's hat with a wide brim that cast his dark eyes and skin in shadow. His coat was dark blue with gold trim. *What is someone in such a uniform doing with a bunch of lowly hunters?*

"Selkie." He spat the word as if it were an insult. Unable to fight, I glared at him wishing the daggers in my gaze would actually cut him. "You have put up quite a struggle, haven't you?" He reached forward, grabbing my chin and forcing my mouth open. He gazed curiously at my seal teeth, his grip tightening on my jaw to keep me from talking or biting. He examined my teeth with a sense of near admiration as he forced my head to turn, like a hunter might admire its kill and imagine it on their wall before shooting.

I managed to spit in his face.

He reared back, letting go of me to wipe his face as he stepped up. Anger and disgust filled his eyes.

"You won't be able to keep me for long," I snarled.

He made a ball of cloth from part of the shirt, and smeared dirt on it before shoving it roughly into my mouth and giving one of the hunters the other strip of shirt. As it was quickly tied around my mouth, he leaned closer and stared hard at me.

"We shall see about that." He smiled.

Instead of then being immediately put into another glorified box, their strongest man held my bound arms and walked behind me. With two hunters in front of me and a total of three behind me, bound and gagged, I was walked up the gangplank of a ship. The adrenaline was wearing off. I was exhausted. Putting any weight on my ankle made my leg want to buckle, so I limped and was shoved onto the large ship. I gazed down over the edge at the waves. It was getting dark, the sunset blocked by a forest behind us. The water below was grey, like the sky, and was beginning to hit the land with more force. I yearned with all my might that I could simply dive in and swim away. Away from the hunters and pirates, away from any ship, away from all of it. Towards home. But the only thing successfully jumping into the ocean would get me was a real possibility of drowning. Bound or not.

The hunters took me below deck. Down the hall. Into a tiny empty room that might have once been a broom closet. They shoved me to the ground, and then bound my ankles together too. The door closed, leaving me alone as the lock clicked shut. Darkness again.

Except for the tiny stream of the last bit of weak light coming in through a small porthole on the wall above me.

We set sail shortly thereafter.

<u>Adrian</u>

I sat up in bed and yawned, stretching my arms. I lifted handfuls of the blanket from my lap up to my face and rubbed my cheek against it. *How do humans make these things so incredibly soft? It is wonderful.* I glanced over to the other side of the room, where a giant lump under a blanket rose and fell slightly with Miles' breathing. He was still asleep. My stomach grumbled at me with hunger. I wrapped the blanket around my shoulders and got out of bed with it trailing behind me.

I shuffled out of the tavern room Miles and I were sharing, and down to their mess hall with the blanket still around me. People looked at me as I entered, but I simply headed for the large plates and containers of food. I did not really recognize any of the strange substances. I grabbed two of the light brown soft disks, and found a seat, wrapping the blanket around me. As I was getting settled, Miles walked in. He scanned the room, and when he saw me, he hurried over.

"Adrian, ye not supposed t' bring those outta ye room, bud," he tugged on the edge of my blanket. "And what are ye doing with those pancakes, where's ya plate?" he asked.

"... I can not keep my blanket?" It fell down to the floor as I let go of it to sign. "And I thought the small circle food was eaten by hand." Pancakes, he had called them. Miles chuckled to himself.

"C'mon bud, I'll show you how t' make those circles taste even better," he signed back, then gestured for me to put the blanket on the chair and follow him.

A while later, Lorelai groggily came and sat with us with a plate of food.

"Velia's gone," she said gruffly. She shoved a note at us. It read;

'Sorry if I caused any trouble last night. Hope you're okay. Don't look for me— you won't find me. But we will meet again, dear fellow witch. Best wishes, ~Velia."

I looked back up at Lorelai. She ate, and her eyes never lifted from her plate. I frowned. Lorelai seemed unhappy. I hesitated. Then I held the note out to her, pushing for her to pay attention to me. When she glanced up at the note, at me, I underlined with my finger the words 'we will meet again' and tried to give her a reassuring smile. She gave me a brief, weak smile in return. We all returned to our meal.

After a few minutes of eating, Lorelai said that we should head off. She reminded us that we had to keep moving, and could not settle, if we wanted to find Morgan in time. After packing up our very meager belongings, we left the tavern and walked out of the village. As we left, Lorelai turned to us, holding out two pieces of old yellowed paper with drawings of plants on them. I recognized them, she had shown them to us before. One was an image of a flower with thin pink petals pointed down around a large, round, reddish center, which Lorelai and I had at one point been looking for in a different town. Before Morgan was taken. The other was a flower with orange petals.

"We still need to look for these. We may be able to find them in the plains we will be walking through." Lorelai paused. "I guess I might as well tell you *why* we need them. They're for a spell to heal Morgan's sister-- it's what she gets out of our deal once we rescue her."

"Morgan has a sister? Who is hurt?" I asked, surprised, but my words were never translated.

"Oh! I almost forgot!" Miles exclaimed instead, dropping his small knapsack on the ground. After digging through it for a moment, he pulled out a similar paper to Lorelai's, that depicted a flower with pink triangular petals and bits of yellow, and a center of many tiny yellow circles put together to make one. Then— he held up an identical flower. It seemed to be wilting a little.

Lorelai's eyes went wide. She leapt forward, snatching it out of his hands. She waved her other hand over and around it, and dark blue and dark green swirls appeared around the plant while Lorelai focused intently. Slowly, the curled brown edges lifted up, life and colour flowing back into it.

"Wow."

I glanced over. Miles was in awe at the simple display of magic once more.

Lorelai

We ended up having to walk for half of the day until we reached the cavern where the Informant was living for now.

"We're almost there," I told the two of them. I looked back, expecting tiredness or boredom, but instead the two were chatting animatedly through hand signs.

It wasn't long after that until the cave was finally before us.

"Now wait here for a minute before following me, I'll make sure he's here." I entered the cave alone, and had to walk for a minute in total darkness before the dim amber glow of an oil lamp began to flicker against the rough stone walls. He sat on a blanket, sharpening a dagger. He had a small, scraggly beard that he had always insisted on growing despite the fact that he could hardly grow one. The scar across his left eye that he had gotten in a particularly nasty fight years ago had faded to white. He showed his age more now though, than he had the last time I had seen him. He looked up at me, unsurprised at the presence of another person in his middle of nowhere cave. He jumped to his feet, setting his dagger down on the ground.

"Ma- I mean, uh, Lorelai! It was Lorelai wasn't it dear, it's been so long since you've found me, you look incredible! You've changed so much, I hardly recognize you! You do always have that special little weapon kept in your boot though, and you've been wearing that jacket for decades at least," he exclaimed.

"Yes, hello John, it's been quite a few years hasn't it… holing up in caves now, are we?" I said, giving him a brief pat on the back as I let him hug me for a second.

"Ah, well, y'know…" he stopped. "Who have you brought with you there, Ms?" he asked me, suddenly a bit on guard.

"Trust me, they're harmless."

I then groaned and rolled my eyes as I heard Adrian bumbling around, stubbing his toe, struggling through the darkness. I put my hand over my eyes and shook my head.

"He couldn't sneak up on *anything* in the dark, huh," John said— clearly convinced of my point.

Miles appeared first, slinking silently out of the darkness. He smiled and waved. Then Adrian walked up.

"Miles, Adrian, this is The Informant," I said, remembering in time that John prefers that those outside his inner circle only know him by his title. He sat back down on his rough and worn blanket.

"What do you folks need to know?" He asked.

"We need to know where The Meeting Place is," I said. John stared at me. I returned a hard stare back. "It's urgent," I insisted.

"Lorelai. What is your intention, travelling with *these two.*" His voice was ice cold now, the previous warmth gone. He jerked his head in Adrian's direction in particular. I bit my lip. So it was true then— John really could see it. Past the human facade.

"I made a deal with someone that would help solve my biggest problem in life and I will find her there," I said through gritted teeth.

John nodded, his brow furrowed.

"It will cost more this time," he said.

"Fine. Name your price."

He hesitated. He looked at me, at Miles, and then looked a confused Adrian up and down slowly. He stood, approached me and looked up at me sternly.

"I need a golden dagger," he said. "It was stolen from me. The hilt is solid gold with small gemstones in it, and even the blade itself is gold plated. You know the one. But it *cannot* fall into the wrong hands, Lorelai, you hear me? It's magic should not be corrupted." I nodded solemnly.

Oh John, but how do you know that the wrong hands aren't my own?

John thought that bandits had come in the night and stolen it from his locked box. I figured though, that it was more likely that pirates or hunters— potentially the very hunters we were after now, ironically the ones we needed his information to find— had been the ones to steal his dagger. Particularly since it was monetarily valuable *and* magical. But he wouldn't listen to me this time. The company I was keeping was probably to blame. A civilian, who isn't supposed to know of this life, and a monster. But Adrian… despite all the damning evidence of his reaction before and both Nico *and* John seeing or realizing it… how could he possibly be an evil monster?

We left John's cave and walked through the woods. Adrian and Miles were following me towards a reported bandit camp, since John insisted we check out the bandit angle to find the dagger. The criminals supposedly hid out in an abandoned warehouse in the forest outside the small town that had been having trouble with them. John's cave was not too far from it either.

I looked back at Adrian and Miles. They were communicating to each other with their hand signs, too enraptured in their conversation to notice my glancing back at them. Both Adrian and Miles were so determined to rescue Morgan--this girl they both hardly knew--that they left whatever life they may have had previously to follow a known witch that they also didn't know well into likely dangerous unknowns. *Are they just stupid and naive… or genuinely incredibly selfless?* Either way, that did not sound like any monster I had ever run into. And I had had multiple hunter lifetimes worth of encounters.

Abruptly, I stopped and turned to face the two men who walked with me.

"You don't have to do this," I told them. "It could be very dangerous. What do you even have to gain?" They both looked quite surprised at my sudden comments. Adrian started signing immediately. Miles translated for me.

"I have nothin' to go back to, no other home… I must do what's right, and I can't let someone innocent be, uh, killed, or worse, if there's somethin' I can do about it," Miles said for him. "That's mighty noble of ya, Adrian," he added. "As for me…" he paused, collecting his thoughts. "I do have a nice home to go back t', but all I've ever wanted was to sail and go on an adventure. Now I've got one. And honestly, don't tell her I said this, but Morgan kinda reminds me of my niece back home and I'd be sick with worry if I didn't know what was happenin' t' her."

I blinked.

"You're… both seriously putting your lives in danger for a se-- *girl*, you hardly know, because… it's the right thing to do? *Really?*" I said. I could not remember the last time I had known someone who wasn't doing what they were doing for monetary or personal gain. Much less someone who would put themselves in danger for someone they barely knew.

"Uh… yeah? Yeah I guess so," said Miles. "Eh, good on us!" He turned to Adrian and offered him a high-five. He stared at his raised hand in confusion. Miles grabbed Adrian's hand and showed him what to do. I rubbed my face and eyes and sighed. Turning, I kept walking.

John seeing what Adrian was, and questioning why I was with them, came to mind. *I should have found a minute to ask John exactly what monster or creature he had seen Adrian to be… but does it even matter what he is? A monster is a monster… Right?* But monsters weren't stupid. They weren't naive. They certainly weren't friendly, or cheerful, or selfless, or giving. Monsters were ruthless, destructive, cunning, killing machines. Enemies of people. Wanting nothing but bloodshed. I had seen evidence of that first hand, countless times before. But there, right behind me, Adrian and Miles continued to mostly-silently converse, with big gesturing and smiles on their faces. Following me against all better judgement. To save someone they barely knew-- with no *real* gain on their end. But John was never wrong about what he saw.

I simply *couldn't* make sense of it. It defied everything I had ever known.

Miles

The three of us stood at a distance, peering out from behind a few trees, eyeing up a wood and stone structure ahead of us. It was a box really, with small square sections poking out as lookout spots with short walls. The roof was uneven rough stone and the door was giant and barred. The entire thing looked like it may have been an abandoned post that a monarch had built decades-- or maybe even a century or two-- ago. My old Pa had said he had seen a few things like this dotted around on his travels. It sat surrounded by tall trees, and had few windows. It seemed to have no activity or people anywhere. *The thieves must only go on out stealin' at night I suppose. There's gonna be a bunch a them in there though, I bet.* I looked over at Lorelai with unease. *She best not be thinkin' 'bout just stormin' in there…* I thought.

"Ms. Lorelai, there might be a lot a people in there, we shouldn't just run in…" I tried. She turned her gaze to me. Seemed to be thinking.

"Hmm… You're...right," she said. *I am?! Is she agreein' with me?* "You're right that I would have, in the past, charged in with magic and swords and done away with them," she continued. *…Oh? The past?* I wondered, giving her a puzzled look. "But today is not that day. We will survey them for now. See if we can spot anything that could lead us to the dagger," she declared. I smiled.

"Adrian an' I can go 'round the back, check for back entrances or anythin' strange," I suggested. Lorelai's eyes drifted toward Adrian with a hesitant look.

"He'll be fine, I'll watch him and make sure he don't make too much noise, I swear," I said.

"Fine. I'll take the front, see if I can find a way past the door or see anything through the windows. No matter what, don't get caught. Scream if you do," Lorelai warned before heading off.

Adrian and I stayed within the treeline, sneaking through the edge of the forest around the criminals' base. I looked at Adrian, then checked the ground for any twigs or anything, maybe low hanging branches, to make sure he wouldn't trip or make noise.

There was no one waiting in the forest for us. No guards around the back, but no back entrance either. I could see several people milling about inside through a small window, though. For a couple of minutes, we hid behind tree trunks and watched them… But eventually, I noticed something. A rope ladder. Strung down the side of the building, partially hidden by vines and leaves, and it led up to one of the currently empty lookout posts. *Hmm…*

I headed for it. Until I was stopped by the top of my shirt being pulled back with surprising strength, that is. I turned back to Adrian as he let go of me.

"What do you think you are doing?!" he asked.

"It's fine. There's a ladder, no one is up there, I'm gonna check it out," I signed back.

There wasn't time to argue or disagree. Stepping out of the treeline, I hurried for the rope ladder and began to climb it. After a moment, Adrian carefully followed me. As I reached the top and pulled myself up onto the stone floor, the wind messed my hair. I climbed up, and approached the side. An ocean of green was laid out before me. The forest continued on for miles and miles to one side of me before it met the sky. On my other side, the trees went for a ways before turning into grassy plains. The part of the field I could see was, surprisingly, not empty even though we were in the middle of nowhere. Trekking through it was a group of people. Maybe five or six. The sunlight hit off the metal of their armour and weapons… I realized they were heading west, away from the direction of The Informant's cave. There wasn't anything else nearby to the east that I knew, as the town Lorelai mentioned as being attacked by these bandits was south of here. Something about the group gave me a very bad feeling-- even though they weren't headed towards us. *Where're they coming from? … They're not coming from The Informants cave, are they? Is there red on one a those blades? It's hard to see from all the way up here...*

A tap on my shoulder. Adrian.

"I would ask you what is wrong, but I think we need to get out of here *now,"* he said quickly, with fear in his eyes, before pointing back at the door that led into the building. Commotion was beginning to build behind it, sounds of many people thundering up stairs and talking. We left in a hurry down the ladder, retreating back into the forest before circling around in an attempt to find Ms. Lorelai. We found her-- squeezing as fast as she could through a broken window with a small bag in her hand. She spotted us quickly, and ran towards us, only to keep going fast right past us.

"Come on boys!" she called back. Adrian shook his head in disbelief, and we started running as bandits started spilling out of the front door of the base.

I took off right behind Adrian, following him as much as I could keep up as he moved through the trees. I could hear the group of bandits not far behind me, as Adrian moved up to catch up with Ms. Lorelai and created space between us. The bandits were rowdy, some hooping and hollering as they chased us through the forest. I jumped to one side with a yelp as a dagger landed in the ground next to me, just barely missing my leg. Adrian glanced back at me-- I forced a weak smile, but it must not've been very convincing as he slowed a little to run by my side. I was already starting to breathe heavily. *Geez, how long have we been runnin'?* I looked back and blinked in surprise; I could still see bits of the building we had left between the trees. But blocking most of my view of how not so far away it was, the group of maybe four or five men all had weapons in their hands and I could see more tucked away. Devilish grins grew on their faces when they saw me looking. I gulped. Facing ahead again, I tried my hardest to run faster, as my legs ached. Adrian kept up with me easily. I hadn't realized how fit the guy was before. I could lift just about anything and climb easily, but running? Not so much.

"You okay?" Adrian asked, looking concerned. He had no problem signing while running. I was breathing so heavily, focused on trying to stay ahead of the bandits and not trip over roots and sticks, or run into trees, I couldn't really respond. I thought about just nodding, but I didn't really want to lie. Truth be told, my body wasn't handling this so well. I wasn't sure how much longer I could keep ahead of them.

"Hey Miles, Adrian?" Ms. Lorelai called back to us from a bit ahead. I wished Adrian could respond for me.

"...Ey?" I called back, between my heaving breaths.

"Move." Suddenly Ms. Lorelai stopped in her tracks and faced us. She pulled a ball of water out of her canteen. Adrian and I jumped to either side just in time as Ms. Lorelai sent water not only splashing all over the bandits, but with enough force to knock them all onto their backs!

"Does th--" I started, planning on asking if this meant we could have a quick break, but Ms. Lorelai took off running before I could get the words out. Adrian waved for me to follow, and then ran after her. The bandits were starting to get up-- I took off after them.

After more running than I think I'd ever done in my life, following Ms. Lorelai and Adrian as fast as I could through the woods, we had *finally* lost them thanks to the lead Ms. Lorelai's water magic had given us. Maybe they had just decided that whatever Ms. Lorelai had stolen wasn't worth this much effort. I stopped, and leaned against a tree, heaving and gasping for air. Adrian and Ms. Lorelai were breathing heavy too, but they did both recover faster than me. Adrian tried to communicate, but it was too bad for him that he couldn't say anything to Ms. Lorelai until I had decided I had enough air back. I sat on the grass leaning on a tree trunk, and translated.

"Why the heck did ya do that," I said for him. The words sorta lost all of their energy when they went from him to me. Lorelai smiled, for once with a touch of cheerfulness, and shrugged.

"What can I say, old habits die hard."

Inside the sack she had stolen was not the dagger, but a pile of gold coins.

"I didn't have much time, so no dagger-- the people were *everywhere* in there! But I did get us some money for our troubles," she said.

"I also may have spotted somethin'..." I said.

I explained to her what I had seen; the men in armour and with weapons, that might have had blood on them, heading away from the East. Away from where The Informant's cave was. Her eyes widened. I had seen that look before. She made sure that I was sure about everything I had seen, asked if I knew what colour they were wearing, and then just like that she ran right off. I heaved a big sigh, and clambered to my feet. Adrian and I took off at a jog. We managed to keep her just barely in sight, or, well, Adrian did, until we made it back to the cave The Informant was in.

Right away I knew that my hunch had been right-- something terrible had happened here. Bloody boot-prints left the cave's mouth, and as Adrian and I slowly entered the cave through the darkness, I heard a tiny, quietly wavering voice from up ahead.

"...*John?*" It was Lorelai's voice, sounding choked up. What we found when we finally entered the light of the oil lamp… was horrid beyond any nightmare of mine. The Informant lay there, in Ms. Lorelai's arms as she sat on her knees in a pool of blood. I couldn't stand the sight of so much blood, I had to look away from the man. Lorelai was clearly holding back tears, but I couldn't help a few of mine escaping. The dagger he had when we arrived lay next to him, both the handle and the blade covered with blood. I abruptly realized, when I let myself really look at him, that blood continued to pour out of the man's mouth. He was also laced with cuts and gashes.

While biting her lip, Lorelai raised one hand, and waved it over his mouth multiple times. Adrian went to her, and knelt down with her, an arm around her shoulders. But I couldn't bear to get any closer to all that blood. After a moment or two of her casting magic, the blood stopped coming out of his mouth. Adrian moved around Ms. Lorelai, and carefully put his ear above The Informant's mouth. Abruptly Adrian's head shot up, a smile on his face, and he signed to me excitedly. I was shocked, but so happy, I was speechless at first.

"What, what is it? What is it?" Lorelai urged.

"H--he-- he's breathin'. Barely."

"Really?" Lorelai perked up. "John, John, can you hear me? It's Lorelai, they're gone..." There was no response. She took a deep breath. And then slowly put him on his side, facing away from her. There was a pause, then she leaned forward and put two fingers in his mouth. She scooped out some blood-- and he started coughing! He was coughing up blood, but he was coughing! And his eyes fluttered open.

He blinked up at Lorelai, and a strange garbled sound came out of his mouth. He tried to sit up then, but Lorelai kept him down with a firm hand on his chest.

"It's me John. You're going to be okay," she said.

"Why...why isn't he sayin' anythin'?" I was hesitant to speak myself. Lorelai looked down at him. They looked at each other for a moment, and then Lorelai raised her head, stared me in the eyes, and said;

"They… they cut out his tongue. I noticed for certain when I cleared his throat."

At that, The Informant sat up, and then stood up, ignoring and pushing away Lorelai's insistence that he should stay lying down. Approaching his bag and rug, which were both stained with patches of red now, he dug around until he found two mostly clean pieces of paper and a pen. He scrawled on the uneven stone floor.

'Those bastards did this to me because they don't want you to lead civilians to The Meeting Place, and they think you want to steal their selkie for profit. They think you were hunting it first. Told me so. I figure none of that is completely true… but you should watch your backs carefully.

As for me… I'll tell you where The Meeting Place is for free so that you can kill those bastards for me.'

Chapter Ten - Black Spots

<u>Morgan</u>

I was stuck in near complete darkness. The slight movement of the floor beneath me soon became more normal than a still one had been. My eyes began to see things in the dim light, in the shadows caused by the small amount of muddled sunlight that streamed through the tiny window during the day. Swimming lines and shapes. A person standing in the dark just out of view. Sometimes I would close my eyes to be rid of them. But then I would fall asleep. In my dreams and nightmares there were people, and seals, selkies, and tritons and chaos and magic and blood. I could never remember the details. Hunger began to gnaw at my insides. The pain and empty feeling of hunger grew and grew, like a tiny monster in my stomach that was consuming me from the inside out. Creating painful holes. Sometimes it would go away for a little while, but leave me feeling drained. It would only come back stronger.

Regardless, I had to try to escape. Or at least not be bound.

For a long, endlessly long, undetermined amount of time, nothing really worked. It wasn't that hard to find motivation to continue, though. All I had to think of was Adva, or of the men who had me captured. I couldn't let them do whatever it was they wanted to do with me.

Eventually, after many tries and what felt like days, I managed to get the rope off of my hands by getting an old nail on the wall in between two pieces of rope and loosening them. It was hell. I temporarily gave up several times. But with my hands free, the rest of me was quickly unbound as well. I spat the disgusting ball of cloth out of my mouth immediately, and spit several times in a corner, cursing. The spit came out dark brown thanks to that damn pirate captain. Or whatever he was, I wasn't sure. An enemy. I could be sure of that.

I sat on the floor in dim light. Tried picking the lock with the nail I pulled out of the wall. Laid down. Paced in circles until my ankle or side hurt too much to continue. Slept erratically if at all. Spent hours gazing out the small porthole at the dark, empty ocean. I sighed. Wondered why they wanted me alive when hunters just like them had mercilessly slaughtered my whole pod without a second thought. Why was I supposedly different? Wondered what the little group from the island that I had left behind were doing. If they were even still together. Wondered what Adva was doing. If she was okay. Wondered why I had ever let go of my seal skin for even a second. Thought about whether I was even going to live to see anyone I liked or cared about again. And about what I was going to do to those damn hunters as soon as I had a chance.

I stood there, looking out at the sea from below its surface. We were moving, I knew that to be true, but you almost couldn't tell looking out of there. There was rarely anything to see besides a school of fish every once in a while. Which meant that when a group of strange dark shapes appeared in the distance, ahead of the ship and to the side, I noticed. As the ship and the creatures moved closer to one another, they came into view.

A pod of seals swam peacefully together under the waves, their tails moving back and forth. Little ones moved around the pod in between the adults, playing with each other under the watchful eyes of their parents, grandparents, and other pod members. If only I could have heard the children through that tiny ship window, I was sure they would be laughing. Then, to my surprise, they saw me. Not only did they see me, they decided to come a bit closer.

And that was when I noticed. I couldn't believe I hadn't realized sooner, but at the same time what I was seeing was impossible.

The pod was made up of mostly white seals--the family--with black spots. Which was a common sight; spotted seals, leopard seals, harp seals, many different types of seals could likely have that colouring, except they would also have significant grey areas on them as well. Not only did this family not have any grey on them… their black spots shone. Glowed. It was often hard to see, especially from a distance, and most would think their eyes were playing tricks on them but. I saw it, and in that moment I knew.

I was looking at a pod of selkies.

But not just any random pod of selkies.

They were related to me.

I was shocked. I couldn't understand how such a thing was possible and yet, seeing them, their patterns of spots, their colouring… I knew it to be true. Someone must have… I don't know. Left the family, years and years ago. Found a mate and left with them instead of simply growing our pod. It could happen, surely. It must have been when I was very young, or even before I was born, since I had no memory of it. I waved to them. One of the little ones moved his flipper back. Maybe the child was simply swimming, or mimicking me, but I believe they had waved back. *Is there any way I could-- could show them, prove that I'm one of their own before they get away? There is no way in hell I could get my ankle--injured or not-- up to the porthole to show them my spots…*

So instead, I tried speaking. Not any natural marine animal, not even Seal.

I spoke Selkish.

And I said hello, and introduced myself.

They swam closer! One of the adults, parents, moved closer, forcing their children to stay next to them. Their head was tilted, as if their interest was piqued. Or maybe they were just trying to listen. I continued speaking, my voice bubbling out of me in happiness even though the words were a bit odd on the human tongue.

But then the face of the one trying to listen fell. They all stared at me, the entire pod. My voice trailed off. The one in front seemed… sad. Disheartened. A few of them made noises back at me, and none of the sound could make its way through the glass… *Oh.* But, at the same time, I could tell by the movements of their mouths and fins that they were speaking Selkish. The language is rarely ever spoken on human tongues, as actual humans cannot speak it. Hopefully they could read the movements of my mouth and know that I was speaking the language of the selkies too. The way they were acting, I felt that they did. But we could not hear each other.

Suddenly the biggest one of the pod started ramming himself against the porthole glass. The others backed up as the wall shook with the force. He continued to do it too, again and again and again, one or two others joining in to try to help. The boat shook. The wood creaked as they thudded heavily against it. Nothing showed any sign of breaking. Little did they know, even if it did, I might just drown. Or nearly so. Regardless, the gesture moved me. My hand rested on my heart as my eyes welled with tears. I couldn't believe they were doing this for me.

"What the hell is going on in there!" I stopped. It was a distant yell, from above deck possibly. I made sweeping, shooing motions with my hands at the selkies, even though it pained me greatly. They didn't understand. But it didn't matter, because spears began flying down at them from above, barely missing as they panicked. They fled quickly. It didn't look like any of them had been hurt, but it was hard to be completely sure.

I scrambled, grabbing for the cloths and rope that had bound me. One strip, two, dirty ball of cloth hidden in my clothing. One strip around my mouth. Rope, wrapped around my hands, behind me. I sat on the floor against the wall just barely in time before the door burst open. Only for me to realize-- I had forgotten the blindfold.
The one with the blue and gold coat and the wide brimmed hat stood towering above me. He glared.

"*What* exactly have you been up to, my pretty?" he asked. I shuddered. "I was told that *selkies* had been seen throwing themselves against the side of my ship…" He walked up, and crouched down in front of me. Peering into my eyes. Not seeming surprised that they were not covered.

"I wonder if you can contact your kind from a great distance… create sounds we humans cannot hear…" his voice trailed off, but gears were clearly turning behind his eyes. *You know a lot less about selkies than I would've expected. Idiot.* He smiled. "Well, either way, soon we will find out every single one of your kind's little secrets, won't we." He stood up, a look of delight edged with malice appearing on his face as his hat cast it back into shadow.

Lorelai

I left the boys alone in an Inn in the nearby town. I walked around the town after nightfall, alone with my thoughts as I liked it. Miles had been *quite* distressed at John's request, but I would be happy to see it through for him. That is, except for the fact that they are hunters. Hunters killing other hunters in cold blood… meddling in other hunters' business… all a very big *no* in the community. If you could even call hunters' way of interacting amongst one another a community, of all things. But, I had to tell John I would do it. I'd never get Morgan back-- never get our deal fulfilled-- otherwise. I'd hate to break my word to John though…

Abruptly I spotted something out of the corner of my eye. A shadowed figure, quickly disappearing behind a building. *Hmm.* I kept walking. More alert now, I noticed when the figure moved swiftly out from behind the one building, moving closer towards me, only for them to hide again just before I turned a corner. I was being followed, it seemed. *How interesting!* I didn't even bother moving one of my weapons to my hand: I could withdraw one fast enough for that to be null. Not that I couldn't defeat someone without them anyway.

I flattened myself against the corner of the building I had rounded. *An old trick but a good one.* As the cloaked figure turned the corner to follow me, I threw myself at them, intending to have my hand to their throat against the wall. To my utter shock, the assailant grabbed my arm and flipped me right over onto my back on the ground before I could get a chance! I glared angrily up at them, ready to jump to my feet and fight-- only to recognize the face under the hood.

"You *left*!" I exclaimed angrily.

Velia chuckled, pulling the hood off and taking its shadow with it.

"I also said we would see each other again, didn't I?" she said, offering me a hand. Begrudgingly, I took it, letting her pull me to my feet-- only for her to pull a little too hard, and have us end up *very* close together. She came up to my shoulder. We gazed at each other for a split second, only for her cheeks to turn slightly red as she sheepishly stepped back. *What a dichotomy in her…*

"So, um, anyway, uh, you, uh, probably--" she began.

"Yes, why exactly *are* you following me?" I finished her thought. She gave a small smile up to me.

"I was in the area, delivering a package, when I saw you… I wanted to see if I could sneak up on you. It's my specialty, but I knew you'd be a challenge. As for the flip…" her voice trailed off for a moment. "Uh, instinct?" She said sheepishly. "I'm not really sure what happened there, honestly. Sorry." She stuck her hands into pockets that were almost unnoticeable in the black cloak. I raised an eyebrow. *A package delivery in the dead of night… and she was able to get the jump on* me *by, what, just simple instinct?!* I had a number of questions for her. But as she looked up at me, her green eyes twinkled in the dim light of the lamps that dotted the streets. I remembered how flustered she had become a moment ago from simply being so close to me, and I wanted to see it again. Because it was cute, and silly, and so innocent of a grown woman with such a mysterious past. Perhaps also to prove to myself that it had been real; it had been quite some time since I had 'played the field' so to speak. I smiled at her, and slid one of my hands under the cloak to her shoulder.

"Well, you snuck up on me-- you succeeded. Now what?" I slid my hand down the length of her arm while drawing even closer to her. Her cheeks began to flare red once more. My hand lightly brushed against hers, and our fingers gently intertwined in the darkness under her overcoat. She tore her eyes away from mine.

"Lorelai… We barely even know each other," she said quietly. Our hands were still together.

"Then talk to me," I said, taking a half step back to give her space. "I have plenty of questions, and I suspect you have more for me as well." I tilted my head a bit to one side, trying to regain eye contact. She lifted her gaze up to meet me. There was a pause, as our hands were loosely entwined, and our eyes each staring into the others', where all I saw was her.

Then a loud CLANG of something metal was heard from down the street and Velia broke away from me, stepping back. She exhaled, and stuck her hands back in her pockets.

"This isn't what I had meant to talk to you about tonight. But the package delivering is a side job, for people who need it done discreetly. To pay for my spell materials and food. And years ago when I was taught how to use my magic, I took a few martial arts lessons as well. That's all," she said. She looked right at me when she said it, and she seemed to be honest-- but was leaving some things out. *That's fair. I understand not wanting to tell your whole life story.*

"Okay, then. What *did* you want to talk to me about then? Were you not just trying to get the jump on me for fun?" I smirked playfully.

"Well, when we met…" she hesitated. "That fight wasn't the most *fair,* with you ambushing me where I lived. Still, I seriously doubt that that was the best you could do. I want a rematch, of sorts." Her smile grew. It was a pretty smile. We weren't going to head out again after Morgan until morning anyway...

"I would love to have a rematch with you."

In a grassy clearing, we decided on ground rules. Agreed no weapons, for one-- a show of magic only. Alright. We stood a few feet apart from one another, hands at the ready. Velia had a belt with several holding compartments in it, for spell components. I myself had a small canteen of water in my jacket pocket. I needed nothing else. Though I would have preferred to be able to use my weapons, but I understood. She was fascinated with my atypical magic, and I would happily rather use it to show her instead of being asked questions about it again.

Velia began by trying to blow a strange powder at me. I pulled a rope of water out of my canteen and deflected, washing the powder away. Her eyebrows raised and her eyes widened, and we made eye contact. She winked. A small crystal flew at me. I caught it in my hand. The talisman around my neck under my shirt warmed, and that warmth travelled immediately through my arm into my hand. Velia stared, pausing, but the rock had no effect. She swore under her breath. I smirked. The rock fell to the ground. But as my opponents hand hovered over one of her pocket belts, everything went dark. Now it was my turn to curse— she had done this before, when we met. Blindness. I lashed out with my whip of pure water, and it struck nothing where she should have been. *Damnit.*

But my other senses were still keen. I heard her extremely quiet muttering of a spell from behind me to the left, and I spun around, bringing the water with me. *Thwack!*

"Ugh!" I smirked. It had connected. *Don't fight a sea witch and expect to stay dry...*

However, she must have already been holding the components she needed, as suddenly my arms snapped to my sides, pinned.

"Not another old trick again dear, show me something *new*!" I cooed as my talisman warmed further, spreading through my arms and face. I pushed, and my arms broke out of their prison as my sight returned.

Velia stood before me, dripping wet and frowning, eyebrows furrowed. My rope of water hovered in the air next to her.

"Your components are soaked, ready to give in yet?" I asked, smiling. She laughed.

"Would *you*?" As she said that, she waved, curling her fingers with her palm up. I felt an ice cold, ghostly invisible hand stroke my cheek. I grimaced. It left me, and I felt it speed away towards my water. Abruptly, it broke apart, the water falling to the ground with a *splat*. Velia smiled.

"Well that's new..." I said. I moved my hand, gathering it back up, and the water on the ground was pulled towards me, where it levitated and reformed.

Abruptly, my feet began lifting off of the ground, as I was pulled up by the collar of my jacket. The ghost hand was back— and it was strong! I was lifted higher and higher, as Velia smiled at me from below. With another same wave of her hand and curl of fingers, as her other hand crushed a leaf from her pocket, my canteen of water floated out of my pocket and soared downward before I could grab it. I hung there.

"Ready to give up yet?" Velia called up, quite pleased with herself.

"*Please*, I don't need to have the container on me to contr—" I stopped.

We were barely out of the town. I could now see over the small buildings... and what I saw was definitely not good. People, crowding out into the dark streets with torches and lanterns. Weapons glinting in the moonlight. I knew what I was seeing, I'd seen it before.

"Velia, put me down *now*, we're both in serious trouble th—" I started.

"I'm not fooled nearly that easily."

A group of people appeared at the town's edge a small ways behind Velia.

"See! She's a witch!"

"I saw the other one controlling water with her mind! They're *both* witches!"

"What are we waiting for?" said a grinning, tall, broad man.

They ran at us. I had never fallen faster. Only to be gently placed at the end.

We took off. Hand in hand, we ran together, towards the woods. We glanced at each other, smiling. Giggles and little laughs escaped us.

We lost the mob quite quickly in the woods.

Adrian

Lorelai had left us in a room she paid for in this little town's… what had they been calling them? Taverns? Inns? I was not sure what the difference was. Before she took off, she left us a few gold coins for food, which was nice of her-- we spent a few copper's worth of it on a deck of cards. By the time we had made it to the town from The Informant's cave, obtained a room, a meal, and cards, the sun had set.

Since his initial strong protests at The Informant's request of murder…
Miles had fallen very unusually silent. He had hardly said a single word
since. Not that I was surprised. My friend valued life and compassion
above all else, it seemed. And I couldn't help but have my old dark
secret spring to mind in light of everything. One that not a single being
knew about, besides me. *Miles would probably hate me if he knew.*

We sat on the floor, playing cards half-heartedly in near silence.

"Miles…" I waited for him to look up at me as he noticed my
hand movements. "We're not going to kill anyone. We don't have to.
You know that, right?"

"Lorelai just might. And we have to find Morgan." He looked
down, dejected.

I hit the ground in between us to get his attention back more
forcefully.

"Do you really think he is going to check and make sure that his
attackers are dead? Really? Who *knows* where any of them could be by
then," I insisted. "And he already told Lorelai where we need to be
headed, remember?" Slowly, a look of realization dawned on Miles'
face and his usual happiness flowed back in, a big smile growing back.

"You're right!" He exclaimed, breaking the silence for the first
time in this conversation. "We can go get Morgan out and no one has to
die!" I'd never seen anyone say something like that so excitedly before.

Oh buddy, I think you are majorly underestimating the difficulty of breaking a selkie out of a place swarming with hunters...

The next morning, Lorelai came back wearing a black cloak with a large hood up instead of her usual jacket. We questioned it, but she brushed us off. We left the town that morning, and spent most of the day walking. This time, since we were heading to the ocean as the crow flies-- as the ship's crew would say-- instead of winding around, town to cave to town, we would get back to the sea much faster. We likely were not even *that* incredibly far away from the coastline.

When we finally reached a tiny, secluded beach, Miss Medea was waiting for us with Nicodemus aboard. Once all three of us were on deck, Lorelai and Nicodemus immediately headed for the Captain's Quarters. Nicodemus' stride was stiff and quick, his face stony. Everything between the two of them was tense. I was curious, and bored, so I silently followed after them once they were inside. Leaning into the closed door, I listened.

"You could have *told me* you were going to be on land for *days,* galavanting around--" Nicodemus' voice.

"You of all people should have expected me t--"

"I didn't even know one of them was goddamn *taken,* Lorelai! And she's a selkie, a *monster*--"

"Hey! You don't even know any of them!" Lorelai interjected. I was surprised.

"And you *do*?! Why are you still helping them?!"

"Nico, the deal, you know I ne--"

"It is not worth helping *monsters,* Lorelai! Need I remind you how your parents died?"

I stepped away from the door, the room, the yelling. This was clearly not my conversation to hear. Not my information to know. But it certainly unsettled me. Nicodemus' opinion… terrified me. Most importantly… Why had Nicodemus said 'not worth helping monster*s*' *plural?* Was he becoming more sure of the fact that I was not human?

When the two left the room several minutes later, they quickly parted ways and hardly spoke from then on. We set sail, heading towards The Meeting Place.

I stood at the front of the ship, relishing in the feeling of the wind in my face and the spray of sea salt and ocean. The ocean stretched out before me, touching the horizon. There was nothing but water in every direction, and I felt… nostalgic. Melancholy. Happy, and loving the ocean that, despite everything, still felt like home even when I was on top of it, but the feeling was edged with longing. I felt at home and out of place all at once. I missed Myrddin and simultaneously never wanted to leave that moment.

The wind began to pick up. But I didn't realize anything was wrong until the ship's crew began hurriedly piling below deck. I watched them, they seemed frantic and… scared? I looked past them, and saw Lorelai and Nicodemus talking in hushed tones while-- while she wrapped rope around him and the mast? *Why on Myrddin is Lorelai tying the ship's Captain to the mast?! What in Myrddin is going on?!* I began running down towards them, but suddenly, I stopped. I had been hearing it for several minutes by then likely, but it had shown up so subtly, crescendoed so slowly, that I had not registered it until too late.

A lilting, melodic tone was drifting across the waves. The sound swayed with the rhythm of the seas, the rock of the ship, and it entered the ears and wrapped around the mind.

Sirens had come for them. For the humans on the ship.

I sprinted across the deck.

Nicodemus was tied tightly to the bottom of the mast, as he sat on the deck. Thick rope wrapped around him and the post multiple times, and several knots were tied. The ship's crew had all disappeared below deck. The sky was grey, and the deck felt like a ghost ship as Nicodemus' eyes glazed over and he began struggling. Fighting, wrestling, trying desperately to get free. An expected response, but he seemed to be well secured. The incredibly interesting thing, though, was Lorelai. She stood a couple of feet away, holding her palms to her ears. Her face was tight and scrunched, and she shook her head crazily. I had never even heard of such a response-- humans are not able to fight off the call of a siren. It takes only a couple of seconds, a minute at most, upon hearing until they are taken over.

Knowing this, Nicodemus and Lorelai were not the ones I was most worried about.

Where, dear god, is Miles?!

The deck was empty, and he was nowhere to be seen.

The ladder that led below deck creaked. Slowly, the trapdoor above it opened. Miles' smiling face appeared.

"Ey, Adrian, what's goin' on? The crew's a mess down 'ere!" he called over to me.

"Cover your ears! Get below deck! Hide! Leave! It's not safe!" My hands moved frantically, urgently. I had never before wished harder that I could speak human. Miles stared at me confused, and I saw his eyes begin to glaze over as the magical song entered his mind.

He climbed up onto the deck methodically, slowly, his face completely blank. I ran to him, and grabbed his arm. I pulled and tugged with all of my might, but it only slowed him as he grunted with the effort of dragging me next to him as he headed towards the edge of the ship. I could not stop him. I was panicked, my mind racing, and I had no idea what to do. I ended up clutching onto his arm, trying to stop him with all of my weight and strength, until we stood before the railing. Miles shook me off with relative ease, and then jumped into the waves before I could do anything more.

I was shaking, restless, panicking. *I cannot even swim in my human form, I do not know how! I almost drowned the last time I ended up off of a sailing ship! ... But Miles saved* me *then.* The presence of a person next to me abruptly caught my attention-- it was Lorelai. She had been exposed to the siren's song for possibly multiple minutes by then. When I saw her there, standing at the edge, her eyes were glazed over. She was shaking. Until she dove into the waves.

I knew what I had to do in that moment. There was no other option.

I closed my eyes.

I had only ever done this once before, and I still was not incredibly sure how to make it happen. All I knew was that I focused, until the smell of the sea increased. I could hear swimming beneath the waves, smell fish that were miles away. I took a deep breath, and my lungs filled my chest.

I jumped into the waves.

Water caressed my scales. The salt water flowed through my gills. My eyes shot open. I could see Lorelai, swimming quickly through the waves, heading forward and deeper. Miles was ahead of her. I could hear the siren's song. They sang of... love. Belonging. Home. Being a ship's Captain. Others sang of revenge, violence, retribution and... more love, belonging, home, friendship. The sirens were not very far away, and they were beckoning them deep into the sea where they would surround them.

I pushed my arms back, and kicked, soaring through the ocean as my muscles worked and my fins propelled me even more. Quickly, I caught up to Lorelai. I grabbed her in one arm, restraining her as best as I could, and she struggled against me. I managed to grab some seaweed, and launched both of us towards the surface. When we broke back into open air, I tore the kelp in half and stuffed it into Lorelai's ears. I held her shoulders, my arms outstretched, and stared at her eyes, waiting for only a moment. Her eyes began to clear. She began kicking to keep herself afloat. With that, I left her and sped as quickly as I could back down in the direction the siren's song was coming from.

I pushed and swam with all of my might, my muscles aching and I kept going stronger. Finally, I was getting near. But Miles... was becoming far too close to the waiting group of sirens. Their hair drifted along in the current, and razor sharp teeth protruded from their open, singing mouths. They had yellow, or brown, or blue eyes, but all of their dark eyes were slits. I couldn't help but notice that one of them, a bit smaller than the rest, wasn't singing. He was hanging back instead, watching. Watching me. Then another one of them who had a flower in their hair tore forward towards Miles, and I burst forward with enough speed that I reached my friend. I threw myself in between him and the siren, and was faced with the snarling, scaly face. The siren clawed at me with their long, sharp nails, and I dodged and weaved away from one hand, while grabbing the other tightly by the wrist. The siren hissed at me, biting and thrashing-- as Miles tried to move around us, heading for the group of them that were waiting, watching, singing. I knew it would be a struggle to get him back up to the surface. And any second now, he would open his mouth and start drowning. I clawed back at the attacking siren, until suddenly I noticed something. The flower in the attacking siren's hair had small yellow petals, and I recognized it. *Lorelai's flowers!* I grabbed the creature by the hair, tearing the flower out of their curly locks. Earning myself more anger from them.

I launched myself into Miles, knocking him farther away from any of the sirens. I gripped his forearm, and began swimming back up. My body ached, my muscles yelled at me, Miles struggled against me. Luckily, my triton form was stronger than my human form, and with the amount of fear, resolve, determination, and care for Miles, there was no way I would let myself fail.

With one arm wrapped around Miles' arm, I used my other to push back against the few sirens that followed me. They did not like me stealing their meal. I punched, clawed, and kicked them, doing everything I could to get them to leave us alone while still holding onto Miles. After several hard punches to the face and kicks to the stomach, the sirens decided that this meal was not worth fighting for. *There is a reason sirens use magic to make their hunting easy...*

That was when all of the sirens stopped singing, and swam away. I pulled at Miles, as his eyes began to clear. Suddenly, he began thrashing, choking-- drowning. I pointed him upwards, and continued to help him get to the surface quickly, except now he was working with me instead of against me.

We made it to the surface. Miles coughed loudly, sputtering and spitting out water. I helped him get back to the side of the ship, where Lorelai helped him back up onto the deck. I stayed in the water for a moment, looking back out over the waves. The siren man who had not been singing came to mind. *Why had he not been joining in? Why had he been staring at me like that?...* I glanced back up at Lorelai, who crouched on the edge of the deck looking down at me.

"I will be right back!" I said, before diving downward. I could defend myself, and would only be gone for a minute.

As I headed towards where the group of sirens had been, I relished in the feeling of the water flowing past me. Cool, calm, soothing. There was nothing like it. When I neared where they had been, however, I slowed and focused. There was a reef here, colourful corals all along the ground as they poked out between long, tall tendrils of seaweed. There was a cave not far away. I did my best to stay on the outskirts of what appeared to be their current area, and hid low down in the seaweed. I hesitated. *What am I doing? How will I know that he will hear me before anyone else does?*

A hand appeared out of the green and tapped my floating hand. I reeled back, staring, but all I saw was plant life. Before I could decide whether or not to leave or try to find the owner of the hand, I felt another tap on my shoulder from behind. I spun around, and heard a small chuckle drift in the waves.

"...Who's there?" I asked tentatively, my voice coming out in a sing-song tiny burst as I spoke the language of sirens and mermaids. Being so incredibly out of practice, as I had not spoken to a siren in years, my voice broke at the end of my sentence.

The small chuckle, or perhaps giggle is a better word, happened again. This time, the owner showed themselves, as a young siren male with very short red hair peeked out from between the thick seaweed. Seeing me, he slowly came closer, revealing a beautiful long, crystal blue tail. He was definitely the non-singing siren from before, but at the time his tail had been hidden in the shadows and plants. He looked at me curiously, and swam around my left side, his tail curving through the area around me, as he checked me over and hesitantly ran a light hand over the scales on my arm.

"Never met a triton before?" I asked, trying to not feel uncomfortable at all the attention. He moved back so that he was in front of me again, his tail curling beneath him. I swam a little higher to be of equal height. "What's your name?" I asked. He said nothing, only blinked. "I-uh, I'm Adrian. Nice to meet you," I tried. He pointed to his mouth, then his throat, and shook his head, looking apologetic. I stared. "You… you cannot speak?" I realized. He nodded. Then, he turned part way around and pointed to the long blue fin on his back. He pointed at his chest next. "You… you are, um, Fin?" He nodded excitedly, smiling. I smiled back.

Something drew my gaze back towards the ship. My friends.

When I looked back to Fin, he gave me a knowing smile, waved, and then disappeared back into the seaweed.

I paused.

Then swam back towards the ship.

I hope we meet again, Fin. Preferably under better circumstances though.

I didn't have much on my mind when I climbed back onto the ship with Lorelai's help. That was until I climbed aboard and saw a crew member pointing a sword at Miles, while I was faced with Nicodemus. He glared at me, a sword unsheathed in his hand. A large group of his crew stood behind him, also armed.

"*You.*" he seethed. "I was right all along. You are a wretched monster." His offhand was curled into a tight fist. He was tense, and raised his sword. I had n0t even had a second to change back to my human form.

"Nico, he just *saved my life,*" Lorelai said.

"It only wanted to kill you itself later." His eyes stayed locked on me. Anger flared behind his eyes. I gulped, and started scanning the nearby area. Looking for a weapon. I did not want to hurt anyone. But I was not about to die. Not like this. Not now. But my muscles screamed at me. My entire body wanted to collapse. It was taking considerable strength simply to continue standing after all the energy I had used.

My vision blurred as swirls of air and light filled the space around me.

And suddenly I found myself sitting on cold stone. Miles stood next to me, still soaking wet. Lorelai stood before both of us, glaring.

We were on land, in a cave somewhere. I could see a forest outside the entrance behind Lorelai.

"There's a town with a harbour not far away east from here." She turned her hard gaze directly onto me. "You saved my life, now I've saved yours in return. We're even," she said, and snatched the orange flower out of my hands. I had forgotten that I was still holding it. Pausing to kneel before a pile of rocks, she unearthed a hidden crystal and replaced it with a different one from her bag. With it hidden once more, she walked out of the cave, and off into the forest. She did not turn back. Just like that. I did not think she was *ever* going to turn back.

Chapter Eleven - Sick Bay

<u>Morgan</u>

When the ship finally docked, I didn't even realize it at first. But then I heard noise from outside my room, people moving about and talking. I still managed to hear the slow, steady, thump of his boots on the stairs as he descended towards me. I wanted to fight back, but this time they were more prepared. Men stormed in wearing thick black gloves that I couldn't penetrate, and long sleeves. They were so quick, a group of them running at me, my arms were grabbed and pinned behind my back before I could blink, and they stayed out of the reach of my bite. As I was re-gagged and tied, tighter this time, the man with the large black boots and the blue coat finally strolled into view. He stood in the doorway, the light from outside my dark room making his silhouette cover me. He towered over me, his hands behind his back and a large, sinister smile on his face. He regarded me-- the weak, exhausted, bound mess of a creature that I was.

"It is time," he said. "We've arrived."

He turned and left, and I was dragged and pushed after him.

They led me up above deck while I was still not blindfolded. Before me was an island. Mountains rose on its furthermost edge, forest covering the rest. That is, except for the building that stood there, a sore thumb in an otherwise seemingly untouched land. It was largely made of stone, walled in and with blackened windows.

Then the blindfold suddenly covered my eyes, wrapping around my head and tied tight. I had no choice but to limp as they pushed me in front of them, off of the ship and onto cold, hard ground. As I left the ship and stepped onto land for the first time since being captured, I found myself hoping that I'd be able to one day find those selkies I had seen-- who were somehow related to me. *If I really do still have family members out there, I need to find them… But first I need to survive this.* Through a sliver of sight at the bottom edge of the blindfold, I could see that they were making me stumble across a vague gravel path that hardly existed. The walk was agonizing, my ankle screaming in pain as my injured side gave a sharp pain when I moved. I was moving too slow for their liking, as they prodded me in the back with something that had a blunt, hard end. Occasionally they would shove me, chuckling to themselves as I stumbled and struggled to keep my balance. But as the long walk went on, they grew more and more agitated-- finally, one of them pushed me a bit too angrily, a little too forcefully, and I fell forward. My hands were tied around my back, so though I tried to catch my fall with my knee or leg, I was *so* tired. I didn't have the reaction speed I should have, and my nose smashed into the ground. Gravel stuck in my face, and as I tried desperately to get up without hands, blood began to run from my nose. The hunters didn't care. They simply watched me, until one yelled at me to get up already. I found myself wishing that I could simply stay here lying on the ground, until the earth swallowed me whole.

When I was ordered to stop walking, I tried to put as little weight as possible on my injuries. I heard a door loudly creaking open, and managed to peek under my blindfold and just barely see a very large set of metal double doors slowly swinging open. They led me inside, and unlike the stark silence of the rest of the island, this place was buzzing with activity, people, talking, movement. And noises of the occasional other non-human creature. I didn't recognize most of them. As I passed by, sometimes people would go quiet. I could feel their eyes on me, hear the edge of their whispering. I wondered what they thought I was; what this place was.

We entered a smaller room-- I could tell by the change of lighting, the pause to open the door, and its sound. If it hadn't been for the thin sliver of sight at the bottom of my vision, I definitely would have fallen down the stone stairs. Stairs were hard in my condition, I nearly fell down them anyway a few times. If the hunters had had a problem with my speed before, I could only imagine how annoyed my stair taking must have made them, considering that I had to move my

good foot down one stair, and then bring my bad one to the same step.
There was a railing, and I used it to support my weight and assist. But I
could hear the hunters grumbling just behind me. I kept waiting for
them to prod me again, surely sending me tumbling down the stairs. But
it never happened. Abruptly I realized something-- I hadn't heard the
pirate captain's voice or bootsteps since soon after leaving the ship. I
hadn't really been paying attention to him then, but thinking back I
realized he had gone on ahead of us. *So am I heading to his dungeon
lair, or someone else's?*

When the stairs came to an end, the room was lit, although
dimly, except for one bright white light ahead of me, maybe roughly in
the center of the room. To my surprise, my blindfold was taken off, and
I saw what would become my room of torture in full view.

The bright light in the center of the room hung over a large
table— that had straps on it. *You have got to be kidding me. There's no
way in hell I'm getting strapped onto that thing.*

Surrounding it were counters and shelves and cupboards, with
many different sharp things and bottles and tubes of unidentified liquid.
Oh god. This is going to be fun, huh.

I only noticed the door at the opposite side of the room when it
opened, and light streamed in. Standing there was him— dark blue coat
and all.

They started dragging me towards the table— I kicked the closest one in the shin as hard as I could. He swore and stood on one foot, while the one on my other side strengthened his hold on me. I tried to kick him too and get free from his grasp, but he saw it coming this time.

"Now now, no need for any more desperate attempts, dear," my main captor said from where he still stood, watching, from the other side of the room. *Why don't you come face me yourself and see how my attempts feel, you bastard.* I wished I didn't have a disgusting gag still in my mouth. The man walked towards me slowly, circling around the table, and trailing his fingers across the bottles on the shelves as he passed them. "You're quite a little fighter, aren't you?" He turned to face me, smiling darkly. "That will no longer be the case by the time we're done with you," he paused. "Assuming you even live." He closed in on me then, his eye contact never wavering. He crouched down so that our faces were at the same level, and he had gotten so close that I could smell his breath, his clothes, him. I wrinkled my nose.

"If only I had your seal skin," he continued, musing. "I could make you walk in here unrestrained and strap yourself to that table." He stood up straight, and stepped to the side with a nod to the ones holding me. They began dragging me again, forcing me forward with all of their might up to and onto the table. I fought and squirmed and kicked, only to suddenly be slapped across the face as hard as the man in the blue and gold coat could. I reeled back, stunned.

"That. Stops. *Now.*" he said.

I was put across the table, and strapped in. When I tried to fight back, I was threatened with a knife.

They… they did things to me that I tried to forget. For brief, merciful parts of it I would fall unconscious, only to be awoken by screaming pain. Someone screaming. It was me. My own voice, I realized. Creating a sound of agony that even I didn't recognize. One of his side men covered me in wounds slowly, and occasionally they would force something down my throat. A liquid that made internal fire spread throughout my body was one of them. I didn't understand what they were doing. I was poked and prodded, injected multiple times, even had magic cast across me once or twice.

They used mostly typical human blades, but at one point my main captor left for a few minutes. They decided to toss a bucket of water over me while he was gone-- perhaps to keep me awake, I don't know, but I did know that it was saltwater. Ocean water. It flowed across my skin and entered my wounds, soothing and cooling them, and it was incredible. But the men seemed very disappointed; as if they had hoped so much more would happen.

When he came back, he ordered the others to stop what they were doing to me for a moment. He held a wooden box, and when he opened it, his eyes lit up and danced. Slowly, carefully, he pulled out a dagger that was richer than anything I had ever seen. It's blade was made of gold, and several large gemstones were in its handle. It shone and glittered, near blinding in the bright light that hung above me. He wrapped his hand around the gemstones with near reverence on his face.

When it cut into me, it moved as if I was butter, and sent a searing painful heat throughout that limb. I screamed, the sound flying out of me with all the force it could. The screams felt as though they were from someone else. I was not there, I was not anywhere. I was not even a being. I existed only as pain. Tears fell down my face. I stopped paying any attention. I couldn't. I slipped in and out of consciousness, unaware of most of what was happening from that point on. My heart raced and my chest heaved with the effort of wanting to keep me alive, but my mind was not present.

When they were finally satisfied with enough of my blood and screams, and had taken enough blood samples, injected enough things, and had someone come in to cast a few unknown spells, I must have been--surprisingly-- bandaged up and put in a cell. I didn't remember anyone putting bandages on me, or being moved and put in a cell… it was as though I had either passed out or blocked out the memories when I was on that table, only coming back to when I was relatively safe.

Chapter Twelve - We're All Thieves Now

<u>Morgan</u>

I rested for a while; I knew I would need all the strength I could muster. Sleeping was always difficult, but even just lying with my eyes closed was helpful. My mind drifted as I lay there, wondering about how Adva was doing, what Miles, Adrian, and Lorelai were up to-- if they were even still together. But eventually my mind drifted back to those selkies again. I hadn't seen other selkies besides Adva in… ages. The idea that our family could be--or was--more than the two of us again was hard for me to fully wrap my head around. They could even have answers, about why I never knew of them and where they had been during the attack on my pod. Finding them would be, realistically, almost impossible though. I had nothing to go on. But I had to try. I always had to keep trying.

Finally, once I felt more rested, I got up in the middle of the night. A small groan escaped from my lips as pain coursed through my body as I stood. I paused, one hand on the wall with no pressure on my bad ankle, until the pain subsided a little. I couldn't give in to the pain, I couldn't focus on it, I had to try to escape. I peered through the bars of my cell, scanning the area. There was only a single guard, sitting in a chair a few feet away from me. He was large, broad, and strong, and had a lump of some sort of hidden weapon. A desk with papers piled messily on it sat to one side.

But I slowly brought myself back to lying down. I waited. I couldn't tell the time of day, but as I pretended to be sleeping, the guard left. I didn't move. He returned shortly, bottles in hand. The edge of my lip twitched upward in the slightest bit of a smile. Eyes closed, I continued to wait. Wait until I heard the clank of empty bottles being put on the ground and tapping against one another, and the guard even began to mutter to himself. Complaining about his job. Then, I peeked. He was slumped in his chair, facing away from me as he continued to drink. *Perfect.*

Slowly, I stood, careful to not cause myself too much pain. I then pulled two hairpins out from under my clothing and eyed the lock that contained me. Something to pick locks with had always ended up being helpful on my excursions onto land before, so I had slipped off to pick up a new set beforehand in whatever that town was— the one they found me in. Humans seem to consistently have a lapse in oversight when doing searches, men especially, forgot to check under my outer clothing.

I knelt on the ground and reached through the bars, before bending my wrists and elbows to point the hairpins back at the lock from the outside. Doing it like this was tricky of course, I'd never had to pick the lock from inside before— I'd never been caught for anything before. I did everything I could to remain quiet, and took a deep breath to steel my nerves and focus. Eventually, the lock opened. *Yes!* I stood, and pushed the cell door open. Picking up one of his bottles, I approached the guard from behind. *Hopefully this won't make too much noise, but there's nothing else around here to use…*

THUNK! I swung the glass bottle as hard as I could over the man's head, and he crumpled, falling forward onto the floor. The glass remained unbroken— I was surprised, but very glad. The last thing I needed was the sound of smashing glass to alert more guards, plus leaving this one bloody wouldn't exactly help me.

I quickly glanced around the room to see if there was anything I could take that might help me. Unfortunately, the room was mostly empty. Except for a desk, with a few papers laid on top of it. I glanced at the limp guard. Technically, no one knew I was free yet, and he probably wasn't going to wake up anytime soon after that. My curiousity getting the better of me, I scanned the papers to see if there was anything interesting. Some of them were filled with words I didn't really care for, talking about evading sheriffs. But one of them caught my eye. It was a letter from someone called Captain Samael Williams, to the entire guard patrol. Telling them to keep a careful discreet watch on someone named "Velia Curran", that this captain was apparently suspicious of her for some reason. I shrugged. *And here I thought a message from the Captain of this place would be meaningful or at least intriguing...*

I had been here too long. Someone might come to check on me or my guard soon. Realizing I still held the bottle in my hand, I put it down and ran— well, half ran, half hobbled.

There was a staircase in the opposite corner of the room that I took upward. *By the length and seem of it, this might be the same staircase I took down to the room with that table...* As a result of this thought, when a door appeared mid-way in the staircase, I was hesitant to take it. But I couldn't hear any sound of footsteps or anything else from behind it, and this was my one and only chance to potentially do some snooping on the strange hunters— not to mention the man in blue and gold— who had brought me here. A once in a lifetime chance to get some answers. I went through the door.

Finding myself in a hallway, lined with more doors. *Whichever one I pick... could mean hunters and guards, or answers...* I snuck carefully through the hallway. None of the doors had any indication of what was inside them— except for one. "Library", the plaque said. I scoffed. *Hunters don't read! I, however, have found books helpful in the past.* After trying to first listen through the door and hearing nothing, I entered. The room was small, shelves of books lining the walls. In one corner, sat an armchair and a small table with a locked box on it. The room was otherwise empty. I began to wonder if this place was deserted. Approaching the locked box, I saw that it had a glass top.

Inside, cleaned and polished, sat the golden dagger with encrusted jewels that had torn into me.

I was right, he doesn't read, he just sits here and admires his treasure, I thought.

And what a tempting lock it had. However, taking it would only make me more of a target by tenfold. Instead, I picked up the book that lay on the lower section of the side table. It was the only one not neatly on a shelf, and it was with the dagger. Turns out I was right to be curious about it. '*The Dagger of Corruption, by E.S Locklire*' the cover read. It sounded like a deranged storybook, but I immediately flipped it open anyway.

'Warnings' was the first chapter, or section. After a foreword by the author, urging the reader to destroy the golden dagger if they found it. *Okaayy then...* I opened the first chapter.

'As you may have guessed by the title of this book, the dagger (an artist's rendition of it is pictured bottom right), corrupts. Well, perhaps that is not the most accurate. It, magically, reviews the wielder's moral essence and amplifies to the extreme, always leading to the same ending—' I slammed the book shut.

Despite how much I may have wanted to read on, I couldn't. It felt as though every second I held the book, every letter I read… made me more and more worried. Incredibly so. When I shut the book, my heart had been racing by that point, my hands clammy, and my mind was filled with anxious thoughts that soon I would be caught. When I put the book back down, my heart began to slow. *Thank god…* I turned and left. I wanted nothing to do with that blade, or that book, ever again.

I heard talking behind a few of the other doors in the hallway. I quickly continued back up the stairs I had started on.

When I found another door that the stairs continued past, I hesitated. Nearly didn't enter it at all. But, I still hadn't been discovered. Maybe I was pressing my luck. But that tends to lead to discovery. I opened the door.

Only to find myself back in my worst nightmare.

The table and its straps were mostly covered in blood.

Many different kinds of sharp things, with my dried blood on them, still lay next to it.

But, to my horror, I was not alone.

At the side of the room, stood a woman with chin-length brown hair, digging through some of the drawers. I froze in place, my heart began to race at the idea of being caught again. But before I could leave, she turned around. She wore black robes with green edging and fancy purple details. She didn't look like she belonged here, but regardless my guard was up. As I scanned her, she noticed the fresh wounds and cuts that covered my body and were only beginning to heal.

"Are… Are you…?" Her hand waved gently towards the table with my blood on it. I gulped. Said nothing. "You are, aren't you. One of their experiments," she stated simply. I stared at her, trying to decide what to do. "Come in, close the door before someone else sees you. I can help you," she continued, insisting. Slowly, hesitantly, I closed the door behind me and checked that it didn't lock. She turned back to the drawers and cupboards that lined the room and began to open all of them. When she found something, she smiled, and took a clean dagger out of the drawer. I glared at her, one hand on the door. I was prepared to find a way to bring out my seal teeth and fight her tooth and nail if I had to.

"Drop it. Now." My voice had more strength in it than I felt. She placed it on the counter and stepped away from it.

"I-I'm sorry, I didn't think-- it's for you. I, uh, assumed they would have something like this here, I want you to have it. So you can defend yourself better," she said. Surprisingly, she seemed slightly nervous. I narrowed my eyes. *What is her game? Who the hell is she?* I eyed the dagger, then began walking forward. As I moved closer to the dagger, she moved farther away from it. *Good.* When I reached the counter, I picked it up while keeping an eye on her. It was actually decently nice. Dark wooden handle on it. But simple, plain. *Not to mention sharp,* I thought, lightly running my finger quickly across the blade. I liked it. I turned slowly towards the woman, holding it out in front of me.

"Why are you being so *nice* to me? I won't fall for any tricks," I said.

"No tricks," she said, putting her hands up. "In fact, I know how you can escape. I can't help you directly, I still have some work to do here so I cannot be seen with you. But when you get outside, sneak around the edge of the outer wall. Head away from the main entrance. There will be crates piled up against the wall. You can climb them and scale it that way. No one would expect it, and then it's all forest you can hide in," she said, gesturing to help explain all of her points. *Hmm. This sounds like a trick to me,* I thought. My new dagger stayed pointed at her. There was a pause. And then I turned to leave.

"Wait," she said, just before I reached the door. For some unknown reason, I stopped. "They don't feed you, do they?" I didn't move. I didn't speak. "I, I um, well, I don't know if you can eat human food, but you look pretty human. Is cooked chicken okay? I keep some pieces for my dog as treats." Suddenly the smell of meat made me turn around. The woman was holding a small bag that was emitting the aroma, and my stomach began to scream at me. I approached her, and put out a hand. She gave me the whole bag. I eyed her suspiciously, despite my yearning for any food.

"It is *just* chicken?" I asked. "No toxins, no--"

"No, no, of course not. Just chicken," she said, half smiling.

I opened the bag and sniffed the contents. Suddenly I was gobbling them down, unable to stop. When the bag was empty, I looked up sheepishly. *Well this is embarrassing.*

"Go now, go, you don't have much time," she said, shooing me towards the door with her hands.

I crept out back into the hallway. As I was about to turn and head up the stairs, I saw two guards on the other end of the hall. They had been heading in my direction, and had immediately seen me.

"HEY! What th—" they yelled, but I was already off running up the stairs, my new dagger tucked into my blood-covered jacket. The guards yelled behind me, and loud bangs rang out. They only spurred me to go faster. I took the stairs as quickly as I physically could, half running half hopping. When I reached the door at the very top of the stairs, I stopped. I could still hear yelling behind me, more than two people now. But I knew I needed to take a second, even if I didn't really have one to spare. I tried listening through the door for a moment before carefully opening it a small amount. Peeking through, I saw a lot of people who were probably hunters walking about. The sun was setting. Crates and boxes lined the giant room, and there were a few cages scattered about. People, or should I say hunters, conversed in groups and showed off items to one another. Several other small buildings, like the one I was about to exit, also lined the sides. The room wasn't really a room to be truthful, more so a stone wall surrounding other ramshackle little stone buildings. Spotting a lull in foot traffic near where I was, I tucked my hair into the back of my shirt and slipped out of the door. I ducked away around the corner and behind the building just as I heard the footsteps of several people come charging after me from below.

Hurrying again, I ran as light-footed as I could along the wall of the place, dashing and ducking behind buildings and crates. A few hunters swarmed out of the dungeon I had left, and the noise in the place became urgent as others were quickly told of my escape. *This is not good... Where to now?* The building I was now behind had a back door with a window in it, so, pressing my luck for the millionth time that day, I stood on the tip of my toes and tried to see inside. It seemed to be a place where a few people were staying— but was currently empty. Ironically, they had probably left to help look for me. I stepped inside, closing the door behind me. I grabbed at the first few articles of clothing I could find until I had a shirt, pants, and a sweater. Then, I took all of my blood-covered torn clothes off and put on the clothing I had found. Kept my own shoes though, and transferred the hairpins and the new dagger. I scrambled to find some kind of headwear— and managed to find a hat and scarf. With my hair and most of my face covered, I slipped back out the back door.

I could hear that a lot of activity was being created as everyone became aware that there was a selkie on the loose… More people were moving about, calling to each other, talking excitedly, and searching for me. There were places to look before coming back here, but not very many. Security would be too high on the main entrance now, and I likely only had a minute, if that, before hunters began circling the edge or checking behind everything and found me here.

So I decided I had no choice but to do what the woman had suggested.

I pushed and lifted a few nearby boxes that I could manage to, and created a three high stack of boxes against the wall before my arms would take no more of it. Climbing to the top and crouching on the highest box, I took the scarf off, and threw it at and around a brick of stone that was jutting out of the top of the badly built wall. I doubted it would hold my weight very well, but jumping off of my good foot got me most of the rest of the way up. After that, I was able to use the scarf trick to quickly haul myself high enough so that I could grab the top of the wall. It was a rather thin wall.

An alarm went off. Yelling increased from behind me. I had been seen. In a matter of seconds, I pulled myself up onto the wall--only to lose my balance and tumble off the other side.

"*OWWwwwww,*" I moaned. But, as per usual, there was no time to be in pain. I had no choice, no matter how much everything hurt. I pushed myself to my feet and hobbled off into the forest, while the fact that I was on an apparently otherwise deserted island hung heavily in my mind.

Lorelai

"We're going to steal a boat, I've decided," I said.

"Lorelai *no,* we can't just—"

"Do you *want* to save Morgan? Because the name J-The Informant, I mean, gave me is a tiny uninhabited island!" I turned to Adrian. "Do you want to try your luck with Nico?" He shook his head vigorously. "That settles it then." I looked to Miles and crossed my arms. He grumbled something about morals. *Sigh.*

"What if... " I hesitated. "What if I don't hurt anyone when we take it and I return it later?" They both eyed me dubiously. "*Hey* I didn't hurt anyone when they attacked me in that town! That's new, right? I swear. We *need* it. Morgan needs it," I insisted. Adrian made a bunch of strange gestures. I glanced at Miles.

"He's askin' if ya know how t' captain a ship."

I had never stolen a ship before, so I thought it best to start small. It took me a few minutes to come up with a plan that didn't hurt anyone. *No wonder I never did this before, it's a thousand times harder and slower!* However, I still eventually figured one out.

We went around the outskirts of the village I had been recognized in until we made it to their harbour. It involved not only skirting the edge of a forest and ducking behind trees, trying to avoid the branches that reached for my hair, but also carefully traversing past areas where the ground gave way to the splashing sea. When we neared their docks, I made Miles and Adrian hide while I moved closer to the merchant's ship. If I had to pick I would say the ship was a sloop, with it's single mast and headsail. I eyed the people who stood aboard the ship from a distance, trying to analyze their clothing. Favouring a sloop suggested they might truly be pirates, who liked them for their maneuverability.

The people aboard wore loose fitting plain shirts tucked into their pants, dark coloured long pants and belts. But I couldn't tell if they had weapons sheathed from the distance I was at. *I suppose it does not really matter. The plan stays the same either way, and if merchants are anything like hunters, most of them are probably also pirates anyway.* My magic would afford me a full disguise, but it wouldn't last long before exhausting me, so I had to hurry. The man who stood by the docked ship was a bit shorter than me, though not by much, and was wearing simple but typical merchant salior's attire. *Here goes nothing,* I thought. He was not the kind of man I normally went after. He was shorter than me, quite plain, and not very attractive. And almost worse, he was probably a lowly *merchant.* Hopefully I was a good actress.

Still hidden, I cast the spell giving me my magical disguise. It altered my face slightly so I wouldn't be recognized, and hid my protective metal choker from being seen. As for an outfit, it made it seem as though I was wearing a very low cut white sparkling V-neck shirt, exposing part of my breasts, that was see-through enough to show a bright pink lace bra and my midriff. The look was complete with very short, tight black pants and matching high heels. And, of course, a full face of makeup with dark eyeliner and red lipstick.

I steeled my nerves; none of this was real anyway, so what did it matter?

I strode up to the merchant, swaying my hips slightly. *I hope he's a certain kind of sailor.*

"Hello handsome," I began, putting my hand on his shoulder and leaning down and into him. I moved my face to his ear and whispered. "You look like you could use some fun…" I moved my other hand down his front slowly-- and he shoved me off of him.

"What the hell lady, get off me!" he exclaimed. But I couldn't help but notice that he was glancing around, and back towards his ship, with a worried look. Moving my gaze down from his face, I saw a bulge in his pants. I smirked. *He just doesn't want to be caught.* I leaned down and pushed my chest forward.

"Don't worry sweetie, if we go to one of your rooms now no one needs to know. No one will catch us, I'm very discreet... And I'll be gone as soon as we hit the next town, and won't say a word," I kept my voice quiet as I spoke. I reached up and stroked down his arm. I stepped closer, and gave him my best sultry look. His crew were starting to peer over the edge of the ship at us, wondering what was going on. *Now is my last chance.* It was time to switch tactics slightly. I fake shivered.

"Please let me on board, I promise I'll keep to myself and make it worth your while," I moved as close to him as I could, my breasts nearly in his face. I ran a hand down his back slowly. He was taking in my appearance, and liking what he saw. Cogs turned behind his eyes as he tried to decide.

"... no cost besides the ship ride to the next town?" he whispered, nearly disbelieving as he raised an eyebrow. I nodded, smiling. "Then definitely," he said. He took off his jacket and threw it around my shoulders as he said this. I was quickly ushered aboard and directly into a private quarters. It was a small, dimly lit room with a hammock to one side, a desk at the back, and a small area for storage. He said that once they set sail he would be back, and then left. I smirked.

Now, to drop my disguise for phase two or keep it... I wondered, sitting lightly on the hammock. *What the hell, I'll give this small town a better thing to remember me by!* With that, the disguise fell away, bringing back my own green jacket, white short sleeved shirt, and long black pants. As well as my own face, chin-length dark hair, and many hidden weapons underneath.

I grabbed my dagger from my boot, flipped it into my favourite sword, and burst out of the room. I charged onto the deck— much to the surprise of everyone there, who quickly pulled out their own weapons. *Ah. It's been a while, hasn't it?* I smiled. Two of the bravest came at me first for trespassing, and I blocked and parried both of them. The facial expressions of men who first realize that this girl can fight *better* than them is always a wonderful sight, a mix of shock, confusion, and anger. It made me smirk. I lifted my free hand up high, and a stream of water from the ocean below us raised up higher than the deck of the ship. I hadn't even realized I had missed using real ocean water until I was doing so, but it listened so much more… *naturally.* The ocean water listened to my every request as if we were one organism, whereas other types of water were simply obeying orders. The men before me were mystified. With the stream of water following my motions, it grabbed the end of some rope.

They tried attacking me again— I fought with one for a minute while the water hung there with the rope trailing down from it. I blocked, and then swiped and jabbed at a skill level far below my own on purpose. He blocked each one, his smile growing more and more pompous and arrogant each time. That was alright; it would be erased soon enough. Through my attacks, I managed to get him to back up, step after step, until all but one of the merchants were on the same middle section of the small ship. To their surprise and glee, I sheathed my sword. Only to wave my hand across the air in front of me, smirking. A brief flash of confusion appeared on a few of their faces, followed by dread and fear as a wave of water lifted up from the sea and washed across the deck. It was strong enough to knock all of them over, but not wash any of them overboard. Then, my other little stream of water used their own rope to tie each of them up in a matter of seconds.

I flopped to a sitting position on the soaking wet deck.

"Come *on,* guys!" I called out.

With Adrian in the lead, Miles and Adrian quickly skittered aboard nervously. I got the two of them to, together, pick up each swearing sailor and deposit them on the dock before I cut the rope that kept the tiny ship tethered. The vessel was already prepared to set sail, so we immediately set off. *Looks like that makes all of us thieves now. Almost pirates.* I smirked. I'd stolen from and battled my fair share of pirates. *Speaking of which.*

"Stay low, in case anybody on shore has a gun," I told the two already very nervous and scared men. "Oh also, one more thing," I said. "This ship is tiny which means it will be fast, but it will definitely *not* make it all the way to our destination's shore. According to The Informant, the seas are rough around there and there are plenty of large rocks. I hope neither of you are against swimming after those sirens." As I spoke, I raised my voice against the wind that was getting stronger, facing forward at the helm. Regardless, I could still easily imagine the look the two of them must have shared at my news.

Chapter Thirteen - Capsize

<u>Miles</u>

We had been sailing for quite some time before we finally neared the island. Rough waters were rocking the small ship back and forth, tossing it around. I had picked up a little bit about how sailing worked along the way by watching Ms. Lorelai, but now the seas were too tough— and the island had caught my attention anyway. Mountains struck up out of the earth from its far side, as if trying to hit a hole in the sky. The rest of the hilly island was covered in trees, and a dark stone structure stood out of the surrounding green.

"I am going to try to get as close to the shore as I possibly can, but we may have to abandon ship! Wait for my order!" Ms. Lorelai was yelling to be heard over the wind as water splashed onto the deck. I looked over at Adrian while I held onto anything within reach to stay on. He was sitting in a corner, holding the edge of the boat so hard his knuckles were white. He stared hard, with wide eyes at the island.

"Are ya okay?" I called out, even though he was a few feet away. He simply shook his head and said nothing, too busy holding on with all his might. *That's not a good sign...*

Lorelai was doing everything she could to keep us up and going, but when I saw her eyes... the sea was reflected in them. Her eyes ain't grey, but the rough grey waves and the cloudy grey sky could be seen in there. She seemed cautious, even worried. *What was the word Adrian had made a sign for? ... Apprehensive. That's what she is right about now. Also not a great sign, huh?* As I watched her I could've sworn out of the corner of my eye I saw her eyes turn startling bright blue for a split second, but it was so fast I must've been seeing things. I rubbed my eyes and looked back at the island.

A surprised sound from Adrian made me turn back 'round just in time to see the water rising up above our heads as a huge wave crashed down upon us. Caught off guard, we all tumbled into the sea, the little ship overturning with us. The water swallowed me whole and I couldn't see a thing, fumbling around blindly as I felt myself sinking.

Suddenly I remembered something. Split second images flashed through my head from many years ago— when the wave taller than the trees flooded my village. I hadn't been able to remember much of that day, but as I saw the wave lift above me on the tiny ship I realized that I had been through this before. The crushing weight on my chest as I struggled to hold my breath became scarily familiar. I remembered that I had been outside, playing in the yard when it happened. Everything was fine one second, and the next, I was under water. Thrashing and sputtering. My Ma had managed to pick me up and get me out of harm's way before the worst of it, but I had nearly drowned. How had I never remembered that before?

My heart was racing and my legs felt shaky and weak as I tried desperately to find my way up. Suddenly, a hand grabbed my arm and pulled me up. When my head broke the surface, I coughed and spat out water. Adrian held onto one of my arms, keeping me afloat. I splashed wildly, attempting to stay up, only for another wave to push us both down. I shoved my way back up, only to take a single breath and have a new wave cover me again. *I dunno if I'm gonna make it in this! I can't swim!* Just as the thought crossed my mind, I was yanked back up.

Adrian was in front of me, holding onto my arm. His eyes met mine, and in them was a steeled sense of determination. He nodded his head back toward the island. But then, I looked behind me just in time to see a huge wave coming for us. Adrian tugged on my arm urgently, and when I looked at him, scared, he lifted his arms outstretched to either side, and then motioned pushing them downwards with force. I watched him, and he watched the wave, and I did as he had shown when he nodded to me, pushing upward with all my might and holding my breath— and though this wave did go over my head, I stayed much farther up than before and was able to get my head back above water more easily. Adrian looked to me after it had passed. I nodded; I felt a tad better about myself after that.

"It's now or never!" Lorelai yelled at us over the wind and the waves from several feet away, and then began swimming strongly towards the island. With Adrian beside me, we followed.

We crawled up onto the island and ducked into the trees right away. I collapsed on the ground, breathing heavily as my heart was still going too fast. Adrian knelt by my side and made sure I was okay. Ms. Lorelai said people might be watching from the building. So once I was good to keep going, we walked quietly through the trees towards it, trying to stay somewhat hidden. Neither of which were things Adrian and I were very good at, but we made it just barely.

When we got near the place, Lorelai stopped and turned to face us.

"Remember the plan, okay? Let's go over it one more time. I go in first, and distract a few of them. You both hide out here, and when you see my cue-- when you see a whip of water fly up past the wall, one of you sneak in and make a distraction. Miles, I think, do that. Adrian, you then sneak in and help me sneak Morgan out. I will then come back to get you out, Miles." We nodded. I wasn't very happy about my role in this plan, but it was what we were going with.

It was time for Lorelai to begin the plan. After I quickly checked to see if the picture of my Ma in my locket was doing okay… it wasn't really, but, uh, there was nothing I could do about it right now.

Adrian and I snuck off away from the main doors to wait in hiding until it was our turn to help, while Lorelai stopped trying to hide and directly approached the main entrance.

We found an untouched patch of dense trees and bushes a little ways away, hid ourselves, and waited. And waited. And waited. We waited for the *longest* time. I was hiding in a few bushes I had wedged myself in, and the position I was in was growing more and more uncomfortable by the minute. Sticks scratched and poked at me from every angle, and my foot was falling asleep. *It doesn't even seem like any a the hunters ever leave those damn walls... Why am I sittin' in here tryin' to hide from people that ain't around?* Slowly, trying not to get too many knicks and scratches, I backed out a my hiding place and stood up, nice and tall. I put my hands on my lower back and stretched leaning backwards, and gave my sleepy foot a shake, and I felt good. I was stretching my arms as an acorn hit me in the shoulder. I looked up at Adrian, who was hiding up in a tree.

"What are you doing?! The hunters are going to find us!" urgency and fear filled his face and his hands.

"Do *you* see any hunters 'round here? Have you heard any while we been waitin' forever? Seen any sign of a single one out in the forest?" I asked out loud. *I am certainly not 'bout t' go back in that bush, Adrian. And I can't climb a tree t' save m' life.* "Come on buddy, let's do some scoutin'! Be more helpful," I said. With that, I started walking and waved for him to follow. Before long he was by my side, as we walked a little ways from the wall in the trees, heading around it away from the doors. Adrian kept always looking around nervously as we went.

We had walked for a bit when I spotted a tree— it had fallen down or maybe been struck down, and was now laying to the side with its branches propped up against another tree. I looked between the tallest bit of trunk of the fallen tree and the top of the stone wall. The fallen tree still went quite high up...

"Miles..." Adrian gave me a look.

I hesitated, looking between Adrian, the tree, and the wall.

I hurried towards the tree with Adrian chasing to stop me.

I have trouble climbin' a tree when its standin' up, but I could probably scramble up one that's leanin' over! I thought. *I just want a peek at what it's like in there, that's all.*

It was a bit difficult and nervous getting up the thing, but when I reached near the top I found out that the corner of a smaller building that stood inside the wall was blocking any view I could've had! I leaned over, towards the wall, holding onto a branch of the tree we were on. Adrian tapped me many times very quickly, no doubt trying to warn me to stop. But I'd never been anywhere so far from home before, all I wanted was to see what the inside was like…

Snap!

The tree branch I was holding onto broke off of the tree, and I began falling towards the wall! I scrambled trying to find something to hold onto, but I landed on the top of the wall rather hard. For a moment nothing happened, and I sat up and looked back to Adrian who was still on the tree— until loud, angry alarms began blaring. I was so startled by the noise that I lost my balance and fell. All of a sudden, I found myself hurting as I lay on the ground, inside The Meeting Place. The alarm blared even louder, coming from everywhere and nowhere. I sat up— only to find two dozen hunters racing towards me with weapons.

THUMP!

"Ughhhhhh…" Adrian was suddenly on the ground next to me, groaning. "What happened to the plan?!"

Lorelai

When I strode up to the main, large double metal doors of The Meeting Place, knowing that hunters I had not seen in years would be behind them… and I was here to technically steal from them and spy on them… it left me uneasy, to say the least. Though none of them were as good as me with the weapons, they did all know how to fight. If there's one thing hunters hate, it's backstabbing; otherwise known as violating our Code in any way. Oh well.

I knew they would have someone watching the main door, so I waited for a few seconds in full view in front of the doors, nonchalantly, until I heard the sound of a few people gathering and talking on the other side of the door. I had been spotted, and reported.

"I would like to come in, please!" I called sweetly.

Slowly, the double doors opened wide. Revealing a large group of presumed hunters— a few I recognized, many I did not. A few of the likely newer recruits whispered in surprise amongst themselves. An older man stepped forward.

"Lorelai! Hello! We were told you weren't going to be coming, uh, this time around?" he said. I smiled.

"Surprise."

Upon entering, I was pulled aside by a few hunters I knew— and were never particularly fond of— and questioned. I assured them that I was not, in fact, travelling with any civilians like they assumed me to be. *Regardless, what you did to John was a nasty trick, my friends...* my fingers twitched near the secret pocket in my jacket where I kept a smaller type of dagger. When I was next accused of wanting to steal their human-form selkie though, I had to also resist a smirk.

"We know you were hunting this one before us, Lorelai, since you were around there but—"

"A hunter's catch is that hunter's batch, boys, I get it. You caught the selkie that was stupid enough to go see a human doctor, *congratulations,*" I interrupted. That stopped them in their tracks. There was a pause.

"Why are you here?" one of them asked bluntly.

"Well… *friends,* I would like to buy the selkie off of you, fairly," I said, giving them a wide smile and offering my hand for a shake.

"It's not for sale 'till tomorrow." A gruff response.

"Can I at least see the specimen then? Confirm the catch?" I smiled and batted my eyelashes. I was good at getting what I wanted, this time would be no exception. "I need to at least be sure that you do *have* the specimen before I invest, surely?"

They lead me through the main hub of activity and trading, full of hunters of varying ages and abilities. Not to mention crates and crates stacked high with supplies— both of the hunter and mundane variety. A few cages with other live creatures were also around, rare and deadly things that would cast quite a price to the right seller. Through a door of one of many small buildings, down dimly lit stone stairs… only to enter a room with three small cells. Three. Small.

Empty. Cells. *Where the hell is Morgan?!* I felt an angry warmth begin to spread from my chest. *I cannot lash out, I have to play this carefully if I am to ever find her...* I spun on the other hunters.

"Oh? What do we have here?" I asked in mock intrigue. "Can selkies turn invisible now, or could you not even keep a *weak, powerless* selkie contained?" My fury reached my eyes. Albeit not for the reason they would think, but it could still be used to my advantage. Two of them looked at each other in shock, sputtering and turning on each other in an attempt to appease me. But my gaze was soon more preoccupied with the form of a man entering the room behind them. He had a short, neatly trimmed dark beard to match his combed hair, with a jagged scar across his left eye. He walked with purpose and authority in his step and posture, and wore not anything a hunter would wear— but a Navy Captain's dark blue and gold coat. Albeit a tiny bit run down.

He had obviously aged a bit since I had last seen him, with salt and pepper speckles in his beard, but I still recognized him immediately.

"Did you fools not hear of it? The alarms blaring the day before last? The selkie has escaped," he said plainly. The other hunters in the room immediately stopped and paid full attention to him when they realized his presence, which intrigued me, but there was no time to wonder why he had respect from hunters as anger welled in my chest at his words.

"What do you mean she's *escaped?!*" I blurted. He slowly turned to look at me, eyeing me up and down. He smiled cooly.

"Lorelai," he said, drawing out my name as if he was tasting it. "It's been a long time, though you have not changed a bit. What brings you here?" His dark eyes glimmered. "I've heard plenty about your exploits these last several years from *many* hunters… they say you have defeated an army of pirates alone with one hand tied behind your back." Despite the anger that still burned embers and small flames in my chest, I almost half smirked. *Sounds like something I might try. Haven't yet, though.*

"*Captain* Samael Williams." I nodded curtly, a touch of anger embedded in his title. "I am here about this selkie of yours, how exactly could you let such an asset *get away?*" My teeth were gritted tight. He remained calm as ever.

"An oversight of a few guards, one in particular, but we will find the monster soon enough," he said, shooing the matter away with a wave of his hand. "Until we do… is there anything else I can help you with?"

I strolled through the open centre of The Meeting Place, trying to remain calm as my mind raced trying to decide what to do about Morgan being missing. But the least I could do in the situation I was in was gain some information. I looked at Samael who was walking with me, about to give me the 'Official' hunter tour. His navy blue coat with yellow trim and buttons had a frayed edge, and the colours were a bit muted.

"What is a Navy Captain doing on an island with a bunch of hunters? Where's the impressive ship, the crew…?" I asked. There was a dense silence. He smirked, but didn't look over at me. I stared hard at him. "What Captain gets to keep the coat when he leaves the Navy?"

"I did not *leave* the Navy, I am doing specific work for them here," he looked at me. "Important secretive work, you understand," he said mockingly. I knew what he was referencing; occasionally I used to choose to break a few of their rules while I did jobs for them. Including the secrecy ones.

"Hey, just because I was willing to go to lengths you wouldn't to do the job, doesn't mean you have to hold a grudge," I replied flippantly. "I got the job done, every time."

Slowly, he stared hard at me. An evil, creepy smile stretched up his face.

"That was years ago. You would not *believe* the lengths I am willing to go to now to get any and every kind of job done… The Navy has been branching out their services, Mrs." His eyes were dark and cold and empty and his smile was wide. His words were precise and slow. I was thoroughly unsettled, in a way I never had been before. So when he almost immediately switched back to his calm self, claiming to have forgotten something important he had to do, then handed me off to a random hunter for the tour and hurried away… My relief covered my suspicion.

It wasn't hard to lose the practically novice hunter that I had been assigned to. When he turned a corner and realized abruptly that I was nowhere to be found, I think he was secretly glad. I could tell he was intimidated, to say the least.

Picking the building that had the most guards hovering near it, the one with the most heavily-armed people pretending to casually walk by, I headed towards it. With a smile to the nearest guard and a confident stride, I walked in like I owned the place. No one stopped me. No one had been told that I definitely *wasn't* allowed anywhere, and I had been seen talking with the Captain. Not to mention that hunters had seen that we knew each other. The door squealed closed behind me.

I was immediately bathed in silence. Lanterns hung from the ceiling every so often, a little too spaced out. The light dimmed noticeably between the lanterns. Cold, dark stone surrounded me like a tomb, and at the end of a small hallway, stairs led down to a door. My heels tapped loudly on the stone as I slowly descended. Reaching the door, it seemed thick and was locked. At the top of the door was a square opening, filled with small metal bars. I peeked through the gaps… and saw something I really hadn't expected to see.

There was a woman, tied to a table… I couldn't bring myself to look at her for more than a second. She was clearly dead, and it was horrible. Lining the wall behind her were three large glass tanks filled with water. One had a man floating in it. His eyes were closed, and his expression was calm, but long sharp teeth protruded out from under his top lip. The other two tanks had selkies in two different forms of being mid-transformation. They were *ugly*. Only one leg had turned to a tail on one of them, with its face a garbled mess with an elongated human nose, no ears, and patches of grey skin. Beside the tanks was a workshop, cluttered with scraps and bits of metal, and a simple wand. Something magic users of a more *typical* variety could use to help focus their magic. But what really got my attention was the small table off to the side with nothing but a flower vase sitting on it. The flowers in the vase were a bright orange with dark tips, and long, thin stems. Despite having never seen them in person before, I recognized them immediately.

They were the third and final flower I needed to be able to keep my deal with Morgan.

But they were behind a locked door.

A loud, annoying blaring seemed to erupt from the very stone around me all of a sudden. An urgent alarm was going off, and I shouldn't risk being found here. I gave one last look at the flowers, at the confusing room, and then forced myself to turn and run up the stairs and back out into the blinding sun.

Only to be greeted by the sight of a small grouping of hunters all clumped together on the other side of The Meeting Place near the wall. A negative knowing feeling settled in the pit of my stomach. *If this is because of who I think it is… Those two must truly be idiots if they decided to find a way inside instead of waiting for my cue… I hope I'm mistaken.* But, no, of course not, I was right. In between a true rock and a hard place, Miles and Adrian both were standing between hunters and a stone wall. As I ran towards them, the hunters turned around, and greeted the Navy Captain as he strode up as well. But I didn't have time to think, as one of the hunters caught my eye and a look of recognition appeared.

"Hey wait a minute, weren't you around *with* one of these guys near where they caught that selkie? I think it was the longer haired guy, yeah! The hell is he doing here?" he said, growing slowly more angry and defensive as realization set in. A few other hunters approached from behind me.

"Yeah I was on that team, I definitely saw both of those guys around there! That one was with this witch, and the other punched me when we were taking the selkie! He wanted to save it!" One of the men called out. The group of interested hunters was growing, as did the volume of voices and anger as they began wondering what I had been doing with a civilian that was now trespassing with the same person who had defended the selkie. It would be moments before they grew far too suspicious, and realized my true intentions here.

"They're here to steal the selkie!" one shouted. *Shit.* That was quicker than I thought.

"The selkie isn't even here anymore!"

"*They* didn't know that when they got here!"

The group began turning on the three of us as a whole. Hands hovered over hilts, eyes flicking away from me to the weaker links at first. Adrian and Miles were backing against the wall.

Wrong direction, boys! I thought, as I swooped in with my dagger in my teeth, grabbing the collars of each of their shirts with each hand, and then tossing them away from the wall. I took my dagger into my hand. With my free hand I swiftly grabbed a spare dagger from its sheath hidden inside my jacket, and tossed it hilt-first towards them in one smooth move. Miles flinched as Adrian caught it safely.

"Run!" I yelled, flipping my dagger quickly in the air and watching as the men around me took a step back as it grew to its full size. I turned on my fellow hunters.

"Anyone willing to take me on?!" I yelled at top volume, finally letting the anger flow. "Got to get through the traitor to get to the civilians, come on who has a backbone?!" I continued to yell. The crowd of hunters around me, all of whom could fight and wield a sword by trade, was giant. And every single one of them hesitated— my reputation preceded me indeed.

But it would only be a moment before they realized they had strength and even skill far against me in numbers.

Chapter Fourteen - Compassion

<u>Morgan</u>

It felt like I had been limping through that forest for *days*. No matter what I did, every single movement hurt. I couldn't even put the slightest amount of weight on my injured ankle anymore. I was sure I had made it worse, it had to be broken by now. I hadn't had any other choice. Before long, I found a soft, sheltered little spot at the base of a tree next to the shore, and there I fell immediately asleep to the sound of the waves crashing against the island. It was the deepest, longest, and by far the best sleep I had ever had in human form. I only awoke briefly once, in a panic after a nightmare, only to realize that I was alone and somewhat safe. I simply covered myself in leaves for better camouflage, and fell back asleep easily.

When I finally, actually woke up, I had no idea how much time had passed. Every single muscle in my body seemed to ache and moan, everything was stiff and sore. *At least they didn't find me. At least I didn't reopen a wound and bleed to death in my sleep.* I thought. *Although then again if I had, the best sleep of my life sounds far from the worst way to go.*

I lay there, staring up at the trees hanging above me. The waves were my company. I didn't want to ever move— partially because every move caused pain, and partially because I had no idea where else to go. Surely moving about the island would only make me more likely to be recaptured by a hunter. I sat up and looked at the glistening ocean. I couldn't even swim away.

But I *was* growing more and more hungry. *What's a severely injured almost-human supposed to do to get food on an island while they themselves are also being hunted?* I wondered bleakly. I could even smell fish, presumably from the ocean below, and it taunted me.

"I am doomed to starve to death, bleed out, or be caught by killers…" I whispered to the sea. "Is there no hope for me?"

The waves did not change, or respond.

I continued to sit there, staring out at the waves. The white froth of sea foam, the sound of the rushing waves. Feeling nice and concealed in the dense trees, at the very least. Trying my hardest to not think. Not think about my situation, or my fate. Simply let the sound of the waves and the wind in the trees fill my mind instead. But I didn't realize how incredibly void of the sounds of birds, or any animals at all, that the island was until I finally heard one.

The sound of fluttering through the trees, as a black crow landed on a branch above me, standing out in the green leaves. In its mouth was a small white pouch. It looked directly at me, cocked its head, and squawked-- dropping the white cloth pouch in the grass next to me. When I looked back up at the branch, the crow was gone. The pouch was made of a few layers of a thin perfectly white fabric, and tied shut with a small bit of rope. A piece of paper was attached to the rope. Some kind of liquid began to seep out of the bottom of the bag, and suddenly I realized that the fish I had been smelling wasn't just because of the sea. I tore the rope off of the sack and it fell open, revealing cut chunks of raw *fish!* I popped one in my mouth and relished in the familiar delicious feeling of slimy juicy fish in my mouth. I enjoyed the rest of the few chunks more slowly, sitting in a spot of warm sun. After I was done, I remembered that there had been a paper attached to the rope, and I quickly grabbed the rope before it flew away in the breeze. I opened the note.

> *I hope Sammy found you rather quickly, and that this ends up in your hands, young selkie. I could not come looking for you myself, as I would likely be followed by hunters. I think you should know… I heard that a few people came looking for you today. Caused quite a… stir. They escaped into the forest, same as I heard you did. Though hunters are still looking for you. Congratulations on the escape, and good luck. I'll see if there is anything else I can do for you in the meantime.*

~ The woman who gave you that stolen dagger

I stared at the words quickly scrawled in a curved, loopy hand-written font. I reread one of the sentences over again: 'I heard that a few people came looking for you today'... People who weren't allowed in there, but found a way in and a way to ask about me… People, or a person, who could figure out where I had been taken. A foolishly large smile grew on my face as my cheeks turned red. Happiness burned bright inside me, and a small tear fell down my face. *They actually came looking for me... They came to save me! They came!* I hugged the note to my chest and fell back onto the grass, smiling. Sunlight peeked down at me through the leaves above.

Miles

"We have t' find Morgan as fast as possible. If those weapon-happy hunters are lookin' for us at all, they're lookin' for her three times as much," I said to the group, standing before them. "And lucky for us, I know how t' track her."

"I also know a thing or two about tracking large prey— and about selkies. I guarantee you right now she will be as far away as she can get from The Meeting Place, and as close to the ocean as she can be while staying hidden," Lorelai said. Adrian blinked in surprise, and Ms.

Lorelai noticed. She shrugged. "Selkies prefer to stay near the ocean if they can help it."

We decided to walk around the edge of the island until we found either Morgan, or the farthest point outward, and then look around there. If that didn't work... we would have to try to search for her throughout the forest. *This island ain't very big, surely we will find her.*

We walked through the forest, careful not to make too much noise so the hunters wouldn't find us. A few feet to my left, the ground fell away suddenly into sharp rocks and crashing waves. The trees around us were perfectly still and silent, except for some few and far between small animals. It was as if most of the animals that lived on this island were avoiding us. Or even, for some reason, maybe there were hardly any animals on this island at all. Maybe the hunters had killed them all. *That's not a very happy thought, now is it?*

We walked for what felt like an hour or two, skirting around the inside edge of the mountains when we reached them, figuring that it was pretty unlikely Morgan had scaled them. It was a mostly very quiet trip, until we suddenly stepped out of the trees into a small gap between the closely standing trunks, only to find a woman standing there, pointing a dagger at us.

The woman was covered head to toe in deep cuts, wounds, and bruises. And she barely put any weight on her left foot-- because it was so swollen it had *doubled* in size! Her face was dirty and bloody just like the rest of her. But what gave her away was the colour of the tangled mess of hair on her head. *What on earth—*

"M-Miles? Is that really you?" Morgan lowered the dagger. "W-where are the others?" Before I could answer, Adrian stepped out and waved, and Lorelai walked into the clearing with her arms crossed.

"You have caused quite a lot of trouble for us, haven't y—"

"I can not *believe* you came all this way for me," Morgan interrupted, staring at all of us. *I'm confused. Why is she so surprised? We couldn't just leave her.* Adrian shared my confusion. Suddenly, Morgan threw herself forward and hugged Ms. Lorelai.

"Thank you," she said simply. "I'm sure none of you would've made it here without *you*." Lorelai stood there, frozen, not hugging her back. Her eyebrows were furrowed and her mouth was slightly open, as if she wanted to say something but had no idea what.

"I—um, well, uh, we, we had a deal, you know," Lorelai said, as Morgan let go of her. I'd never heard her stutter or sound unsure before in my life. But really, Morgan was *covered* in wounds—

"Morgan, what on god's green earth did they do t' ya?!" I cried, no longer able to contain it. Everyone stopped and looked at me.

Since Morgan had somehow managed to stay hidden for something like two or three days now out in her little spot, we decided it was probably the safest spot we would find, and stayed there. We all needed some rest, most could use some healing magic if Lorelai would, and we had to decide what to do from here.

A big problem on the table was Morgan's injured ankle. She couldn't put any weight on it, and it was all puffed up and black and purple, all bruised... Painful to the touch. The poor girl could hardly walk— how she had escaped was beyond me. Even after she told us how she had escaped, I found it hard to believe. But I was *so* glad we had finally found her. I was so happy that she was back with us, safe and sound, that every time I saw her I smiled.

"What?" she said, when she noticed. "What are *you* looking at?" *Ah. Her sass is starting to return, I see. That's nice.*

Ms. Lorelai moved over to us, still covered in scrapes of her own that were closing with magic. I stared in awe at her arm as a small cut closed and disappeared before my own eyes. After getting Morgan to move her injured ankle towards her, Lorelai checked it out closely. Whenever it was touched, Morgan would wince. Lorelai took a breath, before quietly and very quickly chanting a string of very odd sounds as she gently waved her hands over and around the ankle. *Light* drifted out of her, flowing and shining, falling onto Morgan's ankle. After a minute, she washed the light over the rest of Morgan as well. When she stopped, she pulled a small container out of inside her jacket. She warned Morgan that it would sting a bit, and took some kind of cream or something out, and applied it heavily all over the swollen ankle. Morgan grimaced, but refused to take my hand when I offered it. Finally, she wrapped the last of our bandages around her ankle.

"Adrian, please go find a large branch about as tall as just below Morgan's shoulder when standing, she will need something to assist her to walk," she said, sending Adrian off with a wave of the hand before going off to sit on the edge by the water without another word. I turned to Morgan, sitting by her shoulder as she lay on the grass.

"How're you doin'?" I asked. She gave me a look, frowning.

"Everything hurts, I can't walk, and now we are all completely *stuck* on this goddamn island full of hunters because of me," she said. "So in a word, *bad,* thanks for asking." *Those last words woulda been nice if you hadn't been so sarcastic...* "Miles, what if I can't walk normally again? It has to be broken, the last time I saw a selkie who had an injury *this* bad, they were eventually left behind by their pod when a shark came hunting them," she said, more anger in her tone than anything else.

"Aw Morgan, we won't ever dare to leave ya behind, no matter what happens, and I'm sure your selkie pod will take good care of ya too!" I smiled. Only for my face to turn to a frown when she rolled on her side to turn away from me. Somehow I had only made her more upset, which was confusing. *What did I do wrong? What can I do t' help?*

<u>Lorelai</u>

I sat on the grass with my feet dangling off the edge of an island cliff. Below, large waves crashed against the rocks and the cliff face. As the wind coming off of the sea blew my hair behind me, I had plenty to ponder. My identity as a hunter, for one. *I am not one of them anymore, there is no longer any use denying it.* With a sigh, I stood up, and headed back over to where Morgan lay. I sat neatly next to Morgan, opposite Miles, so that as she lay on her side Morgan was facing me. Adrian was standing near Miles now. They all looked at me curiously. I looked Morgan directly in the eye.

"I overheard that you have been quite upset, angry at the world about your predicament?" I nodded down towards her ankle. She opened her mouth to respond, but I decided not to let her. "I understand where you are coming from. I have been angry at the world for a long, long time." My voice grew serious, and in the pause that followed, no one else even attempted to speak. We sat in that silence for a lengthy moment as I tried to come up with the words.

"Morgan… you have a sister, yes? A younger sister, the one who is the reason you came all this way. She's heavily injured and you want to do everything you can to save her, right? I suspect she is also the reason you were able to endure what you have, the thing motivating you above all else to escape, to live, to continue?" I asked. Morgan nodded, biting her lower lip. Still no one else spoke. I leaned closer towards her face. "Morgan." I said, very seriously. "The world is a terrible, cruel place, but if you do not continue to fight, what will become of your sister?" I paused. "And would she really want you to come back angry and bitter?"

I watched as Morgan swallowed, and then began trying to push herself into a sitting position. Miles helped her, and as she sat there, looking straight ahead, instead of at any of us, a few small tears fell down her cheeks.

"You're right," she said, her voice breaking. "If we don't keep going, if *I* don't keep going, if I let this anger at the unfairness of it all get to me…" She shook her head. "I want Adva to be proud of me."

I smiled, and looked up at the entire group.

"Well then we better get going," I said.

I contacted Nico. We didn't have any other choice-- I at least had to *try*. I was quite surprised when his ship pulled up near the island

and Captain Nicodemus himself rowed to the shore, back down where we had first come onto the island. But apparently he had the wrong idea about why I had told him to come.

"Lorelai, I will take you and you alone off of this island-- to any city on this side of the coast and we can both continue with our lives," he said. "But the rest of them are not allowed on my ship ever again." He stood on the rocky shore, as poised and as confident as ever, with the sea behind him. And behind me… were Miles, Adrian, and Morgan.

"Nico, they are not monsters, they--" I tried.

"A *selkie* and a *triton* are not monsters?!" He exclaimed, incredulous. "The Lorelai I knew would steal a selkie's skin, cut off a triton's scales, and sell both without a second thought."

Out of the corner of my eye, I saw a look of horror cross Adrian's face at the words, and I felt my heart sink. Morgan stared at me wide-eyed, until she looked down at the sand frowning, with her eyebrows furrowed. Arms crossed. I forced myself to turn back towards Nicodemus.

"But, Nico, they-- they aren't like what we have always thought monsters were like! Adrian is sweet, helpful, kind, and *selfless!* Morgan is smart, and would do absolutely *anything* to save her family!" I insisted. Out of the corner of my eye, I saw both Morgan's and Adrian's heads lift and a small smile graced them both, brightening their faces. Until--

"Yeah, including *killing humans*!" Nico retorted, his volume growing.

"How do you not *hear* what I've been saying, he *saved my life* Nico!" I yelled back, my anger blossoming. "Doesn't that mean *anything* to you?!"

"Of *course,* I am so thankful you're alive, but they cannot be trusted!" he said, throwing up his hands.

"How can you be so sure of that!" I cried.

"Because I grew up with one!" he yelled. "*Goddamnit* Lorelai, they might seem okay but they'll only stab you in the back and drag you down to a watery death in the end," he said, his voice lowering but losing none of its anger. "And I am not going to just wait until that happens." He turned and left. Throwing his small rowboat back onto the waters, climbing aboard, and leaving as fast as he could. Refusing to listen to a word I said as he did so.

I stared at Nico as he moved farther away, and boarded his ship. I stared and watched as the ship began to leave. I stared out at the waves. And collapsed into a sitting position on the sand, ignoring the water lapping at my feet. First with Miles, then Adrian, then Morgan with her new walking stick, the three of them slowly came and joined me on the sand, sitting by my side. Trying to be there for comfort.

"Nico and I…" the words fell out of my mouth. "We've been friends first for many, *many* years. And he was always the one who was there for me. But now…" I stopped speaking as my voice began to break. The three of them moved a bit closer to me. A hand on my shoulder-- Miles. Another hand, on my other side, holding my own-- Morgan. Slowly, arms wrapping around me from behind.

I have no idea how long we sat like that, without moving. But we all stayed that way for quite some time. Until finally, I nudged all of them off, and stood up. Before I could speak, Morgan did.

"Lorelai…" she began. "When we made our deal, you said you wanted help finding someone and then help with--"

"Yes, and?" I interrupted.

Morgan hesitated before continuing. "Um, if you don't mind me asking… you said you have been angry at the world for a long time. Who… Who is it that you want help finding, and...*why?*" *Mm. At least she's leaving a certain detail out for me. That's good.*

I sighed. And looked at the people before me. Who had either saved my life or I had, for some reason, risked my own for them. Normally this was a question I wouldn't ever answer.

"Morgan, what was done to you in there…" I nod up towards the building. "It pales in comparison to what was done to me. I. Need. *Revenge.*" I said. Anger began to grow inside me at the mere thought of The Taker. "But for now, right now…" I continued, trying to push my anger back down. "It is time to get off this god-forsaken island."

And with that, as I already had the spell prepared and enough energy stored up, I snapped my fingers and all four of us disappeared suddenly from the island's shore.

<u>Adrian</u>

To my left, ships sat in a harbour and crates and large nets lay to the side. Miles, Morgan, and I quickly got to our feet as a few people began to look our way-- but most ignored our sudden presence. They did not even notice that we had literally appeared out of nowhere.

I stared at Lorelai. *How did she…?*

Lorelai smiled proudly upon seeing three expressions of shock and surprise on her travel mates' faces. She turned and walked over to a tree that sat on the edge of the beach, and, after moving handfuls of sand, unearthed a small wooden box. Opening it, she took out a dark purple rock that glimmered in the sun. Pocketing it, she placed a similar green stone back in the box before burying it back where she found it.

"Now, come on, I think we all need some new clothes…" her voice trailed off as she looked at all of our soggy, dirty, worn clothing up and down with disdain. "*And*, I doubt any of you have ever seen a real city before, hm? All towns and villages in your lives, I'm sure…" She began to turn away from us as she spoke, and after regarding the edge of the city for a moment, she strolled towards it. We all, of course, followed.

"Woah, wait, hold on one second!" Morgan exclaimed suddenly, before stalking up to Lorelai and getting her to face her, only to lower her voice and angrily say, "*What the absolute hell* just happened and where the hell are we?! How did you possibly *do* that?! That island was nowhere near any city!"

Lorelai smiled.

"You know full well what I am, darling. Get used to it," she said, turning and continuing to head into the city. Morgan reluctantly fell in line beside me. She looked at me.

"Has she… done this type of thing before?" she asked. I nodded. "Huh. And here I thought she just played with the seas." Hearing this, Lorelai glanced back over her shoulder and glared at Morgan, and Morgan simply gave a smirky smile back to her.

As we entered the city on a smooth stone road, the buildings were sat oh so incredibly close together, a network of large and small stone streets stretched out in front of us, weaving in between buildings and disappearing to continue around corners. In the distance, buildings stretched taller than I thought possible. It seemed everything was made of wood and stone. Small lights, currently not illuminated, were on the outside of each one. Most noticeably, was the major volume of *people.* People walked and rushed around everywhere, filling the streets to the brim. The crowds only parted when those strange, tall creatures pulling wheeled wooden carts insisted on coming through. *Horses*--and carriages, Miles had called them that before. I still found them quite odd. I glanced over at my companions; Lorelai strode forward without a care. Morgan, on the other hand, had her arms folded and was looking around cautiously. Miles, though, was staring around at all of the buildings and people with his mouth open in awe.

"I ain't ever seen so many people in one place before, or any buildings so tall!" he said to me. "My village was so small…" his voice trailed off as he again became wrapped up in our surroundings.

Lorelai moved through the swarm of humans with ease, it was as if they parted for her as well. The other three of us squeezed into the space created behind her. As we moved further and further into the city, the crowd became easier to traverse through, until the space opened up into some sort of … town square? *Do cities have town squares?* I wondered. It was a large open space between buildings, scattered with small outdoor tables. At one of them sat an extremely tall, broad, muscular man. A bright, large sign stood near him, challenging any onlookers to try to beat the man in an… arm-wrestling match? *What is that?*

Lorelai stopped and glanced at the sign, and scoffed quietly to herself but did not share any thoughts. Morgan, however, had a mischievous look on her face as she nudged Miles.

"Miles, you should give it a shot," she said. "You might be able to win."

"Oh, I could never! Look at him! I'm dwarfed by 'im," Miles insisted. "And with all these people 'round…"

Morgan brushed him off and marched right up to the man at the table. Despite having to use a branch to support herself to walk, and only being able to put weight on one foot, she held her head high and moved with a measure of confidence and strength now.

"What do you win," she asked him gruffly, force behind her voice.

"Wha-?"

"What. Do you. *WIN*. If someone beats you."

The man burst out laughing, and told her to go home. Called her a little crippled girl, and that she could never win. *Uh oh… Morgan is not going to like that.* To my surprise, she did not react. She simply repeated her question-- insisted that if he was as hard to beat as his sign claimed, there should be a prize. The man stood up, gaining his entire height as he easily towered far, far over Morgan. His muscles rippled and bulged and his shadow blocked the sun from Morgan's view.

"Alright little girl, if you or one of your friends can beat *me*? They can have… uh...um…" he looked around, thinking. "My old ship, I suppose. It's sitting at the edge of the harbour. I have no use for it anymore. That good enough of a prize for you, girl?" he said.

Morgan grinned, and hobbled back to Miles as fast as she could, and tugged on his arm.

"Miiiiiiiiles, you could win a shiiiiiiiip," she cooed in a sing-song voice.

I could see it in his eyes. They lit up at the mere possibility.

Miles sat at the outdoor table opposite the other man, who looked down at him. He stared fiercely, while Miles smiled weakly back up at him. A small crowd gathered to watch-- from what I could gather from their murmurings, they were not sure who would win. The two men put their elbows on the table and locked hands. From what I could figure out as the odd competition began, it was a small show of specific strength to try to force the other man's hand down first. *Human men have such strange measures of worth and masculinity…*

Though Miles was clearly trying as hard as he could, he was soon going to lose by the look of it. *How unfortunate.* But as I watched on, Morgan sneaking away from by my side caught my eye. I watched as she slithered through the crowd, her movements made more awkward than they may have been by her injury. She stopped when she found herself behind Miles' opponent.

The man's elbow slipped. It lost all of its hold on the surface, and Miles' hand went soaring around in the opposite direction, from nearly hitting the table and barely holding on, to slamming his opponent's hand onto the wood. The crowd began loud and uproarious. But Morgan stood behind him, a look of shock on her face. She had moved to behind him, and her motives seemed suspicious, but I had been watching her. She had not done anything to sabotage the silly competition.

Both men's eyes widened in shock. A giant smile began to fill Miles' face, while the other man threw himself to his feet and began to angrily rant that somehow, he had cheated. At that moment, Lorelai, who had been watching this all unfold, strolled up to the strong man while Miles sat there in disbelief. She placed a hand gently on his upper arm, and began to speak softly in his ear. He took a close look at her and then out of nowhere, roughly pushed her off of his arm.

"Get off me! Ughh," he said. He sounded disgusted, and I could not fathom why-- Lorelai was quite attractive. She put her hands up.

"Okay, alright, geez, calm down. Fair is fair, you slipped, he won. Where is the boat?" Lorelai asked, her voice edged in anger. He grumbled to himself, but many people in the crowd were paying attention to Miles instead now. Patting him on the back and congratulating him.

"Fine. The ship is the last one on the far left of the harbour, with no name inscribed on it. It's yours," The large man said. With that, he stalked off and left, disappearing into the city. Lorelai turned to Miles.

"I am sure you are eager to go see your new ship, but let us get a room for the night and a meal, new clothes, and then once we are not so weary, the first order of business will be your ship," she said softly. I had not noticed it before, but now I saw her face seemed tired. Her arms hung loosely at her sides, and her always perfect posture was beginning to stoop. Even her voice was quiet as if she did not have the energy anymore to raise it to normal. *Perhaps her lack of energy is why she did not even try to stop Morgan's effort to get Miles to do the, urm, wrestle.*

Though Miles' face fell noticeably, he knew the logic of her point. There was also always a chance he was seeing in Lorelai what I saw; her exhaustion.

Miles rose to his feet, his smile abruptly returned. He gathered us together excitedly.

"I know exactly what imma name my new, first beauty of a ship," he said. "Compassion." He said it as though it was a sacred announcement. Upon seeing the slight confusion on some of our faces, he explained.

"I- Well, its… Compassion is my ma's middle name," he said, slightly sheepish. "She's the reason I never felt bad 'bout leavin' my village, since she wanted me t' go in the end."

Morgan

Hours had passed since the arm-wrestling tournament I had goaded Miles into doing. We had got fresh new clothes-- which I was especially fond of, having clothes I liked and felt comfortable in again after having to abandon my own clothes on the hunter's island. Then we'd found a tavern, paid for rooms and meals with the last of Lorelai's gold, and Miles had scarfed down his food before taking off on his own back to the harbour. The rest of us slowly finished and followed after him. Being with only Adrian and Lorelai had been interesting-- I could communicate with them both, but Adrian could still not communicate with Lorelai. I had no idea how Miles always seemed okay with being the translator now that, briefly, I was.

When we arrived, Miles was crawling all over the ship he had won excitedly as the sky grew dark. But it was in incredible disrepair. Parts of the ship were rotting, and a large hole gaped in the front. The sail was sitting on the deck of the tiny ship, soaked and torn. Miles waved us towards him excitedly, calling over that he would 'get it all fixed up'... I wasn't sure how to remind him that we were broke. Every human thing takes money, it seemed.

While Adrian stayed with Miles who seemed to not see how damaged the ship was, Lorelai and I sat a little ways away on the edge of an empty dock. We sat with open water extending out as far as the eye could see in front of us, the sunset far behind us, blocked by the city. I dangled my legs over the edge of the dock, my shoes sitting beside me. My toes only just touched the cold ocean. The wind coming off of the open sea made my face cold, and blew my long white hair around everywhere. I busied myself for a few minutes with trying to force a brush that I had, uh, picked up, through its giant knots. A few stars began to appear in the darkening sky above us. Lorelai lounged on the dock behind me, her legs outstretched as she leaned back on her hands. For several minutes, we said nothing. Just stared out at either the endless sea or the sky.

"You must have had a very tough, cruel life."

I broke the silence. Without bothering to turn around, I could feel Lorelai stiffen behind me. "And out of the three of you, I'm sure you certainly have the best idea of what I went through in there," I continued. The air thickened in my pause. "And yet you are so sure whatever you went through was worse."

Silence. Nothing but the soft lapping of tiny waves, and distant noise from both the city and Miles.

"Yes," she said. The boards of the dock creaked as Lorelai stood up. She moved my new shoes back and took their spot, sitting cross-legged on the edge of the dock next to me. "I never meant to belittle what you went through…" her voice trailed off for a moment. "Considering the presence of that man from The Navy I'm sure it was horrid." ... *The Navy? My torturer* wasn't *a hunter?... That would explain his dress. His authority, even, maybe...* I stayed silent.

"I…" she began, only to stop. "In short, I was kidnapped, abused--physically and emotionally-- controlled, manipulated, cursed, and forced to… Well, hunt." She sped through the words as if pausing on any of them would hurt. "Our deal means I will have help finding the man who did that to me."

For several minutes, neither of us spoke. What do you say to that? *No wonder she is so bent on revenge...and is so angry. And she hunted. She killed my own kind. But she was forced to, at least at first. I don't know what to say.*

"Do you miss your family?" Lorelai asked out of nowhere, as she leaned back and laid down fully on the dock, staring at the sky.

"Of course. I miss each of them every single day."

"Me too."

The waves lapped against my toes. I reached behind me and picked up my shoes, before leaning back to lie next to the sea witch with my new shoes resting on top of my stomach.

"I recently found out that I have some extended family," I told her, staring up at the sky.

"Really?" asked Lorelai, glancing over at me.

"Yes. I need to look for them, at some point. Adva deserves to have more family than only me."

"So… what's this sister of yours like anyway? Who I'm supposed to magically save?" she asked. I let out a big exhale.

"She's wonderful," I said. "She is sweet, kind, and shy… and sad, struggling. She used to race around the choral and chase fish and crabs for fun, but now she can't do much more than lie there most days…" I frowned, biting my lower lip. "I have done everything I can think of, and nothing heals her injury."

"I see…" Lorelai replied.

We sat in the quiet pause that followed.

"Can I… ask you a question?" I asked suddenly. There was something that I had been wondering about Lorelai, and I doubted I would get a better chance to ask her. She eyed me cautiously.

"Is it about my *'tough, cruel life'*?" she asked half mockingly, quoting myself back to me with a raised eyebrow.

"It's about earlier today."

"My interest is piqued. Shoot," she replied. *Shoot?! What? Where?* I looked around, a bit panicked. Lorelai laughed. "It's an *expression*, don't worry. It means 'go ahead, ask'." *Oh. Right, of course.* I took a deep breath.

"Why did the strongman throw you off like that earlier? At the arm-wrestling match," I asked, watching her closely. We had all noticed. Not liking her advances is one thing, but going from being fine with it to being disgusted in half a second? That was strange. Lorelai stared at me for a second, then sighed and looked out at the water.

"Most people never… see anything, that I don't want them to. About me. A lot of me has been permanently changed by a lengthy, dangerous spell and a whole lot of magic… but nothing is perfect," she said. She avoided eye contact with me, still staring away from me out to sea as she spoke. I had never imagined that she would be nervous to look anyone in the eye, least of all me. As for what she was saying, I didn't understand any of it. The idea that she had permanently altered herself with magic was definitely new information, and it surprised me, but I had no idea what any of that had to do with my question. Finally, she looked at me. Directly in the eye.

"He must have noticed when I got close that I still have a pronounced Adam's apple," she said. *Wait, what?* She watched me as my mind flooded with thoughts. *What does this mean? What is she saying? Adam's apple?*

"I don't… I don't understand," I said. She sighed again, loudly this time, and flopped into a lying position on the dock.

"In humans, typically only boys and men have a pronounced Adam's apple, Morgan," she said, exasperated. *Oohh!* My eyes widened. *She changed with magic…*

"That's great!" I cried. "It's great that you were able to… change yourself, then. Honestly, I never understood humans' preoccupation with gender."

"Really? You don't, I don't know, think differently of me?" she asked, turning her head to face me. I blinked.

"Why would I?"

There was another pause before she changed the topic. "Well, um, anyway, I saw you steal the brush before, and those shoes," she nodded in the direction of them. "Your shirt too… which meant we could afford your new jacket, and clothes for the others." I shrugged, and said nothing. "You were quite good at it," she added. I smirked. "Also," she said, pushing herself back into a sitting position. She turned to look down at me. "I think it is high time I learn Adrian's sign language." I sat up and looked at her in surprise. Yet, at the same time, it was *about time*. "I was wondering… since the boys are busy, would you be able to give me a basic lesson?" she asked.

I smiled, and the happiness reached my eyes. It was good that she finally wanted to learn it.

Until I looked out towards the waves, and remembered. Remembered that somewhere out there, hunters were probably still after us. My seal skin was still missing. Adva was still hurt, and without me. But at least we could enjoy a moment of peace and quiet.

Chapter Fifteen - Battle Stations, Skipper

<u>Adrian</u>

I helped Miles figure out exactly how many things were wrong with his ship-- or, in his words, 'needed improvement'... Neither of the women wanted to take a single step onto the dilapidated ship in its current state. As for finding the money and skill required to properly repair it? I coaxed Lorelai into finding and using a contact she had in the big city. Someone who owed her a favour of some kind, and that person knew a person who would do some free repairs on the ship for her. We managed to get it so that the dusty pile of wood was able to sail, which was quite an achievement. It took several days, during which Lorelai and Morgan mostly rested; they both seemed to need it. We decided the next course of action, once the ship was fixed up, was to find the third flower for the spell for Morgan's sister, so we set sail to go find a land it was more likely to be found growing on.

I stood on the deck gazing out across the water as Lorelai taught Miles how to sail, how to be a Captain of a ship. Morgan sat on a crate off to the side that had been on the ship when we got it, and held minor cheap foods that supposedly would not go rotten. I stood there on the deck, one hand on the pole that held up the mast, staring off at distant land. I thought about how incredibly far I had come, how far we had all come, since we had met each other on that shore. My thoughts were interrupted as I looked side to side out at the water, and spotted something coming directly towards us. A ship. *Must be heading to the city,* I thought. But as the large ship came closer and closer, a feeling of unease grew sharply in my stomach.

I realized that I recognized the ship.

Gold edgings, a headpiece of a screaming, tied up mermaid.

The ship careening straight for us belonged to none other than Nicodemus.

Who surely wanted me-- and Morgan-- dead on his deck.

I could just barely make out men aboard the ship, many men, all armed with swords and bows.

I turned, and hurried over to Lorelai and Miles.

"Nicodemus is coming! It is not good! He has reinforcements and he is coming for us incredibly armed!" I looked at them in desperation, frantically signing. Lorelai stared at my signs closely, and shook her head.

"Are ya sure?" Miles asked, holding direct eye contact with me.

"Yes," I signed. "Completely sure." He relayed the message to Lorelai immediately, whose eyes filled with fear. My heart thundered in my chest. She looked at us both, gave a heavy sigh, then looked at Miles.

"There isn't a strong enough wind for us to be able to escape in time. Looks like it is time for battle stations, skipper." Her voice and demeanor was steeled. All possible colour drained from Miles' face.

Lorelai pulled the sword off of her back sheath and handed it to me, then handed a dagger from inside her jacket to Miles. Turning to Morgan, the selkie put up a hand to stop her, and showed that she held a dagger with a smooth wooden handle.

"I already have my own," she said.

Lorelai armed herself with a dagger kept inside her boot. She threw it up in the air, and I watched as the weapon grew into a sword before landing perfectly back in her hand. Meanwhile, Miles was panicking. He paced the small deck back and forth, weaving around the rest of us, eyes wide and his breathing already heavy. I stopped him, stood in his way.

"We are going to be okay. We are all here for each other," I signed single-handedly.

Men jumped onto our ship with a thud that startled Miles and I and shook the entire ship, then blades began to clash. One of them engaged me in battle, and I turned, swinging my sword at him only for our blades to clash together. I realized quickly how out of practice I was with a sword; *No better time than the present to improve.* I blocked his attack, only to move my weapon swiftly to his thigh, drawing blood. He made a sound-- something born of pain and anger. There was little to no room to back up or side step with all of the fighting going on around me, so I stayed locked in place, focused only on the opponent before me. I managed to block several moves before my arm that was not holding the sword moved out too far to the side, and I received a terrible gash on my forearm. I cried out, pressing my bleeding arm against my chest on instinct, but still holding my sword at the ready, eyes alert.

That was when I realized something.

These were hunters.

And thus, more importantly, if I did not kill them, they would kill me.

This fight could only end in death. *I always hated having to take lives... but these men and women are not innocent. And I cannot die.*

I began to slash more ruthlessly, my eyes constantly scanning for openings and weakness, my movements and attacks much more careful now. As we fought, blocking each other repeatedly, I heard cries of pain from all around me. Not to mention anger. The smell of blood made me wrinkle my nose. When I saw an opening in my foe's stance, I took it immediately, sending the sword tearing deeply through his side.

He yelled in pain and surprise, his free hand flying to the open wound as the new patch of red grew on his clothing.

Lorelai was next to me now. She gave me a nod, and then flew at my attacker, her short hair blowing in the wind as the sun glinted off of her blade. I swung at him simply to keep him distracted, and watched as his head fell clean off at Lorelai's hand. We made eye contact as his body slumped to the ground. In that moment, an understanding seemed to pass between us. We each faced a different side of the small ship, back to back with only slight space between us. Together, we fought. For a while, we fought quite successfully. Sometimes, one of us would join the side of the other and assist in their battle. Whether side by side or back to back, we helped each other.

The small ship was being lurched side to side as battle raged. When the rain began to pour, I welcomed it, as though the deck was now slick, the red it had been painted was leaving. Our ship stood against the side of Nicodemus' ship, and I realized I had not seen Nicodemus himself at all yet, and Miles and Morgan were also nowhere to be seen. But I had to focus. Block, parry, lunge, all while careful to not slip and fall or trip on one of the bodies lying wet on the deck's floor. An opponent of mine however, lost his footing as the waves began to grow stronger, tossing the tiny ship around. He stumbled, off balance and distracted and-- *shnk*. My sword was in his stomach nearly to the hilt. I pulled it back, the man sliding off of my crimson blade and falling to the floor.

I turned to check on Lorelai-- and saw her dark hair slicked down by the rain and sticking to her face and neck. She breathed heavily, and rain poured down her face and back. Plenty of blood was around her, only very little of it her own. She never slipped. Never hesitated. For me, these were people who had hunted my kind and creatures like me and murdered them mercilessly. They were people who would kill me without a second thought if given half a chance. But for her… had they not been her people once? I began to wonder how much she had truly been a part of their ranks as she now killed them without mercy. Did doing that mean she was less a part of them, or even more so their kind?

It did not matter. She was fighting to save all of *our* lives.

I hurried towards her, and slid into battle beside her seamlessly.

As we cut down the last of Nicodemus' men, lightning flashed in the distance. It illuminated a tall figure standing high above on the much larger ship. His dark brown hair blew to the side in the wind, and the murderous glare in his piercing blue eyes became apparent.

He was staring directly at me.

Climbing onto the edge of his own ship, Nicodemus Galanis leaped down, landing on our deck right in front of me. He stood tall and engaged me in battle, slashing towards my chest. I was able to keep him at bay for a moment, but could not land a hit on him no matter what I did. Lorelai, after hesitating, tried to help, but Nicodemus managed to bat her away each time. He swung, and somehow the sword went flying out of my hand. It slid across the deck and as the boat tipped, it fell into the thrashing sea.

I stared as my weapon, my only means of defense, fell into the watery depths. Gone. A rough hand reached out and Nicodemus shoved me to the ground. He smirked, pointing the end of his blade at my neck. He stepped towards me, his face shadowed once more as a storm raged around us. Rain pelted my face as I stared up at him, lying in a puddle of someone else's blood. A disembodied, panicked female voice drifted over from the side, begging and pleading for Nicodemus to stop as he pressed the sword's tip against my neck.

Morgan

People, hunters, all armed to the brim jumped onto the ship. I pointed my dagger at the nearest one, my other hand on my walking stick. I hissed in his face, snarling.

Only to be abruptly picked up and whisked away from the battle.

Slung over Miles' shoulder, I just barely managed to hold onto my stick as he charged through the battle-- I went flying, suddenly airborne, for a brief moment before landing on the deck of the hunter's taller, much larger ship. I groaned as my still healing body ached with the impact. I pushed myself into a sitting position as Miles quickly hauled himself up onto the deck with me. He picked me up again.

"Hey! Miles what the hell! Stop it! Put me down!" I yelled over the wind.

He ignored me, and I heard the trapdoor that led to below deck open. I looked outwards for a moment, shifting my focus away from Miles, and saw that, as far as I could tell, all of the hunters but one were on Mile's little ship, Compassion. Adrian and Lorelai were there, right in the middle of many blades. The deck of Miss Medea was empty except for one man at the helm, who was facing away from us. The captain's quarters were closed. My view of what was going on disappeared as Miles carried me below deck. He finally put me down sprawled across one of the beds in one of the rooms. He stood before me, breathing heavily, as I noticed that his shirt was torn and turning red.

"Miles you're hurt!" I exclaimed.

"Ah…" he said, looking down at the red. "Must've been knicked as I ran off with ya. Didn't even notice. It's jus' a scratch or two," he said, sitting down next to me.

"Why the hell are we here?" I asked him plainly.

"You're not fightin' in th--"

"What, in my condition? I can fight just fine!" I insisted. He looked at me doubtfully, but didn't argue. Instead he stood up, and headed for the door.

"C'mon," he said. "Let's go find somethin' that could help our friends out there."

We ended up in a room at the end of the hall that I had never been in before. I had not even noticed its existence when I had been on this ship once before. Miles checked a couple of rooms at the end of the hall before finding this one-- and it was locked. He looked at it thoughtfully.

"...Are you sure there will be anything useful in there?" I asked.

"Nope!" he replied cheerily, as he kicked the door with all of his might. It swung open and banged against the wall.

Apparently the big guy's hunches could be trusted. Because the room had crates on the ground, and shelves of bottles full of strange mysterious liquids. Some odd sort of work station sat in the corner, with tubes and glass containers and ingredients I had never heard of.

"*Woaahh…*" Miles said, in awe. "Are these… *magic?* I wonder what on earth all a these can do! And where did they come from?" He then began to look for labels on the bottles, while I continued to stare in shock. *What was all of this doing here? Had it been here this entire time? What* is *all this?* I walked further into the room, looking at the bottles on the wall opposite Miles. I hauled myself, using my stick to help, on top of one of the crates to get a better look. There were vials of bright green liquid, bottles of dark blue liquid, and a few of a white liquid. *I'm guessing that's not milk.*

"Ey! Didn't some sorta medic give Ms. Lorelai one a these green vials when we first met him since she 'ad passed out?" Miles asked. I slowly turned myself around to face him to answer him, but instead was faced with a different man standing in the doorway. Miles was also staring at him now. He was a bit shorter than Miles, but towered over me. He was dressed more like a sailor than a hunter, but had a short, broad, slightly curved blade at his side.

"Well, what do we have here?" he asked, looking us over. "A couple of stowaways escaping the raid? Breaking and entering where they don't belong?" I glanced at Miles. My hand drifted to where my dagger was kept in my new belt. As his gaze turned towards me, I whipped my dagger out of its sheath and launched myself at him with all the strength my good foot could muster, yelling. I caught myself on his shoulder and cut into it a bit, not very deep. My assault distracted him enough, and unbalanced him, so that when Miles slammed his entire body into him, both the man and I fell to the ground. I was scooped up once more, and Miles took off running. I laid over Miles' shoulder as he climbed up the ladder that led to above deck, as I watched the man get to his feet and come after us. I waved my dagger back and forth as he came close, snarling and growling at him, successfully keeping him an arm's length away.

Miles plopped me on the deck and climbed up, as I immediately slammed the trapdoor shut and sat on it to keep it closed. The man banged on the hatch from below. Miles was standing, and looking out over to Compassion.

"Miles, a little help here with this guy?" I asked, annoyed. But… something had his attention. A yell that sounded like a roar erupted from his mouth, full of a fury I never thought he had in him, and he sprinted across the deck and went flying over the side of Miss Medea. I crawled to the ship's edge, since my stick was still below deck, and didn't even hear the trapdoor burst open behind me.

Instead, I saw Nicodemus with a sword to Adrian's throat, and Miles running towards them. I yelled out for him to stop, but Miles ignored me and threw himself at the hunter. Time seemed to slow nearly to a halt. I stared, trying to yell, but only weak sounds came out that were stolen by the wind and rain. Nicodemus heard Miles coming, and slowly turned to face him, his sword held out. I watched Miles' face twist in agony as he landed against the tip of the blade. I saw it enter him, and slice across his chest. Blood began to fall in torrents down his chest and stomach. People crying out filled the air-- Adrian, Lorelai, and I. It was a song of deep sorrow and pain. Miles fell. He hit the deck heavily, the sound seeming to echo throughout the two ships. The crimson colour of blood spread beneath him, too wide, too much.

"NOOOOOO!" I screamed, my voice returned but I heard it as if I was outside myself. Nicodemus walked forward and began kicking, pushing Miles towards the edge of the deck. I hobbled forward--

Suddenly I felt the cool sharpness of a blade to my throat as strong, thick arms surrounded me. I froze.

"You're not going anywhere, little missy." My captor had a deep, scratchy voice. Where had he even come from?! The deck of Miss Medea had been empty… *The trapdoor,* I realized. *He was below deck.* I cursed. I slipped my hand into my pocket, and held the smooth and familiar hilt of my dagger. He began to drag me backwards, further onto Miss Medea, and I struggled to keep my feet beneath me. I purposefully took a too big step towards him-- and slammed my foot onto his. He gasped in pain and surprise, but his grip on me didn't lessen. *Fine then. We'll do this the hard way.* In one fluid motion I took my dagger out of my pocket and jammed the blade towards him. He yelled, releasing me, and I moved away from him. I didn't look back. Hurrying-- but painfully slow-- towards the edge of Miss Medea, towards Miles, I fell forward off of the ship. I landed painfully, with a thud, amongst blood and bodies, attracting the attention of the others near one edge of the boat. I pulled myself to my feet, with difficulty. Nicodemus raised an eyebrow at me, and I saw him mentally brush me off.

With one final kick in Miles' side, I watched in horror as his limp, bloodied body fell off the side of the ship. *Splash.* I hobbled ahead as fast as I could without my walking stick, but when I reached the edge and looked down, Miles was already gone. Into a watery grave. I fell to my knees and put my face in my hands. Nicodemus turned away from me, and I glanced back. Just in time to see him put his sword trained back onto Adrian's neck as he tried to move towards me. My hand went to my pocket, but it was empty. *Shit.* I had left my dagger in the man's stomach. Nicodemus glanced at me, and pulled out a second sword. One pointed at Adrian, one at me.

"Don't get any ideas," he said in my direction.

We were defenseless. At the mercy of a man who seemed to have none. Especially towards our kind.

He could easily kill both of us in seconds if he wanted to.

<u>Lorelai</u>

My mind shut off as I felt the familiar weight of my sword in my hand as people now turned enemies began their charge. I recognized some of the faces that leapt from one ship to the other, aiming weapons at me. That didn't matter. My body took over; it knew how to fight, how to be swift and accurate, how to stay alive. I ended several lives before I saw Adrian and suddenly my brain re-engaged. I felt a certainty in my chest that I would regret the lives I was taking later, but as such a feeling was new and uncomfortable, I ignored it and ran to Adrian's aid. As we fought together, we were like a single organism. Except that he had a slight hesitancy when it came to giving the final blow. The longer we continued, the more that hesitancy lessened and lessened. I had been surprised the first time I had seen him weild a weapon, but now, I was nearly in awe and shock simultaneously. He moved with a fluidity and accuracy I rarely saw in others. His gaze became cold, hard, calculating. The way he fought was beautiful to watch, but the look on his face was… Unsettling. It was so incredibly opposite from his usual goofy grin or puzzled head tilt.

I thought the worst of it all was over at one point. Only to look up and see Nico standing on his ship, glaring down at us. At Adrian.

The face he wore then was a look I had never seen on him before, in all our years together. The closest thing I could think of that I knew of him was from long ago, when we fought against one another in the Arena.

Back then, I went by another name. I looked different. In many ways, I was different. But Nico… had always been my dear Nico. We learned how to spar, how to hold swords and how to wield them, around the same time in the same place. We both quickly rose up the ranks and became the best two fighters in the entire Arena. As a result, we often sparred and competed with only each other. No one else was a challenge. The first time we kissed… had been a surprise to us both, I think. We had spent a long time together, against one another, learning the other person's movements, style, and weaknesses. Staring each other down over sharp blades. We had spent nearly as much time talking in the locker room after each session, before parting ways for the day. There was clearly something between us. It was a tension born of chemistry, and of time spent studying each other. The tension was like a band that stretched each time we were near one another. Then one day, late at night after a hard training session, when the Arena was otherwise deserted… the band snapped in two. We simply fell together.

Since then, he had supported me and cared for me no matter what. We had cared for each other. He was my rock to lean on, my soft place to land when nightmares made me wake screaming. I was his confidant.. It had stayed that way for years, despite wind and high water.

But now, I had to watch him fight ruthlessly against someone… someone I had grown to care somewhat about. Adrian was silly and confused, naive and perhaps not the brightest as a human… but he was also selfless, kind, good. He listened. But as I begged and pleaded to Nicodemus then, with tears streaming down my face, simply wanting him to not take this life… I was the farthest from heard, from listened to, that I had ever been. Adrian's eyes were full of fear, and Nicodemus' were empty of everything but hate.

I began to hear the sound of roaring ocean waves in my ears. The kind that sank ships and drowned cities.

I did not even hear Miles yelling as he ran to Adrian. I did, however, see Nicodemus swing towards him. I saw a red line tear open and stretch across Miles' large frame at the command of the blade he held. I saw Miles's face contort in pain and shock. I saw him fall to the floor, and a dark red grew around him, seeping his life away with it. The roaring in my ears increased. I could feel my own blood, mostly water, speeding throughout my body. When Nicodemus carelessly shoved Miles' body off of the ship, I closed my eyes. But an anger unlike anything I had ever known raced through me. *This is not my Nicodemus. This is not the man I knew.*

<u>Adrian</u>

Lorelai closed her eyes when Miles was pushed off of the ship, my heart crying out in pain and agony as I yearned to help him, but the sword was swiftly pointed back towards me. I saw Morgan go to him… but she was too late. His body dipped over the edge and fell into the seas. My chest ached, and a small cry left my throat as I reached out towards them-- and the sword's tip poked me sharply. Nicodemus took out another sword and trained it on Morgan. *We will get out of this and I will go get Miles. He will be okay. He has to.*

However, both my attention and the attention of our attacker was pulled to Lorelai as her eyes burst open and were now a bright, glowing, *piercing* icy blue. She began to mutter quietly and quickly to herself, in a very old guttural language I recognized but could not fathom how she possibly knew it. We watched in awe as she rose off of the deck, floating in the air. With a flick of her wrist, the wind increased. It lifted her hair to wave around her face, and with a wave of her palm the seas rose and surrounded her. She spun her hands around one another and the water encircled her, moving fast, spinning around her; a whirlpool of her own. Blue light as well as a glowing blackness began to emanate from every part of her, seeping out like ink in water, surrounding her image in a black and bright blue glow. She looked almost... divine in some manner, until her gaze turned sharply to Nicodemus and her pupils narrowed. Lightning crackled in the sky but the waves beneath us remained eerily calm, awaiting her orders.

Nicodemus backed up, only to trip on the slippery deck but continue to try to skitter away. His eyes were wide with fear and shock, but neither of us could take our eyes off of her. A tendril of darkness itself arched away from Lorelai and surrounded Nicodemus, ensnaring him in its grasp. He was lifted up, higher, eye level with the witch who controlled the waves and much more. He squirmed and fought against his restraints, but they did not budge, they did not break. He could not get through.

He began to plead with Lorelai, suddenly his captor.

"You did not listen when I *just* begged to have a life kept safe." Her words ran with anger and were edged with pain. A dark arm branched off of his restraints and forced his mouth closed. *Something terrible is about to happen. Something she will greatly regret for the rest of her life... I cannot let her. She is not thinking right.*

I stood up, but hesitated. Pure power and fury was flowing off of her. If she truly was not thinking right, she could lash out at anyone who got in her way. Without even realizing it was me she was hurting. But I simply could not let her do whatever she was about to do to Nicodemus. In the end, it would hurt her too much. I approached the powerful sea witch. I moved in front of her, between her and Nicodemus, careful to not touch the glowing black that hung between the two. Her gaze fell down to me, and softened almost imperceptibly. I looked up at her solemnly, and slowly shook my head.

"You can not do this," I signed slowly and clearly.

"But, but *he--*" her voice broke. "*He will kill you. And Morgan. He killed Miles.*" Tears welled in her eyes as her voice cracked. It nearly sounded as though she was begging to me now. I had to force myself to not look towards Miles and Morgan. Instead I made a far throwing motion, and pointed out into the sea.

"Killing him will kill your heart," I said, looking deep into her eyes. I used signs with obvious meanings and pleaded with her through my gaze.

"He will live and he will come back, you know," she stated.

"He is not…" I paused. I was not sure how to communicate my thought, considering her limited knowledge of my hand signs. "Come down," I gestured. She hesitated, but decided to slowly lower her feet back onto the deck. The vortex of water around her flew back over the side of the boat, and as soon as I could, I wrapped my arms around her. Despite the fact that the glowing black and mystical blue light still remained. The entire mass of this magical light flickered for a moment, and then was hazy like fog. I stayed there until, reluctantly, she hugged me back. She tried to let go after a brief moment, but I held fast. Instead… her head landed gently on the top of mine.

When I finally stepped back, her ice-like blue eyes began to melt and soften to their usual grey with a hint of blue. The black glowing around her drifted to grey and seemed to meld into the grey clouds above us. The blue light disappeared. The Lorelai I knew was back. I smiled, and a small smile graced her features.

I turned as Nicodemus, now flat on his back on the deck, began to try to say something and stand up. Instead, Lorelai made the ocean curve over the edge of Compassion, and it plucked him off of the deck, and took him riding above the waves very fast and far away.

He left a small, wilting flower behind. It had fallen out of a pocket as he was lifted off the deck. I stared at it in shock; it was the exact final flower we needed, orange petals, dark tips, and all.

Chapter Sixteen - Reunite

<u>Morgan</u>

Once Nicodemus was gone, and Lorelai had returned to the less frightening version of herself-- which I still couldn't quite wrap my head around-- Adrian came sprinting towards me suddenly. I dove to the side as he leapt past me and over the edge of the small ship. As he neared the water, I saw green scales begin to grow on his neck and arms. Then he was gone. Lorelai and I stared at each other, and at the space he had left behind. It was then that I noticed how *many* bodies and how much blood still covered the deck. It was gruesome. Lorelai fell into a sitting position despite the mess, looking exhausted.

A green scaly hand abruptly appeared, splashing out of the water and gripping the edge of the deck next to me. I grabbed Adrian's wrist and tried to help pull him up, but I wasn't much help unfortunately. He pulled himself up onto the deck rather ungracefully, briefly splayed out, and then sat up and used both hands to lug what he had been towing behind him. An arm. Miles' face lifted out of the sea, his eyes closed, mouth open, entirely limp. I immediately began trying to help, and once Lorelai noticed what was going on, she came over and tried to help as well. Frankly, Adrian did most of the work.

Miles' body was slowly pulled onboard, where he laid limp in a large puddle. I stared at him. I could hardly tear my eyes away from his face. *How could a man once so full of life be so quickly turned into… this? Ashen, limp, lifeless. It's not fair! He never did anything wrong, he least deserved to die out of all of us.*

I glanced at the others. Lorelai sat there looking like she hadn't slept for a week, slouching with her eyes half closed as she tucked a flower into her breast pocket. Adrian's eyes were filled with so much sadness… I had to look away or risk beginning to cry. Suddenly I remembered something that might help. I hurriedly started digging in Miles' pockets, trying to avoid all of the blood and not look at his injury or his face. Or at Adrian.

"What are you--?" Lorelai asked, blinking at me sleepily.

"Shhhhh, it's *fine*. He will be *fine*," I quietly insisted. Hoping.

Ah! There it is! Thank god, I thought as I triumphantly pulled three thin vials full of bright green liquid out of his pockets.

"Where did you get those? When?!" Lorelai exclaimed in surprise.

I turned to Adrian. He had gone from a sitting position next to Miles to now on his knees, leaning down to wrap his arms around Miles' frame. He was almost lying down with him. Tears fell down his cheeks. He was silent.

"...Adrian," I said. He opened his eyes, his head already turned towards me. "This… it might help." He sat back up as I leaned past him until I could open Miles' mouth and pour the lime green liquid inside. I poured the first one slowly, and then paused. Nothing happened. *How fast is this stuff supposed to work anyway?* I glanced at Lorelai.

"They… usually don't kick in right away. Give him another. Then I'll do what I can," she said, never looking away from his face. She stared intently, as if scrutinizing him. Watching for the slightest change. I gave him another, and put the last one back in his pocket. All three of us watched him, and waited. After a minute, Lorelai stood up. She looked around the deck of Compassion, and then up at Nicodemus' ship that still floated close by. ... *Are there any survivors even left on that ship?*

"You two start cleaning up Miles' ship," Lorelai said, pulling our attention to her. "We want it to look good for him if-- *when* he wakes up. I need all the energy I have left to do healing magic on him. We also need to make him comfortable. And Adrian," her eyes snapped towards him, where we had his head back on Miles' shoulder. "Do stop moping and help. You aren't doing any good there." Adrian slowly lifted his head and looked up at Lorelai. His eyes were big, sad, and pleading. *Ugh. I hate seeing grief.*

"Adrian, please help me up. I lost my walking stick," I said. His head perked up and looked at me confused. "It's uh… it's below deck over there," I nodded to the side in the direction of the ship that shadowed us. Adrian pulled himself to his feet and started walking away. *Where the hell is he going?!* I watched as he reached the side of our ship and then *jumped as high as he could off of the side?!* Somehow, he just barely managed to grab the edge of Nicodemus' ship and from there he pulled himself up and onboard. I stared in shock at where he had been. *Well… damn. Half falling half jumping down from that ship to ours was one thing, but being able to jump high enough and have enough arm strength to pull yourself back up? That was kind of impressive.*

While he was gone, I busied myself with trying to find a comfortable way to sit that didn't hurt, and then silently watched Lorelai work. White and yellow light drifted gently out of her hands into the deep, wide cut across Miles' entire torso. In the dim light of an overcast sky, as the sun began to set behind them and filled the edges of the sky below the clouds with yellow, orange, and pink hues, Lorelai's magical light seemed to sparkle. She was still doing it, unmoving, when Adrian returned empty handed.

"What happened? Where's my stick?" I asked him.

"The door that led below deck was either locked or held shut from below," he explained. "I tried to get it open but I could not. I will try again in a few minutes, I think there are people below deck. I wanted to check on Miles first." He looked over at Miles, and his face fell. Lorelai was still healing him, the large gash in his chest closing ever so slowly. She was too focused on her work to notice us. I tried to pull Adrian's gaze away from his fallen friend.

"How about we try to clean up the deck a bit so that when Miles wakes up he doesn't have to see his beloved ship like this, okay? Lorelai needs more time," I said gently. He needed a distraction. We both did.

Adrian and I found a bucket and went around trying to wash the blood off of the deck. I focused on not slipping as I limped around, cleaning. When Adrian offered to help me move around, I refused. *I can still take care of myself,* I insisted in my head. I started pushing bodies overboard. It was disgusting. After a while, the deck was as clean as we could get it, but some blood stains still remained in the wood. Lorelai waved us over. The gash in Miles' torso was closed, but a large ugly scar remained.

"He-- he is, uh, still healing slowly," she told us, her words slow as she struggled to keep her eyes open. "We won't know for…" her voice trailed off. "We...we need to wait to see if he will wake up. I have done everything I can." She turned to Adrian. "Is Miss Medea empty?"

"As far as I can tell, there is only the sailing crew. They're all below deck," he said. Lorelai glanced at me, and I translated. *I will have to give her more lessons later. Or maybe Adrian should do it.*

"Mmm…." Lorelai looked towards the ship. "I would like to steal a mattress or several pillows for Miles and I, but I doubt I could get up there right now." She looked at Adrian. I glanced at him.

"Okay, I will be right back," he said, standing up and leaving once more.

Adrian

The jump to get up onto the large ship was getting harder the more time passed-- the ships were drifting apart. Though falling into the waves would not be much of a problem for me, regardless. However, the second time around I barely made it, hauling myself up and aboard. I awkwardly stepped around the body of Nicodemus' first mate, who had a cutlass by his side and a dagger in his stomach. I paused, and bent to look more closely at the dagger's hilt. *Was Morgan not using a dagger just like this one?... Is this her dagger?* I had not considered that Morgan would kill a human, but a lot had been going on. I pulled the dagger out of the body to return it to her, but more blood began pooling.

Ah. Darn. What a mess. I hesitated, looking at the bloody blade in my hand. It needed to be cleaned, or at least wiped off. I did not want to get more blood on my clothing… So, reluctantly, I wiped the blade off on a clean section of the first mate's pant leg.

I stood, dagger in hand, to be greeted by the sight of Nicodemus' crew sheepishly, slowly, coming up from below deck. First three men came, brandishing weapons in shaky hands, pointing them at me. I raised my hands. *Oh no, how do I tell them I do not intend to hurt them? I need to get below deck.* I tucked Morgan's dagger away and then raised my hands again.

"W-What do you want? Haven't you d-done enough?" One of the men asked, his voice admitting his fear.

"I only want a few pillows or something soft, please I--" I began.

"Oh, dammit he's mute. Or deaf," another man interrupted. "Look, buddy, do you need something? Did ya leave a dagger behind or…?" I blinked. Their hostility was disappearing, as well as their fear. I could not figure out why. Hesitantly, I pointed down, then at the trapdoor that led below deck. One of the men told the rest of the crew to come up from where they waited beneath the trap door. They listened, but eyed me with fear in their eyes as they began to go about the deck preparing to sail. No one came anywhere near me.

"Alright, go ahead and grab whatever you left behind, I'll be right down with you in a moment," said one of the first men to speak to me. He seemed to be in charge, at least at the moment. I headed below deck, weaving between the crewmen, and found Morgan's walking stick on top of a crate in a back room. The door had been slightly ajar, so I checked it first. Vials of various potions lined shelves on the walls. A few I recognized, many I did not. *Hm. Nicodemus had someone crafting potions...* I heard someone yelling at me, that I was not allowed in here, so I grabbed the stick, pocketed one more green vial, and one dark blue one, before dipping into a bedroom and grabbing as many pillows as I could carry. I headed quickly back to my friends.

I stopped in my tracks just before jumping down off of the deck. I saw below me, Morgan yelling furiously at Lorelai.

"How *could* you?!" she yelled, loud enough that I could easily hear. "*That's* why you were on that damned island in the first place wasn't it! Did you mean for me to *drown* after you stole the most important item in the world from me?! Was that your plan?" She was holding Lorelai's black bag in her free hand, shaking it around. She dug through it and pulled out a large, long, untrimmed fur. It was white with black spots, and very short fur. As Morgan threw Lorelai's bag to the floor, the fur began morphing and shrinking, until she instead held a soft fuzzy sweater in its place.

I jumped down onto the deck quickly, forgetting the pillows behind me. Lorelai stood to one side, struggling to find the words she wanted to say, and Morgan… as she held the sweater to her chest protectively, doing her best to not put any weight on the one foot… I had never heard someone sound so angry and so incredibly hurt. "I thought we were friends," she said, glaring at Lorelai. Her voice was lower, but held equally as much malice. "Turns out you were my enemy all along." She turned, and hobbled as quickly as she could to the ship's edge, before launching herself into the water as she held the sweater over her back. She vanished beneath the surface.

I stared at Lorelai with my mouth open in shock. *How could she…? This whole time?*

"Adrian, let me explain, I-- I didn't mean for--" she started.

I jumped into the sea after Morgan. I did not want to think badly of Lorelai here, but it was hard not to. She surely had some kind of explanation, but first, someone needed to make sure Morgan was okay.

As the water encased me and I sank deeper, I willed my scales to grow and spread across my skin. My gills protruded from my neck suddenly as my fins grew out from my legs and arms. My eyes burst open and I saw fish hurry away from me. I looked quickly side to side until I saw what I was looking for-- a seal, white with black spots… and half of her tail was limp as she struggled to move through the water with the new handicap. I began to move towards her-- and then realized something that surprised me. Wherever Lorelai had teleported us to, wherever we now found ourselves… was in very similar waters to that which surrounded the island where we had all met. Similar temperature, similar smell and feel… we were likely not that far from there. I caught up to the seal that must be Morgan, and her head whipped towards me, teeth bared. When she saw and recognized who was before her, she stopped, and looked surprised.

"What the hell are you doing? Leave me alone!" Morgan's voice barked out loud and deep as she spoke Seal, remarkably different from the voice of hers I was used to. But the tone was unmistakable.

"Morgan," I said. She stopped swimming suddenly and stared at me.

"Your voice…" she said. "I… never thought it would sound like that." I smiled. "Wait, you can speak *seal?!*" Her tone changed from awe and surprise to near accusatory and confused. I blinked.

"Well, yes, I can speak every language of the sea." I did not understand why she was surprised. *Oh, right. No one seems to know much about Tritons since we never leave Myrddin…* I shook my head. I was not the priority here. "Here, let me help you. Which way to your sister? We are close, yes?" I asked. Seeing she was about to protest my help with her swimming, I interrupted before she could. "You will figure out how to swim with your tail like you learned how to escape hunters and walk with your ankle. For now, *let me help you.*" She gave me a look akin to a glare, but conceded anyway and let me assist her. I wrapped an arm around her as best as I could, making sure to give her fins room, and helped propel the both of us through the water.

We swam for a while under her direction. After several minutes, Morgan told me to stop.

"Do you hear that? It sounds like...*seals*..." she said suspiciously.

Morgan squirmed out of my grasp and began swimming as quickly as she could ahead of me. Her tail moved side to side in small movements in the water, one of her fins flopping uselessly next to the other, as the fins on her side moved more strongly to attempt to compensate.

I stayed back, following slowly and keeping my distance. I watched as Morgan swam excitedly, yet simultaneously struggling, as she approached a group of seals that were frolicking in the water playing with one another. They all slowed to a stop and looked at Morgan curiously, except for one. All of the other seals in the group were fully grey, with tiny barely noticeable darker speckles, but one seal who was smaller than Morgan shared her white coat with black spots. This seal burst out of the group towards Morgan, and I nearly lost track of who was who as they happily barked at each other and swam fast little circles around one another. But the large dark red and black gash across the younger one's side gave her away. *That must be her little sister...* When they slowed, they nuzzled each other fondly. Morgan inspected her sister closely, drifting around her and sniffing, nudging with her snout. When she was finished, she turned to face the group. Only for a few of the seals to bark fearfully-- they were talking about me now. I had been seen, and was a potential threat. I shrank back a little further away; I didn't want to be thought of as that.

Morgan wiggled her way over to me, and nudged me towards the seals. She presented me in front of the younger white seal with the terrible injury.

"Adva, this… is Adrian. He's a triton, and he's my friend," she said simply, glancing at me. I waved awkwardly.

"Um, hello, Adva. Your sister will do anything for you, you know…She is quite strong of will," I said. The little seal with large, dark eyes and a giant gash in her side stayed right up against Morgan shyly.

"I know," she said quietly, smiling. "Also-- Nixie, what happened to your tail? You are okay, right?" She looked worriedly up at Morgan. *Wait, who is Nixie?*

<u>Lorelai</u>

I was lying down on the still wet deck a couple of feet away from where Miles lay, now that the deck was free of blood. I didn't have the energy to magically breathe underwater and go after the other two. So instead I stared up at the sky, my mind drifting and considering all of my many regrets and bad decisions. *Will Morgan and Adrian ever even come back?*

The sound of groaning began next to me. I sat up and stared over at Miles. His eyes were open, and he was trying to sit up.

"Miles stay down, if you reopen your wound I swear to god," I said, and Miles immediately laid back down and stared at me.

"O-okay, yes Ms. Lorelai, sorry! I'll stay here!" he said worriedly. I placed a hand on his shoulder.

"I… am glad you're alive. Relieved. However, that was terribly stupid and reckless of you," I scolded.

"He was gonna kill A-!"

"I had it under control!"

He looked at me dubiously but said nothing. There was a lengthy pause. He glanced around as best as he could while staying lying down.

"... where're the others? Is e'rebody else okay?" he looked at me, a hand drifting to his lengthy scar. "What happened? Did I… *die?*" He stared at me with wide eyes.

"Very nearly." I laid back down next to him. Then, slowly, reluctantly, I explained what had transpired… what Nicodemus did to him, how I sent Nico away on the waves, and how Morgan had found what she had. Then I waited, lying there. I expected him to react, to be surprised, even angry, like the other two had.

"Ye must've had a good reason to hold onto it this whole time," he said simply. I sat up and stared at him. "I mean--" he grunted as he struggled to sit up to face me. "Ye kept it this entire time. Even though ya fought against and *killed* other hunters and helped break out a captured selkie… ye ain't much of a hunter anymore, are ya Ms. Lorelai? And yet ya made sure to keep this no matter what," he looked at me. "Why?" There was nothing but genuine curiosity in his eyes, in his words. No hate or anger. He just… believed that I must have a good reason. *Why would he possibly believe in me? I am a killer, as he said. I am wretched and malicious and have so much blood on my hands. Miles surely despises nothing more than unnecessary death… right? And yet…* There he sat. Giving me a chance to explain myself, and a willingness to believe me. Maybe even trust me. I sighed; this was not going to be the easiest of explanations, and I would very likely have to give it multiple times.

The water splashed unnaturally off one side of our ship. Green scaled hands with webbed fingers curled over the side, as the tiny boat leaned that way. Adrian's head, covered in scales with gills on his neck, appeared as he began to pull himself aboard.

But when he saw Miles, sitting up and very much alive, his eyes lit up like a fire and he smiled bigger than I had ever seen him smile before. It was quite... sweet. He scrambled aboard Compassion as quickly as he could, and ran towards his friend while Miles put all of his effort into standing. The two embraced with the happiest looks on their faces. I chuckled as Miles wrapped his arms around Adrian and lifted him off of the ground without a sweat. *Wait--*

"What did I say about your wound!" I yelled at Miles, who immediately put Adrian down and apologized sheepishly. He went to let go of his scaly friend, but Adrian did not budge from his hold around Miles, his face buried into his chest.

"Uh... buddy? I'm okay, you can let go now," Miles said awkwardly, only to be ignored. I smirked. "So, uh, Adrian, where's Morgan at now? Ye go after her?" he asked. Only at that did Adrian slowly pull himself away and look up at the big guy. He began signing too quickly for me to keep up, so I laid back down and stared at the still overcast sky. Like a grey blanket over us all. Nico drifted into my mind; happy memories, and very conflicted feelings. I pushed it away roughly and instead forced myself to think of Morgan. *I am sure she went back to near where I found her skin, surely she lives around there somewhere… re-connecting with the sister I was supposed to help.* Reluctantly, I pulled myself into a standing position. *I would rather not break my word. Not to her, not like this… Not after everything I have put her through already.* I faced the two, who were signing very quickly to each other seemingly at the same time.

"So, boys, sorry to interrupt what I am sure is a *riveting* conversation, but I think it's time to head off, don't you?" I said, as I walked over to them. I forced a smile. They stopped, looking to me with confusion. I pointed down to Miles' pocket, and when he pulled out our last bright green vial, I grabbed it from him. After pulling the top off I drank the entire thing at once. "Ah, much better. Lead the way Adrian," I smiled at him.

With that, I pushed past them and jumped off of the ship into the freezing cold waters. Instead of cold, I felt *better* now. Warm. Energized. Adrian, perhaps realizing what I was up to, jumped in after me, splashing me in the process.

"Hey!" I protested-- only to see him smile and have my mouth reflect it without thinking. I looked back up at Miles, who stood up on the ship by himself.

"Get down here you, I'll help with the whole *breathing underwater issue.* Can you swim well enough yet?" I called up to him, only to receive another, much larger splash over my head as he landed in the water next to me. There was an anxious moment's pause before he resurfaced, assuring us he could do it.

"It's just…" he glanced at Adrian nervously. "We, uh, we just want to make sure that you're goin' t' make this right, yeah?" Concern, or perhaps worry, filled Miles' eyes.

"*Yes.* I am going to make things right. I am going to make everything right," I assured them both, determination swelling inside me as I said it. I waved my hands around Mile's face and neck, drawing symbols in the air no one else could read as I felt the magic flow out of my fingertips and grace his face, mouth, and throat. It zapped out of me like blue streaks of lightning, and once certain it had taken effect, I dove beneath the surface and swam.

Chapter Seventeen - Release

<u>Morgan</u>

Adva and I talked nearly non-stop as we drifted lazily around the seals. I told her how I had fallen off of a cliff face trying to get something to help her and that was how I hurt my tail. She felt bad about that, which I quickly shushed and reassured her that it was nothing to worry about. I kept the details of my rather harrowing adventure limited, and decided to not tell her yet about the selkies relatives I had discovered. The last thing I wanted was her trying to find them herself, or getting her hopes too high and having them dashed. Instead I repeatedly turned the conversation back to her to get details about how she had been while I was gone. Thomas had come through on our agreement, and instead of only checking in on her, he brought her to live with his pod for a while. She seemed to really enjoy spending time with them, as there were breaks in our conversation where one of the younger seals would pull her into play as much as she was able. She knew their names, and had friends. I, on the other hand, had never really connected properly with seals, and I was glad that my numerous scars hadn't transferred over to my seal form as well. Or at the very least they weren't visible thanks to my fur.

Seeing Adva happy and safe filled me with an indescribable warm, joyful feeling. I could hardly remember the last time I was that happy.

The feeling faded when I heard multiple creatures coming towards us. Their swimming was clumsy, awkward, and rough so it didn't take long for the seals to hear them too and begin to become fearful. I noticed that instead of simply running off they urged Adva and I to go with them. But I knew exactly who was approaching us, their scents were imprinted in my mind. I told the pod to calm down, that the creatures approaching were ones I knew. I promised I would signal them with a flip of my fin if it was better for them to leave; for now, Adva was not about to leave my side.

I turned to face the intruders, waiting for them to finally reach me. Adva hid directly behind me and peeked out. The actual seals stayed a little ways back, on edge and watching.

Adrian was the first to reach me. I nodded to him, and glared at Lorelai fiercely when I saw her. She locked eyes with me. I couldn't help but notice that she and Miles had sprouted tiny gills on their necks. *Damn witchcraft again I see.* I hesitated, thinking my options over. But in the end, I decided that they weren't going to leave until we talked. I looked to Adrian.

"You're going to have to translate for me," I told him in Seal.

"He can understand *seal?!* What is he?" Adva murmured quietly in my ear, sticking her head up over my shoulder. There really wasn't time to explain all that. Meanwhile, Adrian looked between Lorelai and I, uncertain.

"*Adrian.* Do it," my body stiffened as I glared at him, my voice as cold as ice.

"W-Well, what do you want to say to her?" His voice was filled with hesitancy, and he again glanced at Lorelai. I paused. Looking at the witch that had taken me away from my sister.

"Tell her to leave. That I want nothing to do with any of you," I said. I didn't take my gaze off of Lorelai. Adrian pushed at the water in front of him, as if trying to push the words I had said away from him. He moved backwards because of it.

"I am not telling her that. I do not think it is a good idea for me to get in the middle of this, Morgan…" He shook his head, his voice steeled. But then, when he looked at me, his face fell. "Frankly, your words hurt me as well." I let out a small sigh, and closed my eyes. I didn't mean to cause him any pain, he hadn't done anything wrong. I looked over at Miles, who swam there blissfully unaware of what I had said. I knew it would have hurt him too.

"Fine," I said. "Tell her that she will need to cast that water breathing spell on me in a moment if she wants to talk," I told him. He looked confused, but translated the message to the other two.

I couldn't help but hesitate. The one and only time I had been in human form underwater I had nearly died. As I thought of it, memories of being battered and suffocated by the very seas I call home came to my mind. Feeling betrayed, but mostly fear and anxiety. Being disoriented, as the rushing water spun me around and blurred my vision. My chest tightened in pain, darkness crowded my vision-- I shoved the memories away. *I refuse to have my decisions controlled by fear. If worst comes to worst, I have my skin this time. I can change back.* I took a deep breath. And shifted, morphing like I was simply stretching my arms. My vision went blurry for a moment, and then cleared as at the same time my chest tightened. Lorelai hurriedly gestured, casting the spell on me, and I took a deep, refreshing breath. I kicked in an attempt to stay up. Luckily the current was light. *Swimming as a human is so, so terrible and unnecessarily difficult.* My arms held my large seal skin against my front instinctively. *I've spent too much time around humans, caring now about covering up.*

Adva still hid behind me— or attempted to, at least. I glared at Lorelai. *How dare I be forced to leave my beloved seal form so soon.*

"What are you even doing here? And why did you bring them?"
I gestured to Adrian and Miles. "They have nothing to do with this. And
I want nothing to do with *you* and your damned magic ever again.
You're nothing but an evil witch," I spat. "Leave my sister and I alone."
She sighed.

"You're right," she admitted. *Woah, wait, what? This must be
another trick. Another lie of a long string of them.* I narrowed my eyes
and said nothing. "You're right, I have done terrible things. I am a
witch in every sense of the word, and I have also killed more creatures
than I can count, both human and not... I'm realizing, thanks to both
you and Adrian," she glanced at Adrian for a moment and gave a small
smile. "That just because you're not a human doesn't mean you're a
monster." She paused. My eyes widened in shock... I was blown away
that someone who had been a skilled hunter could ever come as far as to
admit that. Even with being around two 'monsters' for so long. *I mean,
look at Nicodemus.* I grimaced. *But I don't know if I can believe what
she's saying. Who's to say it's not more manipulation to get my end of
our deal out of me?*

"You kept my skin, the one and only object that matters to me,
the thing that is why I live, the thing that enables me to be with my
sister, the only person I love, and *despite everything we went through
together*—" I paused in an attempt to hold back what I was feeling, my

anger increasing with every word battling against the sadness that suddenly threatened to betray me by making my voice break. "Despite everything, you kept it from me."

"Morgan..." she sounded almost sad, almost concerned, almost hurt. *I'm not falling for it,* I told myself. "I didn't know the skin was yours until you found it today," she said.
Everything stopped. I stared at her wide eyed. *There's no way that's true. It can't be.*

"B-but the storm was unnatural and you're a sea witch, I was *right there*, you were *so close,* we both ended up on that island, I—" I stopped. "...how?" I asked simply, my tone corrected, forced, to anger.

She moved a step closer to me. Adva flinched. I didn't move.

"I didn't see you," she said softly. "You have to believe me, Morgan, I was so focused on what I thought to be the easiest and best find of my life that I saw little else in those fast moving waves," her voice was edged with pleading. I still hesitated. *That's an awfully convenient story, Lorelai.* "Did you ever wonder why you *didn't* drown in the storm that day?" She asked suddenly. I bit my lip. I glanced at Adrian and Miles.

"I was a little too busy trying to stay alive to think about it," I remarked sarcastically. She wasn't fazed.

"When I did notice you, just before I swam up into a nearby cave, I thought you were a young stowaway on the pirate ship I had been on. I pushed the waves towards the island, and then moved on, hoping the current would wash you ashore. I recognized your white hair when we met but..." she paused. "By the time I found out you were a selkie, the coincidence had slipped my mind— it was a chaotic time." Her voice was gentle and calm. I wasn't sure what to believe. I felt as though he could see the uncertainty in my eyes..

"Remember our deal?" she asked in the silence. I glared at her, on guard. Said nothing. "A selkie's skin was going to help me defeat him, my past abuser. A key ingredient for a very powerful spell. But now..." she glanced at Adva, her sentence trailing off. *Wait, 'was'? What is she talking about?* She looked me directly in the eyes with a seriousness that caught me off guard. "I want to heal your sister, for free," she said. "You are released from our deal. I don't want to make you do anything. At this point... I just want you to finally be happy, friend." She gave me a hesitant smile, and slowly pulled the three flowers we had begun searching for what felt like years ago. The three needed for the spell to heal Adva. *Hold on, surely she's not serious... unless everything she's ever told me was true.* I looked down at Adva, who looked back up at me with giant dark seal pup eyes laced with worry-- and hope. *If there was a chance she could finally be pain free...*

"Okay," I looked back up to Lorelai. "If you really are able to heal her, please do it. And… and I *might* help you find that bastard anyway-- but I'm certainly *not* being bait anymore."

Lorelai smiled when I said that-- a bright, genuine smile.

"Of course not. Thank you. I appreciate it." But then her smile faltered slightly, and she peered past me to Adva, the seal pup staying closely tucked behind me. "The only potential issue for the ritual spell is… Well, we need to be on land. I can't have the materials floating away or moving around."

Convincing my timid, and rightfully so, sister to come on land… took time. It was quite difficult for me. In the end, she was more than willing to climb up onto the rock in the old sea cave she and I used to spend time in, with me right by her side, if it meant finally getting better. Besides, there were no people there. It was the idea of coming onto a proper shore, where there might be people, that she avoided. I watched as she stayed glued to my side and kept glancing briefly at the others, her eyes flicking around. I could feel that her body was tense against me. She kept a flipper on me at all times. She was very nervous with Adrian, Lorelai, and Miles being with us.

We all swam up a path that I knew, but hadn't been down in what felt like a long time. Reaching the surface, we popped our heads above the water and saw a secluded cave open up in front of us. After travelling who knows how far, seeing shores I'd never seen before, and being away… the familiarity of this particular little cave was really nice. I hadn't realized I had missed that feeling; of knowing and enjoying exactly where I was. But with three new people, the space felt small and crowded. Adrian decided to stay in the water to give Lorelai the room she needed. I looked over to Adva, as she laid there with her head up, looking at all of us, on one side of the rock. I remembered the last time I had seen her here-- that felt like eons ago. When I was a different selkie.

Miles squished himself into a corner, and Lorelai began placing each of the three flowers in a row before Adva. One pink and yellow flower that I had found on that cliff face, the thing I had been going after when I had gotten hurt and ended up captured. Then there was a yellow one they had found when I wasn't with them, and finally the orange one with dark ends that Nicodemus had apparently dropped on his way out. *Why did he have it?* I wondered. Lorelai continued, asking Adrian to find six seashells of any kind, they had to be whole, and from the nearby waters since Adva lived around here. He dipped back down below the surface and swam out immediately, without question.

"Um, Lorelai?" Miles piped up as Adrian left. She looked at him and raised an eyebrow. "I, well, it's just, I'm just very curious ye see, um… why do ya sometimes not need anythin' to do yer magic and right now ye do?” he asked. Lorelai turned back to the flowers and I thought she was going to ignore his question, but instead she flippantly said;

“I don’t *need* components for most spells, though they can help, but more *powerful* spells need them.”

When Adrian returned with the seashells, she placed them in an evenly-spaced semi-circle next to the flowers, facing Adva.

Then, she took out her dagger. Adva flinched and fear filled her eyes, and she began scrambling, the ritual items knocked astray, moving as quickly as she could towards the sea, towards me, staring at Lorelai with terror.

“N-n-no, stop-!” she was panicked, breathing heavily. I ran to her, and wrapped her slippery seal body in my arms and held her tight. I whispered gentle, soothing reassurances to her as she held still. I glanced at Lorelai-- the dagger was gone, sheathed, tucked away, as quickly as she could. I continued calming my sister. When she was finally calmed down, I released her to lie back down.

“Adva… what happened? Are you okay?” I asked gently.

“I-I really, *really* d-don’t like blades… after what happened. To… our pod,” she whispered as quietly as she could.

“I’m sorry, I didn’t know, I… I need the blade for the ritual. For my own blood,” Lorelai said.

"Why do ya need that?" Miles asked, surprised. She turned to him.

"It… it'll help. The spell needs a little extra power and I have particularly *potent* witch's blood in my veins," Lorelai said. That didn't seem to make any sense to anyone other than Lorelai, but no one asked any more questions. *It's human magic,* I thought with a shrug. I looked down at my little sister, who laid there in her seal form.

"Adva, sweetie, I'm going to cover your eyes for a minute okay? Think about something happy?" I tried. She nodded, and I did my best to cover both of her eyes with both of my hands. Lorelai understood, and in one swift motion she revealed her dagger, made a cut in her palm, and returned it to its sheath. She pressed around the cut, urging the blood to come out. She then did her best to draw a line of blood on top of the items arranged in a semicircle. Instead of lines, though, we got a series of dots and splashes, and she spent a good amount of time bleeding herself. Adrian told her to stop in seal, that she was going to injure herself. I translated, and Lorelai reluctantly stopped and cast a quick moment of a healing spell on her cut.

Finally, with all of the materials arranged just so, Lorelai sat before them and closed her eyes. She began muttering, in a language that didn't make any sense to me. It was strange, and unlike anything I had ever heard. It naturally seemed to have a chanting quality to it, or maybe that was how she was speaking. As she did this, she held her hands out to either side of her, palms up. A shimmering, golden light appeared above each hand, a small marble of it that slowly grew and grew bigger as she began to chant louder. I sat next to Adva, and kept a comforting hand on her at all times to keep her calm. Once the golden wisps of sparkling light had each become the size of my head, Lorelai opened her eyes and *they were glowing a very bright blue!* It took all of my effort to not interrupt her and ask what the absolute hell was going on there. I glanced at Miles and Adrian, as maybe this was simply another thing I had missed while captured. Miles was staring with his mouth wide open in awe or surprise, apparently doing what he could to stay quiet, while Adrian gazed at Lorelai unfazed. *That… doesn't give me really any answers.*

While I was sitting there confused and a little spooked and trying to hide that, Lorelai turned her hands to hover them palm-down, one over the other, above each of the flowers one by one. She held both hands over the first flower, and focused intently. After a long moment, the flower began to wilt very quickly. As it did so, mist that was the same colours as the flower drifted lightly out of each one as they died, and the magical mist floated up towards Lorelai's hands. It disappeared inside her golden light, which then would get a little bit brighter. After each flower we had spent so long searching for was dead, Lorelai gestured in a wave-like motion back to the seashells, and then forward to Adva. At her command, white light sprung suddenly out of the bloody seashells and created perfectly straight lines connecting back to Lorelai's hands. Then slowly, she closed her eyes once more and placed both of her hands over Adva's injury, hovering just above it. The bright, shining golden light now was almost blinding to look at, and it shot directly into Adva's long, jagged injury.

Then, the golden light and the white lines of light increased to the point that they did become blinding. I wasn't even looking at them directly, but for a moment I couldn't see anything. When my vision soon cleared, Adva lay next to me, and… her injury was *gone.* Completely and utterly *gone* as if it had never existed. The wound that all of my selkie magic couldn't affect, the injury that no poultice or combination of herbs had ever helped, the cut that time had hardly ever affected, and had been disabling my innocent, sweet little sister for months… was actually, truly, fully, *gone.* Healed.

Adva looked down at herself and barked excitedly, only to abruptly begin shifting. I...I hadn't seen her shift in the longest time. When her form was finished, in front of us sat my adorable little sister. Even shorter than I was, with wavy red hair and freckles, and shining brown eyes. I hugged her, and we both had the biggest smiles on our faces.

"Oh my god Nixie, I can't believe you did it! You found a way to heal me, I—" her voice broke with the beginnings of happy tears. "I was starting to wonder if I'd ever see you again, nevermind find a way to be healed." I embraced her to find the fact that my eyes were starting to water too.

When we let go, I looked to Lorelai, who had a small smile on her face and looked proud of herself. I smiled at her.

"Thank you," I said.

The moment didn't last long as Adrian shot out of the water, in triton form, signing in a panicked frenzy. Despite his speed and apparent fear muddying his words, I understood what I needed to.

We were under attack, again. This time by sirens. And it was entirely Adrian's fault.

Our only way out of the cave was, unfortunately, into the sea. But it turned out Adrian was already on it, as he handed two pieces of seaweed to Miles and Lorelai. *Uh, what? The heck? How is seaweed supposed to help anyone in a fight?* But when they stuffed pieces of it into their ears, I remembered that humans had a weakness for the creatures. The odd thing was that Adrian did not have to even try to explain what they should do with the seaweed, they already knew. ... *I must have missed a lot more than I originally thought while I was in hunter custody.*

While I tried to give Adva a little bit of information on what was going on, without panicking her or giving too much information, I also had to keep one eye on Adrian— he was signing again. He told us that he had heard them coming, and felt the disturbance in the water of many of them. ... And he had just run into one. Apparently he had realized their presence, or that they were coming, while everyone else had been distracted by Adva's healing and he had dipped away briefly to investigate. Miles quickly began translating what Adrian was saying.

"He, he uh, Adrian doesn't think we'll be able to get past the group a them with how fast we swim..." Miles stopped translating. He stared at Adrian. "Buddy, that's—" he stopped again as Adrian signed more forcefully, urging him to translate what he had said. Also told him to not be a hypocrite, and remember that he had just thrown himself into a blade whereas Adrian could fight back properly. Miles sighed. "He wants to hold em off on 'is own so we can reach my ship in time."

There was a moment of silence as Lorelai said nothing in response. She turned to Adrian.

"Do you have a weapon?" She asked. He gave her a sheepish embarrassed look. "Ah right, you tossed my only sword overboard," she remarked. Rolling her eyes, she handed him a dagger.

"You should stay with the others, make sure they get back to the ship safely," Adrian suggested. Miles translated a few words for her, and she nodded. Adrian turned to go, but she stopped him with a hand on his shoulder. He turned back, and he and Lorelai locked eyes.

"Be as safe as you can down there," she said. "Do *not* be too much of a hero, or I'll kill you myself." There was a pause then, as one corner of Adrian's mouth lifted, and Lorelai smirked. For a brief moment, neither looked away from the other. Then they broke apart, and Lorelai cleared her throat while Adrian had a sudden interest in the rock under our feet. *...Oh?*

Miles ran in and gave him a hug, only for Adrian to remind him that they would see each other safe and sound again very soon. Then he was gone just like that, submerged in the waves.

"Alright everyone," Lorelai said. "Looks like we better get going quickly."

Adrian

I dove back down beneath the surface of the water, as my body sliced calmly and easily through it. Once deep enough to do so, I kicked and began to swim faster. Stronger.

It was not long before the sirens were upon me.

Long, dark claws reached out of nowhere and ripped at my scales as faces with slitted pupils and sharp teeth filled my vision. They moved around me quickly, trying to avoid the blade of the dagger I thrust at them repeatedly. There were three of them. I saw small badges somehow pinned onto their scales that were of an image I had not seen in what felt like a long time; two swords crossing in an X shape, with a golden jewel-filled crown sitting atop them. The crest of The Crown of Myrddin. Somehow, I was not very surprised to see this. I had broken countless laws of Myrddin during my time away from there, it had only been a matter of time until they hunted me down.

I slashed recklessly with the small weapon I held, becoming surrounded with anguished cries and snarls as the water filled with a red mist around us. They gave me a little more space after that, but were relentless in their pursuit. I made sure I kept in mind which direction my friends were heading in to make sure that none of the sirens got past me, but not a single one of them even tried. Not one of the group of them had even attempted to sing at any point either-- this was much too direct an attack for typical sirens. But I had already known that. They were not after anyone other than me, and if I had let my friends come with me they would have been attacked to get to me. I could never let that happen.

Claws raked down my back suddenly, as I had been distracted by the two other sirens. I tensed and grimaced, groaning in pain, but managed to spin around fast enough with the dagger pointed to create a long wound along the torso of the siren that had been behind me.

Kicking forcefully, I propelled myself out from inside the middle of the group. Streams of mist-like red blood followed me. I could feel my muscles starting to ache. Looking at the three wounded but still fit to fight sirens turn on me once more, I wondered how long I could keep this up. And now that I was bleeding, how could I get away without leading them right back to my friends?

One of them dove directly towards my dagger, hands first, teeth bared, and that was a mistake. They had likely wanted to attempt to disarm me, but instead I sliced along their forearm and up to their hand. They recoiled in pain, holding their arm with their other hand, and hissed at me. I hissed back, equally as angry. We were making far too big of a cloud of blood. Predators would surely be upon us soon. Sure enough, I could hear something coming towards us, the movement of the waves also warning me in advance.

Before I could do anything about it, a streak of bright blue launched itself at us-- and to my surprise, left me alone. All of the sirens hissed and snarled, sounding furious but also surprised. Their questions and shouts were repeatedly cut off and replaced with cries of pain.

When the area filled with blood finally began to be partially washed away, I stood back and stared as I saw the three sirens that had been attacking me now instead turning on a different siren. I immediately recognized the iridescent crystal blue tail and short brown hair, but I could not believe my eyes. Fin, my little siren friend, had found me! He nearly looked completely different now, as his cheerful smiling face was replaced by ferocity and bared teeth. I swam over to help immediately, stabbing a distracted grey siren deep into their tail, as they released a loud cry of pain. With Fin's claws, teeth, and my dagger, we both moved swiftly around the sirens to dodge their increasingly frenzied attacks and get them from both sides.

Before long, they were covered in cuts and wounds, bleeding profusely. They stayed and fought longer than they probably should have, but I was sure they were reluctant to go back to The Crown empty handed. Regardless, they soon had no choice but to flee if they wanted to live.

With the two of us only having gained a few small cuts and scrapes since he arrived, Fin turned to me with a smile on his face. But it quickly fell when he noticed that I was still bleeding, and visibly worn. Urgently, he ushered me to follow him. I nodded, and was led a small distance away, where an underwater sea cave sat shrouded deeply in seaweed and coral. It was so well hidden that if I had not been shown where it was, I likely would never have seen it. Fin brought me to the side of the cave, near its opening, and gestured for me to go inside. Hesitantly, I did so, as he followed slowly behind me.

Standing in the mouth of the cave, I peered inside and saw that there was a light shining from deep inside. I headed towards it carefully. I could hear sounds of quiet talking, but as I neared them, all went quiet. *What is Fin trying to show me? What is this siren sending me towards?* He stayed far behind me, which did not ease my slight nerves. Blood was still slowly flowing out of me, and I grew more and more weary by the second.

"... Adrian?" A hesitant, doubtful voice drifted up to me. "A-Adrian, is that really you, it can't be!" The voice became louder as a female triton stepped out from the depths of the cave and hurried towards me. My eyes widened, and I rubbed them, unable to believe what I was seeing. Her hair was shorter, her voice was louder, and stress had not been the kindest to her, but I still recognized her immediately.

"Whina!" I cried, swimming towards her to meet her in the middle. She wrapped me in a hug, and then stepped back, alarmed, looking at her hands.

"You're bleeding," she said, a bit shocked. "Oh no, look at you, what happened? Come here, come in," she said, grabbing my hand and pulling me deeper into the cave. Fin must have swam up behind me, because Whina glanced back over my shoulder. "Oh!" she said. "Blue, you're back." A look of realization dawned on her face as she looked between Fin-- or, Blue?-- and I. She looked at me. "Do you… know this siren?" she asked.

"I suppose you could say that, yes."

My old friend from times past showed me her new home. Somehow she had gotten her hand on a few magic torches, that lit up the space in a bright warm glow. Rugs and covers laid on the ground, and toys made by hand from coral, sticks, and other bits laid around or floated.

"Here, come in, sit, and I'll bandage your wounds. You can't be bleeding around here, you'll attract sharks," she said, leading me further inside. *Or sirens,* I thought, glancing over at Fin. He still had scratches all over him, but they were closing remarkably quickly. "We also will need to talk about what has happened since we last saw each other-- and the kids will be happy to see you," Whina continued, as she led me forward while holding onto my arm.

Three triton children sat amongst the items playing with each other. The older two were so much bigger and taller than when I had last seen them, with their fins growing in nicely and their scales maturing. When they saw me, they stared, before jumping to their feet and running over.

"Uncle Adrian is that you?!" They exclaimed, excitedly bouncing before me just like they had when they were little. I could not help but smile. As the boys threw a million questions at me, and told me all about what they had been up to recently, I sat down and Whina busied applying bandages to the wounds on my back.

But my eyes were drawn towards the third child, the little girl, who still sat on a rug with a toy in hand. The eldest boy noticed, and asked if I wanted to hold her. I nodded, and he picked her up gently and brought her to me. She had chubby little cheeks, and short brown hair that had grown considerably since I had last seen her. Her dark brown eyes never uncrossed. As I held her, I remarked how much she had grown and how healthy she looked. I smiled. I glanced back up at Whina, who was watching me, smiling.

"She loves to play, and to laugh," she said, gazing fondly at the child in my arms. She raised her eyes to look directly at me, still smiling. "Her name is Adriana."

Happiness and surprise swelled in my chest as I held back joyful tears.

Morgan

"Alright everyone," Lorelai said. "Looks like we better get going quickly."

She then did a quick refresh of the water breathing spell as Adva and I transformed back into seals. Making sure to keep Adva right by my side at all times, we all entered the water with Lorelai leading us.

As I submerged my head under the waves, I could distinctly hear the sounds of hissing, snarling creatures. Several of them, not nearly as far away as I would've liked. We turned sharply away from the direction of Adrian's fight and swam as quickly as we could back towards where we had left our ship.

As we swam, the sounds of battle became more and more distant, and nothing stopped us or got in our way. One by one, with difficulty we hauled ourselves onto the small ship. I transformed into my human form, morphing my seal skin into a simple dress and slipping it on in the water. Reluctantly, Adva did the same. I helped her up with Miles' help from above, and then climbed aboard myself.

Only to find a woman sitting on the deck of our ship, smiling when she saw us. I quickly grabbed the clothing I had left on the deck when I transformed before and covered myself. AdvaNot only that, but it was a woman I recognized and who I never thought I would see again. She had shoulder length brown hair, green eyes, and wore flowy loose clothing. A large black canine-like creature sat by her side, smiling and panting. *How did they even get here without getting wet?!*

"Velia?!" Lorelai exclaimed, running up to the woman. The stranger stood, and the two hugged. *She knows this woman too? Wait-- her name is Velia? Maybe Velia Curran, from that note…?*

"Velia?! Hey! You're here!" Miles exclaimed, sounding surprised. He walked up to greet the woman as he spoke, and bent down to scratch her canine behind it's ears. *Wait, hold on, even Miles of all people knows her? How could they possibly have met?!* The woman smiled at Miles.

"You know you really shouldn't leave a ship unattended like that, you could have easily returned to a crew of pirates instead of me," the woman gently chided. "Also, I was wondering you two— I heard in the city about you winning this ship Miles, congratulations, I was wondering if I could hitch a ride with you all for a bit?" She smiled sweetly. *Huh.* Miles, of course cheerily and excitedly agreed with the idea without a second thought. "Wonderful!" She said, before finally glancing past the others towards Adva and I. She stood, and approached me.

"Well, well, well, I never thought I would run into you again! Glad to see you escaped and are in good hands. I'm Velia," she said, offering me a hand. I shook it.

"Yeah, wow, me neither… I'm Morgan, and this is my little sister Adva," I said, wrapping a protective arm around her shoulder instinctively. "Thank you for. Well, you know. So uh, how the hell did *you* meet these guys?" I asked.

"Woah hold on just a second there, how and when did you two ever meet?" Miles butted in, pointing between Velia and I.

Lorelai explained to me how they had met this Velia person while searching for me. *So she was hiding out in the woods? ... That's odd. I'll have to keep an eye on her. She seems nice, but what do we actually know about her?* I then explained how this Velia woman and I had met, stating the simple facts of how I had run into her while escaping. I turned to her.

"Why *were* you there to begin with? You work for them, don't you?" I accused, causing a shift in mood and a rise in tension that everyone felt.

"Woah there, Morgan, what're you gettin' on about? She's--" Miles started, but Velia held out a hand and told him to stop.

"She's right," she said. I smirked, but Miles and Adrian stared with confused, wide eyes in shock. "I worked for him, in The Meeting Place. But I planned to leave as soon as I discovered what they were really up to." She gave me an apologetic look. "I've… I've left that life now." Suddenly, an idea struck her, her face brightening into a large smile as one of her hands went into a large pocket on her belt. She pulled something out of the biggest pockett, and walked closer to me. In her hands she held some sort of strange contraption, cylinders of metal all piled together with many small metal pieces between. Her hands flew, putting the attached pieces properly together somehow, until she held a cane in her hands. She presented it to me.

"It's a piece of tech that I stole from The Navy. I understand if that means you want nothing to do with it, but the metal is incredible strength and lightweight and--" she stopped herself. "It, uh, has two built-in weapons I can show you how to use later," she offered. My eyes widened in excitement and I grabbed it from her. She smiled as I tried putting my weight on it. "This button here," she pointed to a small bump with a cap on it that was on the underside of the curved part. "It can't be pressed unless you take the cover off, but don't press it unless you want to make a hole in Miles' new boat," she was whispering now, pointing to the base of the cane. I nodded, snickering at the idea of how Miles might react to that, glancing at him. He and Lorelai stepped closer to get a good look at the gift, and Adva shifted to be halfway hiding behind me.

"Wow," Lorelai said, staring at it. She turned to Velia. "You were able to disassemble it to fit into your pocket? And what weapons are in it exactly?" I ignored the two women as they became stuck in a conversation between the two of them, discussing the technological aspects of the cane. I tested my weight on it a bit further.

"Is it… is it gonna help you walk better?" Adva's little voice was right in my ear as she peeked over my shoulder down at the cane. I smiled at her and ruffled her hair.

"Yeah, it will. That's the idea, anyway," I said.

"But…" her voice hesitated as she glanced at Miles' imposing form, who was eyeing the cane quizzically. "But what will help with your swimming?" My smile faltered.

"I-- we, um. We'll figure that one out too Addie, don't worry. But I can swim a little, right?" I tried to encourage a smile from her by forcing my own. It didn't really work.

"What did I hear 'bout this thing havin' weapons in it?" Miles asked abruptly. I rolled my eyes.

We all spent the next couple of minutes doing separate things while we waited for Adrian to come back. I sat and talked with Adva, wrapping my seal skin around us both and cherishing the moment. Miles sat near the edge of the ship, reading a book he had found in the ship's small storage, but he frequently glanced worriedly out to the sea. Lorelai and Velia talked amongst themselves for a bit, with the canine sitting beside them, until Lorelai broke away and approached Adva and I. She knelt down to be eye level with me.

"I'm worried about Adrian. It's taken far too long already. He should've been back by now. And I'm thinkin--"

She was interrupted by splashing sounding from the far side of the ship, as a green scaly hand appeared, tightly gripping the edge of the boat. Lorelai ran towards it and quickly helped Adrian aboard. He had numerous deep claw marks all over his arms and chest, and once pulled aboard, he stood only to stumble and be caught by Lorelai, who helped him stay standing. He lifted his hands tiredly to sign.

"They—they're coming. They're coming after me. We have to go," he said, as Lorelai moved him to sit down, leaning him against the mast.

"Hold on a second, calm down. Where the hell did you get these strange bandages on your back from?" Lorelai asked, giving him a look.

"I ran into a friend," he tiredly signed.

Meanwhile, Velia had been staring at Adrian.

"Is that—?" She asked.

"A triton?" I responded. "Yeah."

"No, I mean, his face, his hair—"

"Oh yeah that's Adrian alright," Miles chimed in, as he went over to check on him, as Adrian lifted a hand to wave to Velia. She walked over and knelt by his side.

"Here, hold on Lorelai with the magic, I have some bandages and poultices he can have," she said as she pulled said items out of pockets in a belt she wore. As she began to bandage him up, I limped over to join the crowd around our scaly friend, and Adva followed me.

But before I could even ask him my questions, Adrian began to explain.

He admitted that the sirens weren't after us. They were after him, only him.

"Tritons are forbidden from leaving our home city," he said. "But when I was exiled, I was told that The Crown has spies and that I was still expected to obey triton law... I didn't think he was serious, I was exiled after all," he looked a bit embarrassed at that now. "I've broken countless laws of our people by being with you all and so now his sirens have been released, sent by the Crown to take me away for punishment."

After Miles had finished translating that for those here that didn't speak his sign language, a thick tense silence hung in the air. Adva tugged my jacket.

"I want to go home," she whispered. I looked down at her.

"To the seals?" I assumed. She nodded.

I had known deep in my heart that this was likely to happen; Adva was no fighter, no adventurer. Whereas I didn't belong with the seals. But now that she was finally healed, she would be safe with the seals. Meanwhile, I... I glanced over at Lorelai. Then to Adrian, and Miles. *I have friends who need my help... And selkie relatives to find.*

We set sail as soon as I had said my goodbyes to my sister. I hugged her as tight as I could. Promised that I would be back soon. And did everything I could to not cry as she jumped back into the sea and disappeared. I stood there staring at the space she had been in for a few minutes. Lorelai and Miles sailed the ship together, as I eventually settled sitting on the deck next to Adrian and leaned against the mast. Velia sat at the back end of the ship with her canine, staring out at the waters behind us. Adrian patted me on the shoulder.

"You did the right thing, letting Adva go," he said. "I'm sure it was hard."

"You're the one who just nearly got shredded to pieces by some sirens," I retorted. He shrugged. There was a lengthy pause. I looked over at the waves splashing against the side of the boat, past Adrian.

"So," he said, his hands lifting for a moment to say the word before dropping. "Your real name is N-I-X-I-E?" he asked, having to spell out the name that we had no sign for. I had nearly forgotten that Adva had mentioned that name earlier. I looked up at his eyes; they were simply curious.

"Ah. Right. Well, Nixie is the name my selkie pod gave me when I was born, yes," I said. I paused, looked out at Miles laughing as he held onto one of the ship's ropes, Lorelai next to him with her hand on her forehead. "But you can all keep calling me Morgan. I'm used to it. I like it," I said.

"Why did you not tell Miles and I your true name when we met?" Adrian asked. I couldn't help but burst out laughing.

"Because you were two humans and I had just lost my skin!" I cried, thinking it should be obvious. But, he still looked a bit confused. I smirked at him. "Humans like to kill us, remember? And I had never been without my skin before," I told him. "Morgan was the first name that came to mind."

Seeming satisfied, Adrian and I leaned back against the ship's mast's pole, looking outward. Forward. The sun began to set in front of us, the sky streaked with lines of pink, and areas of yellow and orange as the sky above began to darken and the sun shone directly in my eyes, making me raise a hand to my face. I glanced at Adrian as I blocked the light from my eyes, and he smiled. We sat there for several minutes, and watched as the first few stars of the night began to appear.

In that moment, I knew that wherever I was, no matter what happened or what life threw at us... the four of us could handle it. No matter what, we would look out for each other. Because of that, we would be okay.

With those thoughts in mind, as the sky quickly darkened, I turned my seal skin into a blanket, leaned against the mast and Adrian's side, and closed my eyes. The sound of the waves gently lapping against the ship soothed me. As I drifted off to sleep, I could have sworn I heard the beginning of a beautiful but haunting melody lifting over the waves.

The End

www.ingramcontent.com/pod-product-compliance
Lightning Source LLC
Chambersburg PA
CBHW071534120726
47907CB00014B/1720